# HER NAME
# IS EVE

# HER NAME IS EVE

A REESE CLAYTON AND EMERSON LAKE NOVEL

BARBARA FOURNIER

This is a work of fiction. All names, characters, events and places, with the exception of some incidental references to real cities, towns and airports, are the product of the author's imagination. Any resemblance to actual persons, living or dead, or actual events is purely coincidental.

ISBN Paperback: 978-1-7366109-7-8
ISBN E-Pub: 978-1-7366109-6-1

Developmental Editor: Crystal Dovigh
Copy Editor: Joan Michaels
Author Photo: Erin Malcolm Photography
Cover and interior design by Caroline Teagle Johnson

# DEDICATION

My Mom had a tough life. Eight children and alcohol-fueled domestic abuse made for a not-very-happy home. She made the most of it, not always making good decisions, but she felt she had to abandon her current lifestyle.

Every year, we made time to watch the Oscars® together—truly a fun, bright spot in our lives. It was our *special* time together to admire the actors in their fancy clothes. It was her time to dream she walked the red carpet. She was somebody. Recognized. **Noticed** as the beautiful woman she was.

She found some happiness with her second husband. Still not the best relationship, but she did get to travel and see new places. When he retired, they moved to Florida, leaving her former life behind.

Both husbands passed before her Alzheimer's diagnosis. She was alone in Florida working in a school cafeteria. I received a call from her co-worker stating mom needed help.

My sister Linda flew to Florida first, to have her admitted to a hospital for evaluation while we planned for her return to New York. Then the two of us flew together to bring her home.

It just didn't seem fair; after all Mom had been through in her life, that this could happen to her. She passed away in 1991 at the age of 74.

This Novel is dedicated to my mom. She had Alzheimer's for at least 10 years, 8 of which she spent in a nursing facility. I wanted to shine a light on her and make her the heroine of this story. *Mom's name is Eve.*

I will always love you and understand everything that you went through. I felt it all. Sending you Butterfly Kisses Mom.

Barbara

# PROLOGUE

Eve Clayton awoke early in an excellent mood. "It's a great day to go shopping. I could use some new hair products. Maybe I'll try that new store on West Main after I shower."

She quietly got dressed. Her beloved Warren was still sleeping. She gently kissed his forehead. "I'll be back soon my love."

He never heard her leave.

She noticed the car keys to the old Buick on the side table. "There they are."

The morning sun streamed through the windshield warming her cheeks. "I think, first, I'll drive through the park; the trees are so pretty this time of year." As she came around the bend, she saw the gazebo. "Oh, this is where Warren and I had our first kiss. I love him so much, even after all these years. Oh, there's the park bench where he proposed." She began humming their song and then blew a kiss out the window. "Okay, time to shop now," she said to the wind before closing the window. She turned out of the park onto Morton Drive. "Huh, when did they move the Pharmacy onto this street? Oh, geez," she laughed to herself. "I must have made a wrong turn. Too much daydreaming about my hubby. Silly Eve! I'll go around the block. No. Maybe I'll turn here. What the hell is wrong with me? This doesn't look right."

She was getting anxious, grabbing the wheel tighter, sitting up, straight close to the steering wheel. Her eyes darted back and forth from the rearview to the side mirrors. She was getting farther away from town with every mile she drove. There was no one around to help her.

"Maybe this is the way back." She turned down a dirt road, not even noticing the frayed rope barrier strung between two posts.

"Oh my God, I don't know this place. I need to get the hell out of here!" Hitting the accelerator, the whine of the engine matched her racing heart. Tree branches scraped the car doors, the sound like fingernails on a chalkboard. The Buick pitched forward and a wave of water crashed over the hood as it came to a sudden halt.

"Where am I?" she spoke as she took a deep breath. The contents of her purse were scattered over the passenger seat. Finding the cell phone she dialed.

"Hair by Design. How may I help you?"

"Yes. Hello. This is Eve Clayton. Can I speak to my daughter, Olivia?"

"Um, hold one moment, please." The receptionist held her hand over the receiver. "Hey Margie, there's a woman named Eve on the phone looking for Olivia?" She shrugged.

"Oh my. Keep her on the line for a moment. I'm going to call Olivia's salon. I heard from one of her former clients that her mother wasn't herself lately."

Waiting on the phone, Eve rolled down the window, inhaling a deep breath of fresh Vermont air.

"Hi Eve, it's Margie. I spoke with Olivia."

"Who's Eve? I don't know you!" She threw the phone on the seat with a thud. "I need to get out of here."

Stepping out of the car, her foot sank into the thick, wet grass, struggling to pull her foot up. The mud claimed her shoe.

She hobbled her way from the car to the main road. One shoe on, one shoe off. She was feeling lost and frightened until a police cruiser drove up alongside her.

"Are you okay, Mrs. Clayton? Do you need help?"

"I don't know where I am." Fear, once again, took hold. She didn't remember her name. Tears welled up in her eyes. But never once crying.

"I'll take you home now. You just made a wrong turn. You're ok. Warren and Oliva are waiting for you. Let me help you in the car."

"Thank you. I appreciate it, James. How is your mother these days? I should go visit her, maybe go to lunch."

"Oh, she's doing fine. I'm sure she would love that," when in fact she had passed away four years ago.

James now understood what Olivia had said to him earlier. It was time.

Her mom needed help—the help she could no longer provide.

# CHAPTER 1

The intense overhead light caused her eyes to ache as she struggled to focus. She glimpsed the white coat floating over the edge of the hard surface beneath her.

"Who are you?" Her eyelids fluttered rapidly as she tried to wipe away the haze blurring her vision, but she couldn't move her arms. "Where am I?"

"I'm your doctor." The voice was almost inaudible to her from the buzzing in her ears. Or maybe it was just the buzzing of the fluorescent light above her, filling her ears and head.

"What happened to me and why am I here?" The anger in her voice was strong. "Where is here? My legs." Struggling to sit up, feeling the tightness in her chest and her upper arms, now realizing something was holding her down. The searing heat, like fire to her legs. Crying out. "The pain in my legs," she repeated. Tears began to fall to the side of her face. "Was I in an accident? Did I have a stroke? Is anyone else hurt? Oh my God," her voice now a whisper. "Did I hurt someone?"

"No, you did not have a stroke." The voice was deep and husky. "What you are feeling my dear, is what most doctors would label phantom pain. You no longer have legs. But don't worry," he slowly injected something into the IV in her arm, "we could make you new ones. Maybe!"

# CHAPTER 2

"Okay, my soon-to-be wife," Emerson Lake said, "is everything packed and ready to roll? The car will be here in 11 minutes to take us to the airport."

"Don't get your boxers in a knot hot stuff. I'm almost done here. I'm excited about seeing Olivia. It's been quite a few years since we saw each other. Our phone conversations have been so far apart in the past year. It's been difficult for her to care for Mom and Dad. All I did was sign some paperwork to agree with the decision."

Emerson just listened, knowing his future bride Reese Clayton and her sister Olivia had to work through this.

"I can't imagine what will happen when she sees me at her door. And how will Mom and Dad feel, having me back in Vermont?"

Emerson could see the tears forming when she spoke of her parents. He walked over to her, threw his phone on the bed, took the suitcase from her, and zipped it up. Then grabbed her around the waist, took a tissue out of his pocket, wiped her tears, and gave her the tissue to wipe her nose. Kissing her with all the affection he had. "Everything will be fine, sweetheart, you'll see. I love you and can't wait to marry you."

She kissed him back. "I know. I love you too." She took a deep breath and gave him a smack on the ass. "Let's move it, detective," picking up his phone from the pillow as she looked at his phone app. "The car is here."

"Emerson, are you sure about traveling nearly cross country to Vermont to visit my family? Is this what you want to do? I'm not sure we discussed the headaches this reunion will cause."

"Reese, think, for a moment, we won't be chasing serial killers, worrying if we are going to be shot, looking over our shoulders all the time. I'd say this trip will be a welcome vacation. Rolling hills, beautiful color, and a drop-dead gorgeous woman on my arm. I've always said your sister was hot."

"Really, Mr. Lake? My sister?" Laughing as she grabbed his nipple and twisted it.

"Yikes! You're a mean woman, Reese Clayton. No sense of humor at all."

"I'd say that was pretty funny," she kissed him on the cheek.

# CHAPTER 3

The plane landed at Albany International Airport in Albany, New York at around 10 a.m. Reese and Emerson headed down the escalator to baggage claim, there stood a man, tall, very good-looking, late thirties, maybe early forties. He had brown hair and hazel eyes with a sign that read, Emerson Lake & Reese Clayton.

"What is this?" Emerson inquired. "Do we know you?" Emerson glanced at Reese. She shrugged her shoulders.

The gentleman said nothing, tipped his hat and then flipped the sign over. It read.

*A gift for your use while in Vermont.*
*Love you both.*
*Dad*

"I am at your beck and call 24/7," the chauffeur replied. "My name is Peter Andora. Your father hired me as your chauffeur and as protection. If needed. I am an ex-Marine with assault training." He handed Emerson his list of credentials and replaced his hat. "I am at your service."

After Emerson looked at the paperwork, he called his dad.

"Hello Son, I take it you received my gift?"

"We did and thank you, but seriously Dad, this is unnecessary."

"Hi, Mr. Lake," Reese said into the phone after Emerson put it on speaker. "We have a car reserved for us from a rental service here in Albany."

"I know, but I thought it would be a gracious gesture after all you have done for me. And stop calling me Mr. Lake. It's dad to you, sweet Reese."

"I did nothing, Pop. It's my job to serve and protect." he raised his eyebrows at Reese.

Reese laughed. "You are a class act, Dad. Thank you. But a bodyguard? Do you think that's necessary? We're going to Vermont. Not exactly a state known for its abundance of crime."

"Well, who would have thought, in our small town, we would have a serial killer? I'm sorry, but I worry about you as much as you worry about me."

"Dad, I'm sorry too. It's a grand gesture. Thank you."

"Well, just enjoy your trip and take care of my daughter-in-law-to-be. Love you both."

Emerson hung up the phone and headed to the nearly empty carousel, their luggage going in circles all this time.

"Okay, Miss Clayton and Mr. Lake, your chariot awaits. There is a bottle of bubbly in the cooler and a few snacks to munch on. We will be in Manchester before you know it."

"Thank you, Peter," Reese said. "At least it's an SUV limo," she said to Emerson as she stepped into the vehicle. "My sister would have a hissy fit if she saw me riding around in a stretch."

"We're staying at the Beckham Hotel, Peter," Emerson said. "It's right on Route 7."

"I got it, sir. It won't take long to get there."

The Beckham Hotel wasn't large, but it was bustling with activity. Guests checking in and out. Very busy time as the autumn hues were just beginning to show their beauty. The décor of the hotel was what you would expect of a high-end hotel in beautiful Vermont—country chic.

Once checked in, Reese turned to Emerson. "Do we need the car and Peter? It's so awkward. My sister lives around the corner from here. We can walk it for Christ's sake in three minutes. We can rent a car while here. It's just nerve-racking knowing my sister doesn't have much and I don't think I should flaunt gifts from your dad in front of her. I'm trying to re-kindle my friendship with the family. I don't know if I can make that happen, but a limo and driver won't help."

"I'll call to have a rental delivered in the morning. We'll tell Peter we don't need his services. We can offer to pay for his accommodation for the weekend and then he can be on his way home. Now kiss me and let's unpack before we call your sis and tell her we're on our way over."

# CHAPTER 4

"Wake up," a voice whispered in her ear. "It's time to eat."

She tried to turn her head, but her neck was stiff and achy from lying in that spot. Suddenly he was staring over the top of her, looking directly into her eyes. She felt the heat from his breath on her neck and then he disappeared, only to whisper into her other ear.

"Wake up. Do you want something to drink?"

"Yes, that would be nice." The words caught in her dry throat. Coughing. "Thank you. Where am I? Does my dad know where I am?"

"No!" he slammed his fists on the metal slab that held her body.

Her body trembled with fear at the sound of his booming voice.

"No one knows where you are, and they never will. I'm going to teach you a lesson and you will listen. Then I am going to make sure no one hears you ever again."

"What is going on? Why am I here? I don't understand." Once again, she tried to get up and, once again, she failed.

"Your first lesson: tell no woman to leave their husband. It's none of your business what goes on in my home."

"What are you talking about?"

"You told my wife to leave me because I was abusing her. You know nothing about abuse until now. For that, you get nothing to drink today."

"I don't know what you're talking about. Please," tears ran down the sides of her cheeks, "please let me go."

"You can't go anywhere. You have no legs, remember?"

"What?"

"That is lesson number one."

"What did you do?" she screamed.

"I will feed you through this tube until I'm done with you. Now it's time for you to go nighty night." He pushed yet another needle into her IV.

# CHAPTER 5

Seeing them walk up the driveway through the living room window, she took a deep breath. "Am I ready to see her again?" Oliva Clayton paused before opening the door a crack, "Oh you're here." Her words lacked any trace of emotion.

"Nice to see you. Liv." Emerson tried to break the tension.

"Oh yeah," Reese choked back tears, "you remember Emerson."

"You bet your ass I do!" She opened the door completely, extending her arms out to him. Come over here, you hunk of a man. Kiss me."

"Ooh, my pleasure Olivia." Grabbing Reese's shoulder, moving her to the side of the stoop clearing his path to Olivia, so he could do as he was told.

"Come, sit down," Olivia grabbed him by the hand, leading him to the kitchen. "I have iced tea, beer, wine, scotch, you name it."

"Wow, I didn't know you drank, sis."

"I don't really, but it's here because my man likes to partake in a beverage now and then. Would it matter to you if I did?"

Reese ignored the sarcasm. "We'll have iced tea if you don't mind."

"Where is he? We want to meet the lucky man that got you." Emerson flattered her every chance he got, knowing Olivia needed a boost of confidence.

"He's out of town but will be back in a day or two. His business takes him away a lot."

"What does he do?" Reese inquired. "I should know that by now, but I don't. I'm sorry Liv."

Olivia bristled. Damn right, she thought. If she came around more often, she would know what he does for a living. Stop it, Olivia! She decided to keep her snide remarks to herself. "He's an investment broker for one of the big corporations on the West Coast. Sometimes he's gone for weeks at a time. But it's okay, I'm always busy with Mom. I don't know where the relationship will go. For now, I will continue to see him. We go out to dinner and then come back here for a few days. His name is Craig Stockton. I told him you were coming to help with the situation with Mom for a while."

"Now, what's the problem with Mom and Dad?" Emerson asked.

"She's placed in the nursing wing of Grace Continuing Care Senior Housing Development a few miles from here. At least she is close. The building is divided into two sections. When a spouse becomes unable to handle themselves in everyday situations, particularly those who have difficulty with memory, such as Alzheimer's, they can transfer to that wing. The other side is for assisted living. That's where Dad is. I tried to keep them here, but they fought all the time, and she would leave the house on her own. I had to call the police several times to find her. At least if he wants to see her every day, he can just walk through the halls to that wing.

"So," Reese said. "He doesn't want to accept the fact she is ill."

"You got it. He thinks the whole thing is foolish. When he goes to see her, he comes back to his apartment, so frustrated. He calls me in the middle of the night. He tells me she is looking for her hairdresser and no one believes her that the hairdresser is missing."

"Aren't you the one that does mom's hair? You still have your license, right?"

"I do, but I stopped doing her hair when we moved her into the nursing wing. She claimed I knew nothing about her hair and wanted to go to this young girl. A booth renter who worked at my salon, The Cutting Edge. What could I say? The girl would travel to the senior facility and do mom's hair at their on-site salon."

"If she rents a booth at Cutting Edge, clearly this girl is not missing," Reese said.

"Oh, she's gone," Olivia took a sip of her iced tea.

"What happened? Did you fire her because Mom chose her over you?" Reese looked puzzled.

"No, I didn't fire her. Jesus Reese," Olivia slammed her glass on the table. A droplet of tea splashed over the side puddling around the bottom of the glass. "Do I look like that kind of person to you? Oh, that's right, you wouldn't know. You've been playing big-shot detective in South Dakota the last few years!"

"Olivia!" Emerson shot her with a disapproving look.

She glanced at him and then at Reese, her head lowering a

bit. "She wasn't my employee. She just rented a booth from me. Renters come and go. It happens a lot. I don't have contracts with the stylists. What's the point of that? If they don't like my salon, I don't want them. I was surprised this girl left though. She was so good with Mom and catered to her older clients. She listened to their problems and comforted them. You know, hair stylists hear so much more than you can imagine. It's mentally overwhelming to carry our client's secrets around with us. Maybe she just got tired of it all and couldn't do it anymore."

"That makes sense. So, Mom still won't let you do her hair?"

"No, she doesn't. The aide at Grace Center gives her shampoo once a week, but that's it. I decided to make a plan with the facility to do my own clients at their salon occasionally. This way I'm able to check up on her and Dad. It gives me a break from having to drive over from my salon after work too."

"Okay," Reese took her last gulp of tea, wishing she had requested something stronger. "Tomorrow, you take a break. Go do something for yourself, shop, massage, go to lunch, dinner, take a couple of days if you like. Call Craig and have him meet you somewhere. It's on me, Liv."

"And me too, Liv" Emerson smiled. "You deserve a break. We got this."

"Thank you, Emerson" Olivia completely ignored that it was her sister's suggestion.

They all cautiously hugged and said good night.

# CHAPTER 6

As they walked back to their hotel, Reese kicked a pebble on the sidewalk. "Well, that wasn't exactly the reception I was hoping for with Liv, but I guess it's the one I deserve. I was hoping for one of her rib-crushing hugs. But what I got was all she could muster right now."

"Well," Emerson tried to lighten the mood. "I'd say she is one hot-kissing woman if you ask me. Those lips. Damn!"

She laughed at him. "Yeah, I'm sure she was hoping for someone hot. Disappointment all around."

"Good comeback my love." He threw his arm around her shoulder.

When they arrived back at the hotel the keys to the rental car were at the front desk as promised.

"Who do you think we should visit first in the morning, your mom or dad?" Emerson threw the rental keys and room key on the dresser as they entered the room.

"I think Dad. Maybe he can tell us something more about Mom's obsession with her hairstylist. It seems very odd that she thinks her hairdresser is missing."

"We find that out in the morning," Emerson gave her a full-on kiss, "but now, let's find each other." Kissing her passionately after making love, he said to her, "You know, sweetheart, making love to you is like having a hot-fudge sundae every day of the week."

"That sounds like quite the compliment, my love. Thank you. Speaking of dessert, I'm starving."

"Does that mean you'll be showering alone?"

"Sure does," she kissed him playfully, her lips scraping against his 5 o'clock shadow. "Ow!"

"Wow! I thought women liked that scruffy look?"

"I do like this look on you, it just seems a bit too long. Do men like women to have that scruffy look? If you get what I mean?"

"Got it," he dug his razor from the suitcase. "I'll call Peter and tell him we don't need his services."

"Sounds good. Oh, just FYI, I have a new nightie to wear to bed." She flashed him a mischievous smile. Then kissed him lovingly as he ran his fingers through her beautiful hair, holding her close, closer than usual.

He suddenly pulled away "Wait, I hope to hell it's not flannel. Is it?"

The next morning, they set out to Grace Center. "Hey, do you still think we should see your dad first today?"

"I'd rather take a walk in the woods and smell this beautiful fall air." She gazed at the beautiful foliage as they drove through town.

Emerson could sense her tension. "What are you so worried about?"

"I'm frightened to see my mom, Emerson. Suppose she doesn't know me? I'm not sure I can face that. If I see Dad first, maybe he can fill us in on what's going on."

"Maybe we can convince him, and you, that this is a new life with her, and you both must accept this is not her fault. It is an illness that doesn't have a cure. He had to have noticed the changes in her memory quite some time ago. Wouldn't you think?"

"This is one disease that is so difficult to accept by anyone. I'm sure neither one of us is alone in our thoughts. The one person he spent most of his life with is no longer there, at least most of the time."

"I know it will be difficult, but you have to come to grips with this honey. Not an easy thing to accomplish. I don't care how many classes we attended Reese, it's your mom. Moms are supposed to be there for you forever, I get it, but this is a fact of life. We know the stages and how this will end. But unlike most diseases, this is not time predictable. Saying an average of 8-10 years isn't exactly helpful. Especially when we don't know when it started. It sucks. I don't know of anyone, even in our age group, that doesn't forget things. I'm not being mean, my love. I just want you prepared. I think a lot of what you are feeling has to do with Olivia. The guilt you feel for not being here all this time. Am I right?"

He noticed the tears streaking down her cheeks. He handed her a napkin to wipe her nose and pulled the car off to the side of the road. "Come on, let's suck in some of this Vermont air." He ran around to the passenger side and opened the door. "Come with me little girl," he teased. "Let's go for a quick walk.

There are no woods, but you get my drift. C'mon."

She had to laugh at him.

Once back on the road to Grace Care Center, Reese thought she glimpsed an SUV in the side mirror. "I think someone is following us."

"Seriously? I don't see anyone."

She turned to look out the back window. Nothing. "I don't know, just me, I guess. I'm probably just tired from the long flight and the emotional reunion with my sister."

"I'll monitor the rearview just in case."

# CHAPTER 7

"My name is Reese Clayton. This is my fiancé, Emerson Lake. We would like to see my father, Warren Clayton. Could you tell us where his residence is, please?"

"I need to see your identification."

It was an automatic response. They pulled out their shields.

"I'll let him know you're here."

Reese's dad greeted her before she even knocked on his door. Teary, the moment he grabbed and hugged her. "I missed you, sweetheart."

"You have no idea how much I have missed you, Dad." Feeling better already, she held onto him tight, like his little girl again.

"I'm so glad to see you both," her dad hugged her again and then shook Emerson's hand. "Maybe you can do something about your mother."

"Dad, that's one reason we are here. To help you understand, Mom will not get better. This is a disease in her brain. It's no one's fault. She will only get worse as time goes on."

"Did the doctors explain this to you?" Emerson asked.

"Yes, they did," Warren choked up. "But what do doctors know? This is my wife, the love of my life, and now most times she doesn't even know who I am. All she wants to talk about is her hairdresser. She thinks something happened to her. I don't know what to say to her anymore. I say something and she says let's go, and then she walks down the halls and back again. Back and forth. She's hard to keep up with sometimes. I don't know where she gets the energy. I ask her what my name is, and she says, Oh, you know."

"Okay, before we go see her dad, can we just take a deep breath, please sit down let's talk. Dad, what the doctors are trying to tell you is she won't get better and this could go on for many years. There is no cure. At least not yet. I know it's the hardest thing to accept because she doesn't look ill, like say a cancer patient or someone with a stroke."

"I know, honey. It's just so hard. One minute she knows exactly who I am and then just as suddenly she pushes me away in fear as if I'm a stranger." Warren hung his head.

Reese held his hand tight. "None of us has answers, not even the doctors. Only medications to help with their symptoms. And now some that might help slow the disease. It's a guessing game. The brain is an incredible organ of the body Dad. People ask us all the time in our field why people turn into murderers? What makes them do these terrible things? Yet, there are no clear answers. I'm so sorry for leaving you and Olivia to deal with all of this. So incredibly sorry." Reese felt so selfish. The guilt weighed heavily on her shoulders as she saw the heartbreak in her father's eyes. She felt incredibly anxious, wishing she had an anxiety drug to take herself. "Let's go see her." She took her dad's arm, holding him close to her side as they walked to the medical wing of Grace Center. Her mind raced. What am I going to see when I get there? Will she know me? I wish I could go back in time and just be her little girl again and not have to do this.

# CHAPTER 8

I have to get away from him. Her mind and body felt like an overloaded garbage can. Keeping her eyes barely open, she looked for a door, a window, anything that might give her a chance of escaping this guy who called himself a doctor. She attempted to check if he was in the room with her. The smell of alcohol and a musty odor made her nauseous. Carefully, she turned her head, attempting to focus. She tried to lift herself on her elbows but couldn't because of the straps that held her in place. There, in the corner, she saw him lurking.

"Going somewhere, are you?" he taunted her. "You should have known better than to try to escape. You are not going anywhere."

"Why?" she sobbed. "What did I do to you? Please tell me why I am here?"

"I told you before you should not have told my wife to leave me."

"I never told anyone to leave their husband. What's her name?"

"Janice. But it doesn't matter now. She's no longer with us, and that's your fault."

"How is that my fault?" She let her head rest back on the table trying to keep what little strength she had.

"You will never do another person's hair, ever again!" He pulled at a piece of her locks. "You were a bad, bad girl, so I took a couple of your fingers. That's lesson number two."

She struggled to look down at her hand. It was bandaged where her fingers would be. She screamed in horror.

"Now, it won't be long before your pain will be over." He poured water into her mouth.

She choked and spit what remained in her mouth into his face. "Fuck you, asshole! I don't know anyone named Janice."

"Now that's not nice," he wiped away the water from his cheek. "Time to go to sleep."

"No, get away from me," she writhed around trying to free herself.

It amused him watching her struggle. He flicked the syringe, a few droplets spurting from the needle. "Don't worry little lamb. This will help you relax."

# CHAPTER 9

Warren, Emerson, and Reese found Eve sitting in a chair with a posy, such a harmless-sounding word for such a dreadful device. She was tied down.

Eve was struggling to get out of the chair, a terrible look of frustration and fear on her face. Trying to stand up but not being able. Why can't I move? Someone help me." She looked at Reese, her face scrunched ready to cry, yet there were no tears. Just a look of "Help me."

Reese's dad went to the nurse's station. "I demand my wife's restraints be removed. Immediately!"

"Sir, it's for her protection," one nurse said. "It's too dangerous to leave her wandering around. She could walk right out the door and get hit by a car."

Emerson took his soon-to-be father-in-law's fist-clenched hand, "I'll handle this." He presented his shield to the nurse. "I would like to speak with your administrator right now!"

"She is busy interviewing families of possible new residents."

"Where is her office?" He slammed his badge on the counter.

The nurse jumped, startled. "Downstairs. First door on the

left." She couldn't care less about this guy's credentials. She didn't get paid enough to deal with this shit.

Emerson burst into the administrator's office. "I need to speak to you right now."

The administrator jumped to her feet. "Excuse me, I'm busy right this moment. You can't just burst into my office unannounced."

Emerson took out his badge and turned to the couple looking sitting across the desk. "If I were you, I would think of another place for your loved ones."

They stood and left the room quietly.

"What the hell do you think you're doing?"

"I'm Detective Emerson Lake. I am demanding an explanation for tying my mother-in-law to a chair when she can walk around unescorted. Don't you have alarms on the inside doors? If not, I suggest you have them installed immediately. Do I make myself clear? If I ever see her tied to a chair again, my next call will be to the state department and have you shut down." He walked out, slamming the door behind him. By the time he arrived back in Eve's room, a nurse was already removing the ties.

Emerson looked at Warren and shook his head. "I'm sorry you have to go through this, Dad. I guess it's part of life."

"Yes, but even after going to the class, I don't want to admit that I'm alone. My hopes and dreams of retirement being spent with my beautiful wife traveling are now gone. I stay in my wing alone. I eat alone. I have no one to speak to. Just alone. Even when Eve does remember me. It's short-lived."

Reese wiped away her own tears as she watched her mom

struggle to get up before the nurse finished. "It's going to be okay, Mom, I promise."

"So, does that mean you'll find Alicia? I know he took her; I just know it."

"Mom, who is Alicia?"

"You know, my hairdresser. She's missing. I know he took her away. I know it."

"Who took her, Mom? Do you know his name?"

"You know."

"No, I don't know his name. Can you tell me?"

A blank stare crossed Eve's face. Her eyes wrinkled, and her face twisted. The look of an old woman who had a very tough life, yet she hadn't had a tough life at all.

"Mom, do you know who I am? Can you say my name?"

"Oh, you know. Come on, let's go." She was anxious. She turned and started walking down the halls. Reese by her side.

My mom doesn't know me, Reese thought. She knew this would happen eventually, but she wasn't prepared for it so soon. It felt like someone shattered her heart into a million pieces.

"Do you think we can find her?" Eve asked. "I don't see her here. Do you think we should go to the salon? She might be in there. Yes, let's go to the salon. I'm already late for my appointment."

It surprised Reese at how much her mom sounded like a detective. Could this be something stuck in her mind, knowing I'm a detective? Yet she doesn't know my name.

"Mom, I don't think the salon is open today."

"Why wouldn't it be? Olivia is probably there."

"So, you know who Olivia is?"

25

"Of course, I do. Olivia is my daughter. You know her too, don't you?"

"Yes, Mom, we are sisters."

"Oh," Eve grimaced. "That would make you my other daughter, right?"

"Yes, Mom, I'm your other daughter."

"Of course, I know who you are. How are you today? Want to go for a walk with me? I'm looking for someone."

Reese found it a tiny bit less stressful; that her mom remembered her. Even if it was temporary.

Eve started back down the hallway. The same vacant stare suddenly returned.

What have I done to my sister, leaving her all this time, to deal with our mom's mind and our dad's anger? How can I make this up to Olivia?

"Mom, what day do you have an appointment with Alicia?"

"Today, of course."

Reese had a plan. "Let's go back to the nurse's station. I want to ask one of the staff if the salon is open yet." They turned the corner in silence, arriving at the desk. "Mom, I want you to sit with Emerson and Dad. I'll be right back." But Eve just continued walking back and forth down the halls, not saying a word.

"Which floor is the hair salon?" Reese inquired.

"It's on the ground floor, but we mark the elevators with a sign that reads Beauty Salon, so the patients that can go on their own don't get confused. I believe it's closed today. Although it's never locked. We just put a closed sign on the door, so the residents know."

"Thank you." Reese jumped in the elevator.

Once in front of the salon's glass door, she saw a man walking around inside. She opened the door, "May I help you?"

"Yes," he said. "I'm looking for Olivia."

"Okay, but how did you get into the salon?"

"I have a key. She gave me a spare one. Who the hell are you and why are you here? You certainly don't look like the cleaner. And certainly not a resident here."

"My name is Reese Clayton, and yours?"

"I'm Craig Stockton, Olivia's boyfriend. You are her sister, correct?" He walked closer to her. "It is so nice to meet you, Reese. I've heard such nice things about you. You're planning your wedding, I hear? Where is the lucky man?"

"Upstairs, with Mom and Dad. When we arrived in town, Olivia said you would be away for a while. I told her to take a break, and that Emerson and I could handle Mom and Dad."

"I texted Olivia that I was back, but she didn't answer so I got worried. I thought maybe she came here to clean the place up after she was done doing your mom's hair. Do you know where she went?"

"No, she didn't say."

"Okay, I have to leave to make a few calls. I'll probably see you later at her house. Nice to meet you and if you hear from Olivia, tell her I'm back for a few days. Also, Reese, if you need anything while you are here, just ask."

"Thank you, Craig. It was nice meeting you."

"You as well Reese." They shook hands.

Reese stood in the middle of the salon. She couldn't shake the feeling that something was off with Craig. Why did he say he had a spare key? The nurse said the salon is never locked.

The door opened again. This time, it was Emerson. "Who the hell was that? He practically ran me over on his way to the elevator."

"It's Olivia's beau. He's back in town and thought she might be here cleaning."

"He was sure in a hurry and nearly ran over the top of me. What the heck?"

"Be nice, Emerson," she warned. "That big oaf might be our brother-in-law one day."

# CHAPTER 10

Reese approached a nurse who had just started her shift.

"My name is Reese Clayton. My mom is a resident here, with Alzheimer's. Eve Clayton."

"Yes, I know her well," she responded.

"I know about the effects the disease has on the patient, and all that's about to come, but I wondered about her, well about her fixation on her stylist. She tells me she is missing. Would you know anything about that?"

"No Miss Clayton. Yet I am a bit surprised she didn't show up for your mom's appointment." She paused. "Maybe a week ago. Don't quote me on that. She loved your mom, it appeared. They got along so well. She would give her a big hug, after escorting her back to this unit. Few stylists care enough to help their clients find their way back to the floor."

"What happens if a resident is too ill to make it down to the salon?"

"Then the stylist will come to the room."

"Are the hair services included in the residents' monthly fee?"

We allow the stylists to come in and do the patients' hair if they wish. You know, keep them on a regular schedule. We don't pay them. The family takes care of that. The owner of the salon comes in, meets with a few people, and then leaves. She pays the facility rent and then collects from the families the amount owed through Grace Center."

"My sister Olivia Clayton owns a salon of her own," Reese said. "Close to here. It's a shame mom won't allow her to do her hair."

"I know what you mean. There is no rhyme or reason. Just the way the mind works. Alicia worked for your sister, didn't she?"

"Yes, she did. We don't know why she left or where she went afterward. But according to my sister, it happens a lot."

"I'm sorry. I wish I had better answers for you."

"Well, thank you for the information." Reese shook the nurse's hand.

Reese saw her mom walking back toward her and took her by the arm. "Let's head back to the room and see if Dad and Emerson are there, okay?"

"Okay."

When they arrived back to the room, Eve headed straight to the bed. "I'm tired." She pulled down the covers and climbed into bed, clothes, and shoes still on.

Emerson looked at Warren. "Are you okay Dad? Can we walk you back to your apartment?"

"No, it's better if I stay until she wakes from her nap. She's less frightened if I'm here."

Reese kissed him while grabbing Emerson's hand. "We'll be back. Are you ready to go, sweetheart?"

Emerson nodded. "Do you want me to stay with your dad,

Reese?"

"No! Please," Warren waved them toward the door. "I am fine. I may take a nap myself, right here in the recliner."

Reese kissed her mom's forehead. "Love you, mom. I'll see you soon."

"Okay, Reese."

Reese smiled from ear to ear. "Mom, you know my name."

# CHAPTER 11

"Emerson, I know you will think I'm nuts, but do you see a black SUV about five cars back?"

"Yes. But there are a lot of SUVs on the road. Not all of them look like the SUV limo.

"I think Peter is following us. I caught just a quick look at him when we got in our car. Not just the vehicle, Emerson, I saw him in it. Take a few rights and lefts and see what happens."

Emerson took a left at the next intersection and then another at Main Street.

"It appears we have lost him," he said. "I don't see him anywhere around."

"No, but for some strange reason, he is following us after we told him his services were no longer needed. Wait! Slow down. I see the limo."

"Where? I don't see it."

"It's parked at that bookstore on the corner."

Emerson glanced in the window as they drove by. "Shit, he's not in it."

"Only one way to find out where he went, sweetheart. Let's

window shop and maybe we'll run into him by accident. Find
out why he's still in town."

After parking the car, Emerson said "Let's go into the bookstore
first and then we can walk to the café and grab a bite to eat."

They walked hand in hand down the quaint street. "It is still
so lovely here, Emerson. I forgot how pretty this town is."

"It really is beautiful." Emerson opened the bookstore door
and motioned his lady inside. "Okay then let's take a walk
through the aisles of others' imaginations."

They browsed the stacks. Emerson stopped to pull a book
with an interesting cover. He thumbed through the pages, then
turned it over to read the back cover. "Must be wild being an
author."

"It doesn't appear our careers will ever allow us free time to
read, let alone write a novel." Reese said.

They continued to look around the bookstore for about 20
minutes. For Reese it was like taking a walk down memory lane
remembering her childhood. The excitement that she remembered was there, as the entire class would take a field trip to the
bookstore or a nearby farm. She recalled the aroma of the books.
Some were like fresh ink off a press. Others had an old, musty
odor. To her, those old ones were the best ones. The smell of
the farms on the other hand, smiling to herself, always had the
same odor. Cow patties.

Emerson found her daydreaming, looking at a row of young
adult books. "Well, Peter is not in here. Are you ready for lunch?"

"Yes, I was just reminiscing about my childhood."

They took the short walk to the café, holding hands, not
speaking a word.

It didn't take long for Peter to appear at their table while they were having lunch.

"I knew you two would stop in here if you saw the non-stretch. May I sit with you? I need to talk to you about something. Something important."

"Have a seat, Peter," Reese replied. "Now, why are you following us when we told you we didn't need your services? Did Emerson's dad insist you continue to do this? You're beginning to creep me out. The truth, no bullshit, got it? I have a badge and a gun but prefer not to use it."

"I got it." He paused for a few seconds before he began. "My name *is* Peter Andora. That is not a lie. I live close to the Cromwell Police Department in South Dakota. I know almost everything about the two of you."

"What?" Emerson nearly choked on his sandwich.

"That's not all. I am a special operative agent. My Marine background takes me to a lot of places where I have to perform some very unpleasant tasks. I've made plenty of enemies along the way. I know your father, Emerson. We crossed paths a long time ago and the FBI was called in to investigate. There was a heist involving a rare artifact that was on loan to your father's gallery.

"What kind of artifact?" Emerson asked. "My Dad never mentioned anything missing to me."

"He couldn't. Not if he wanted to keep his job. Or risk losing his funding for the art gallery. Thieves smuggled the item into a foreign country and my task was to retrieve it."

"So, what does this have to do with us coming to Vermont to see my family?" Reese asked.

"Your mother."

"What the hell are you talking about?"

"I received an anonymous call about a missing girl in Vermont. She was out with a few friends and suddenly disappeared from her group. I had to take the case but had to find a way to infiltrate the area without being seen or heard. I remembered seeing on the news that you and Reese were taking a leave of absence from the Cromwell Police Department to re-think your careers after your last case. The reports also mentioned you were planning a wedding in Reese's hometown. So, that's when I asked your dad for help, Emerson. He's the one who came up with the plan to have me become your chauffeur. He's quite a character. Loves getting into this spy stuff."

"I realized that when he could have died in that last case Reese and I were on. He thought it was a rush of excitement getting tied up and thrown into a van. I was furious with him."

"You couldn't come up with your own cover story? Some operative you are," Reese said, continuing the conversation.

"Listen, I could've found several ways to do this on my own, but the gift chauffeur idea seemed like the best way to get close to you Reese. I thought it would be the best way for me to get access to the nursing facility and speak to your mother without drawing too much attention."

"How the fuck would that help you. My mother has Alzheimer's!"

"I'm aware of her condition. Emerson's dad told me. But there are moments when these patients have complete clarity. I don't understand the reason, any more than you do, but it's my only hope."

"Only hope for what, Pete?" Emerson asked.

"The hairstylist your mom keeps talking about Reese...the fear your mom has that this girl has been taken is real. Her hairstylist is Alicia Holmes Andora. Her hairstylist is my daughter."

# CHAPTER 12

"Leave me alone! I don't want to wake up," she cried "Just kill me and get it over with, you monster."

He thrust his face just inches from her nose. "What would you know about monsters?"

"I know you're torturing me for something I didn't do. Cutting me up little by little until there is nothing left of me. That is what a sick bastard of a monster would do." She realized she wasn't as groggy as she was after the first couple of needles. I have to keep him talking. Maybe he will listen.

"You did a bad thing telling my wife to leave me. Now that is being a bad girl. Now you have to deal with my wife's death. It's all your fault."

"I told you; I don't know your wife. Can you tell me something about her, something that I may remember about her? You keep saying, it's my fault that she's dead and yet I don't even know what she looks like. How is that possible?"

Her ability to remain calm and keep him talking, after going through torture, surprised Alicia. "Maybe I'm more like my dad than I thought."

"Really? And who might your dad be?" the creepy voice returns.

"What?"

"Who is your dad?"

Fuck. Did I just say that out loud? She thought to herself. No one here is supposed to know about my dad. Far too dangerous.

"I just asked you who your dad is. Now tell me and make it the truth, or else!"

"Or else what, asshole?"

He slapped her hard across the face. "How's that for a what?"

Her cheek throbbed and her eyes watered, but she forced herself to look him dead in the eye refusing to answer.

He struck her again. This time, he used his fist, knocking her out.

# CHAPTER 13

"Okay, Reese said, "I'm trying to understand all of this. What you're telling me is that my mom knows someone kidnapped your daughter. How the hell would she know that?"

"I know it's bizarre, but this is my daughter we are talking about. I'm special ops, and if someone found out who she is, then that makes her the perfect bargaining chip. We had her change her name to Alicia Holmes instead of Andora. Holmes is her middle name. I know it's a weird middle name, but my late wife thought it would be so clever since we both love Sherlock Holmes."

"So, being the daughter of someone in your position, I'm assuming she knows how to contact you if there is trouble, right?" Reese asked.

"Yes, she does, but she hasn't, and I think she can't."

"I'm sorry about your wife," Emerson said. "What happened to her?"

"Her car went off an icy road. Two years ago. So, the report said anyway. The gas tank exploded, and she burned to death. Nothing left but ashes. To this day, I don't believe it."

Reese was curious. "What is it you don't believe? That it was an accident, or that it burned her to ashes?"

"All of it."

"So, if you and your wife lived in South Dakota, how did your daughter end up in Vermont? " Emerson inquired.

"About a year before the accident, Alicia took a trip to Vermont. She loved the area and wanted to stay. She said there were booth rentals available at a local salon and opportunities open as a stylist for the residents at Grace Center. She always wanted a career as a hairstylist, especially for older people. She has an exceedingly kind heart. I needed to protect my daughter, but also allow her to have a normal life. So, Vermont was where she chose. Quiet area, not much in the line of crime."

"Does she have a boyfriend here as well? Perhaps contact him," Reese asked.

"Never mentioned having a boyfriend, and I never asked. She's almost thirty. I'm sure she will tell me when she is ready. That's if she thinks something is serious. Right now, I need to find her. Do you think your mom will remember the guy she says took Alicia?"

"I don't know what she will say next. All she has said so far is, I know it was him. I know he took her. When I ask who, she says, oh you know that guy? I can contact my sister, Olivia, and see if Mom said anything more specific to her. Alicia rented a booth at her salon. Olivia just assumed she found work elsewhere when she didn't show up one day. She said it happens a lot with younger stylists."

"That's not like Alicia at all. Besides, she is not a kid, she is a grown woman. She may not appear that way, but she is. She has a college degree in communications but loves hair styling."

"You said earlier that Alicia went missing from a bar. She had been out with a group of friends. Have you been to the bar?" Reese asked.

"No, not yet. It was out of town, and I haven't figured out where yet."

"What about the 911 caller?"

"The 911 call was anonymous."

"She was with a group of people. Maybe they saw her having a drink or dancing with someone. Maybe they saw someone watching her. Have you interviewed any of them? That's the first thing I would do." Emerson said.

"No, I haven't found them yet."

"C'mom! You expect us to believe someone with your skills hasn't already done some of these simple things. Yet, you want to interrogate my mother who barely can remember her family. What the hell is wrong with this picture?" Reese stood to leave. "Mr. Andora, as we told you before, your services are no longer needed here. We are through talking." She shot a look toward the door. "Emerson?"

"Wait. Please?" Peter grabbed Reese's hand.

Reese pulled her hand away and walked toward the door while Emerson went to the cashier to pay the bill. When she looked back, the chairs were empty.

"Where in the hell did, he go, Emerson?" Reese pointed to the table.

"I don't know, but it appears we have a Houdini on our hands."

# CHAPTER 14

"What are you thinking about this whole scenario, Reese?" Reese caught her shoe on the carpet, losing her balance, but righting herself before they walked out the door. "Are you okay my love?" Grabbing her arm.

"Yes, just not paying attention to where I'm going. I'm not sure what is going on. I believe he thinks his daughter is missing and possibly in serious trouble. I just don't want a perfect stranger talking to my mom, Emerson. We have no idea what that conversation would do to her."

"The limo is gone." Emerson motioned toward the bookstore parking lot. "Now what?"

"Call your father hon, I think we need a bit more info than we are getting from our Chauffeur. And I'd like to make sure he is really who he says he is."

"I'll do that when we get back to your sister's house. First, I want to see where the limo came from. I have his plate number. He must have picked it up in Albany somewhere before we landed. Maybe we could get a positive ID on this guy."

"Why would you have his plate number?"

"I got it when you first said he was following us."

"Smart man Emerson!"

"Yes, I have my moments."

Pulling into Olivia's driveway, Reese noticed a car parked alongside the garage. "Now who the hell does that belong to?" Cautiously, Emerson and Reese approached the front door. Emerson with his hand near his gun. The door swung open before Reese could put the key in the lock.

"Hi, Reese! This must be the lucky man you're going to marry. I'm Craig Stockton," he thrust his hand out for Emerson to shake.

Emerson just nodded. "Is Olivia home already? I thought she be gone longer than this, right Reese?"

"No, not yet." Craig didn't budge from the doorway. "I stopped by to see if maybe she had come home. I still can't get her to answer my texts or my phone calls. Where did you send her to relax?"

"I didn't send her anywhere. I just told her to take a break from Mom and Dad for a few days."

"I only have one day left in town. I was hoping to see her before I leave."

"How did you get in here, anyway?" Reese asked. "Oh, never mind. You have a key."

"Right," Craig nodded. "Well, if you hear from her, please let her know I was here and I'm leaving tomorrow for New York City. If she would like to join me in between meetings, tell her to contact me." He pushed past the detectives and headed to his car. "Nice to meet you, Emerson."

Emerson gave him a wave as he mumbled a few letters and numbers under his breath. "Got it, Hon."

# CHAPTER 15

Reese opened the front door cautiously, not knowing if this guy was looking for her sister, or just breaking into her house.

"Emerson, check the bedrooms. I'll check out the kitchen, bath, and living room."

Everything appeared in order.

"Holy shit, Reese. Come look at this."

"What?"

"Who is the guy in this photo? They look chummy, don't you think?"

Reese looked at the photo on the mantle, panic weaving through every nerve in her body.

"Who the hell is that? If that's her boyfriend, then who the hell just broke into her house with us right here while he did it?"

"I don't know Emerson, but he broke into the Grace Center salon too."

"Do you have Olivia's cell phone number, Reese? We need to ask her a few questions."

"Of course, I do. And I'm sure she will answer, knowing Mom's situation." She called her number and put it on the speaker.

Olivia answered on the first ring. "Is something wrong with Mom and Dad?"

"No, they are fine. I need to ask you a couple of questions, though."

"Seriously, Reese? My big, hot-shot sister can't be alone with our parents for a few fucking days without my help. Why did you bother coming home at all?"

Emerson grabbed the phone. "Listen to me, you little shit, this is serious, and it's not about your parents. There's a photo on your fireplace mantle. It's you and a man. Is that your boyfriend, Craig?"

"Of course, it's Craig. Why?"

"Describe him."

"Blonde hair, blue eyes, around six feet tall. Buff body. You guys are scaring me. What is this about?"

"Have you given anyone a key to this house or the salon at the nursing facility?"

"Jesus, Emerson, no, only to you guys and there is no key to the salon at the Grace Center, not that I'm aware of, at least."

"Have you told anyone where you are right now?"

"No."

"Check your phone, see if there are any calls you may have missed that you don't recognize."

"No, I see nothing at all."

"Have you told Craig where you are?"

"No, I haven't talked to him since I left the house, needed some alone time."

"Okay. I'm going to give the phone back to your sister. In the meantime, I am sending a car for you. Tell Reese the address of where you are right now. I'll be back on the line in a minute with more instructions."

"Damn it Reese, what is happening? You just can't leave me hanging like this."

"I'm sorry to ruin your free time, Liv, but this will not be something you want to hear. When we returned to your house a little while ago, a man who claimed he was Craig Stockton greeted us. Looks nothing like the photo on the fireplace."

"What?"

"That's not all. It's the same guy I saw in the beauty salon at Grace Center. He said he was looking for you. Said his name was Craig Stockton, called me by name, and knew I was your sister. Please listen to Emerson, if not me, sis. This is serious and extremely dangerous for you. We need to find this guy now. Mom might be right about Alicia."

"Oh my god, sis! I'm scared."

"I know you are. Me too. Hang on a minute. Emerson has the info you need."

Emerson took down the address of where Olivia was staying and instructed her on what to do and who was coming to get her. "Do not, under any circumstances, get into your own car."

"Please, hurry, I'm so scared." Olivia's shaking hands made it difficult to hold the phone.

"Listen to me, Olivia. Do not call anyone or take any calls from anyone except me or Reese. Not even Craig, do you understand?"

"Yes, I hear you and I won't, I promise."

"We love you. Both of us."

"Me too."

Reese ended the call. "Emerson, who are you sending to get my sister?"

"Our limo driver."

# CHAPTER 16

"Well, well, well. You're awake. Are you going to behave this time? I just want to make love to you now. I'm missing my wife."

"I don't know why I'm here. You claim I told your wife to leave you. I've never had a conversation like that in my life, with anyone, not just my clients. Why do you think it was me?" She tried to remain calm and keep him talking like her dad had once taught her.

"You are her hairstylist, that's why. She told me it was you."

"Who told you it was me, Sir? I don't know how many times I need to tell you; that I don't know anyone named Janice."

"My wife. Or I should say, my late wife, told me her hairstylist's name. That was just before I made love to her one last time. She didn't want me, but I insisted. That was right before I smothered her with a pillow."

"Oh my god, are you kidding me?" Alicia tried like hell to stay calm and talk to this idiot. "If you loved her, why would you kill her? Why would you rape her and then kill her? Why not just let her go, let her leave you? Would you want someone who doesn't want you? I don't get it." She waited for his next move.

"No one gets to leave me. No one ever gets to leave me, OLIVIA. At least not alive."

Alicia fought like hell to control herself. Breathe. "I remember you," she whispered. "Now I remember you. My client Eve has Alzheimer's and she wandered off while I was in the bathroom. I found her in the parking lot talking to you while you were waiting to pick up your wife."

"She said I was a bad man. Why would she say that to me?"

"She must have overheard your wife talking to *her* hairstylist. May I tell you something?" she asked before losing her patience. "I don't know who the fuck you are, but you do not know me either. My name is not Olivia," she screamed. "It's Alicia Holmes. My boss Olivia is your wife's hairstylist, not me."

"Liar!" In a vicious rage, he kicked over the cart next to the table sending objects scattered to the floor. "You should never lie to me, for I will hurt you." He walked around to the back of her head. "You will kneel to me and confess your sins."

"Now you're going to speak to me like you are God. How the fuck can I kneel to you if I have no legs, you moron? You made a mistake. You will kill me too. So do it! Just get it over with. What are you waiting for?"

She saw his shadow on the wall, swinging something above his head and everything went black.

# CHAPTER 17

"Emerson, what were you thinking?" Reese smacked the back of his head.

"Hey! What was that for?" he smoothed down the hairs she ruffled with her swipe.

"Peter is going to get my sister. Are you serious? We know nothing about him."

"We do now. I contacted our friend from the FBI. She knows all about our Peter Andora."

"Are you talking about Carly Brown?"

"Yes. And she confirmed he's telling the truth. He is who he claims to be, and yes, he is involved in a situation right now and fears some extremely dangerous people took his daughter."

"It didn't take long for her to become firmly embedded. Geez, that was fast. Cromwell PD lost a smart young lady when the FEDS offered her a job she couldn't refuse."

"Yes indeed. Anyway. She gave me enough info to trust him. Trust him with your sister's life. I called his cell and asked if he would do this for us and in return, we would help him find his daughter. I also told him we would allow him to speak to your mom. Gave him my word, Reese. Are you okay with that?"

"I'll let you know when I see my sister enter this door."

"In the meantime, I'm going to contact Vermont State Police. Get the forensics team here to take prints off of anything this guy, who claims he is Craig Stockton, might have touched while he was here in your sister's house."

"The Grace Center salon as well, Emerson. Remember, he was there too. I'm going to call Dad and make sure he doesn't leave Mom's side until we figure this out."

"Good idea."

"Reese, there is something else you should know. Carly looked up Craig Stockton for me. I sent her a screenshot of his photo on the mantle. He is a high-tech business executive who lives in New York City. Also owns a home in California."

"So, that makes sense why he's gone a lot."

Emerson wrinkled his brow. "Reese there is something else. Craig Stockton is married with two girls and a boy."

"Shit, I wonder if Olivia knows this and is still dating the sleazy bastard?"

"Just be cautious about bringing this up, Reese. The relationship between the two of you may be in the first stage of repair, but this info could ruin it all coming from you. I say let it be as it is, for now anyway."

"It just makes me furious; she is a beautiful, successful woman. Anyone would be lucky to have her as a girlfriend, or a wife."

"She has enough on her plate right now. Let's get this straightened out first."

"I know. You're right. I'll keep it to myself for now, but I won't leave Vermont until she knows about this creep."

The forensics team arrived as Emerson requested. There were prints everywhere, but the doorknob, on the inside of the front door was the clearest. "We'll let you know as soon as we can, detectives."

Detective Clayton thanked the team.

"What now?" Reese asked. "When do you think Peter will get Olivia back here?"

"I would say a few hours by the time he gets to her and back again. isn't that far, probably about two and a half hours one way."

"I'm famished. Let's order in. I don't want to leave the house unattended. Especially if this guy returns."

Emerson stuck his head in the fridge, "Sounds like a plan since there is nothing in here." Emerson paused as he pulled his head from the refrigerator door and then slowly closed it. He signaled Reese, his finger to his lips grabbing her arm. He led her away from the kitchen, out the back door, looking at the roof line, and around the shrubs.

She glared at him, mouthing the words, "What's wrong?"

"There's a camera inside the refrigerator."

# CHAPTER 18

Reese's phone vibrated. "Peter. That was fast. You made it in good time getting there. Anything wrong? Is Olivia, okay?"

"I haven't gone to the door yet. I don't want to scare her. Call her and tell her I'm outside her cabin. Tell Olivia what I look like."

"I'll do that right now."

Peter waited patiently for Olivia to come out of her cabin in beautiful Lake Placid. When she did, he was star-struck at her beauty. Her eyes penetrating green, hair the color of a blonde goddess. And the tiny little body.

"What's wrong?" she asked. "You are Peter, I presume."

"Yes, ma'am." He showed her his driver's license.

"Are you two ok to travel?" Reese was still on the line with her sister.

"We're ready to leave now thanks. See you soon."

Peter helped Olivia lift her luggage into the car.

"Geez! That's the most significant SUV I've ever seen."

"That's because it's a limousine. With all the bells and whistles," he held the door as she slid in the passenger seat. "Bar in - the back included."

"Is it stocked?"

"Yes, ma'am."

"I should have sat in the back."

"You still have time to change seats."

"No, I'm fine. Just surprised by all of this."

"Sorry to take you away from your mini vacation. May I call you Olivia?"

"Yes, you may."

"It's a beautiful place."

"It is, and the perfect escape from everything that is going on with mom and dad."

"I have not been to Lake Placid. I'll have to return one day to appreciate its beauty. The Adirondack mountains are like giant fences enveloping the town. Protecting it somehow."

"Too bad you're here under these circumstances or I would show you around. Maybe some other time."

"Thank you, Olivia, I would like that."

She turned to face the window, smiling. Peter saw her reflection smile in the side mirror.

"So, this is what my sister rides around in?"

"No, I'm a gift from Emerson's father. Like a pre-wedding gift for a much-needed vacation."

"You think my sister needs a vacation? From what? Sitting her ass at a desk all day."

Peter was a little surprised at how little she thought of her sister's work. "That's the furthest thing from the truth, Olivia. You have no idea the things we see and have to do every day. I'm a special operations agent. Ex-Marine. This was the safest way to get you back home. Olivia, your mom's stories about the missing hairdresser are correct. Alicia Holmes is my daughter. We changed her last name long ago. Some terrible people may have taken her. Reese and Emerson are going to help me find her. I just hope it's not too late."

"Oh my God Peter I am so sorry. I like Alicia, she is a sweet girl and a great stylist. What about your wife? Does she know what's going on?"

"My wife died. A couple of years ago. I just can't convince the right people that her death was not an accident."

"I'm so very sorry Peter. About all of this."

"I need your help too, with your mom. Has your mom ever said a name or described the man that she believes took Alicia?"

"Of course, I will do whatever I can, Peter, but she has never said anything other than *he* took her. I'm not sure what I can do. Are you aware of Mom's condition?" "She has Alzheimer's. The doctors feel the middle to late stages of it. Although I do not know where or how they come up with that stages crap."

"I am aware of your mom's disease. The patients can have moments of complete clarity, and I am hoping we can be there at one of those times."

"Of course, Peter, I am sorry about all of this and certainly sorry I just took it for granted that your daughter, Alicia...."

"What? Go ahead. You can tell me what you thought about Alicia."

"I guess I'm just getting hardened to the way people are these days. Your daughter is a nice girl. We got along great, but I never let myself get close to any of my booth renters. Loyalty is rarely in the cards for me." Olivia started to squirm in her seat. "Why the hell am I telling you all of this? I have only known you for a few hours. If that. And I'm starving. Is there something substantial in the back seat to eat?"

Peter chuckled, "I noticed a restaurant on the way to get you. We are only about one hour away from your house, but let's stop and eat before we get there."

"So, you only saw one restaurant on the way to get me?" She made a face at him. "I thought you guys had all-seeing eyes while on the job."

He shook his head. "A bit of a ball buster, are we?"

She held out her hand, thumb and index finger poised close together. "Lil bit."

He went around and opened the car door for her, escorting her into the restaurant.

The eatery served home-cooked food, nothing frozen, all fresh. "Nice job, Sherlock," she chided him. "Very nice."

Peter looked at her, staring straight into her eyes, a concentrated stare.

"What's wrong? I was just kidding with you. I'm sorry."

The oversized menu dropped from Peter's fingers and his brow furrowed as he gazed at his companion. "No apology necessary. What would you like to eat?"

"I think I'll have beef stew. That looks good and I haven't had a beef stew in years."

Peter nodded to the server and asked her to bring them a red wine.

"Well," Olivia said. "That's a first. How did you know I liked red wine?"

"Because that's a detail someone named Sherlock would know." He said smiling at her.

# CHAPTER 19

Reese was the first to hear the car pull into the driveway. She had her weapon at her side as she cautiously pulled the drapery back. One look and she knew it was them. She flung the door open. The love for her sister overwhelmed her as she charged out the door in a flat-out run toward that gem of a vehicle called a limo.

Olivia jumped from the front seat before Peter could open the door for her—something he was used to doing for his late wife.

Reese and Olivia grabbed each other like long-lost friends. Both shed tears, and both whispered, "I'm sorry."

Emerson joined the reunion and shook Peter's hand. "Thank you for getting her back safely."

Peter gave him a nod.

"Come in and rest for the evening Peter. We have plenty of rooms," Olivia said. "You are welcome to stay the night."

"Thank you, but I can tell you need some sister time alone, with no shop talk."

"Nonsense, Peter. We need to come up with a plan to get

Alicia back. Shit, now I'm sounding like my sister and her handsome beau."

They all laughed.

Reese hugged Olivia again. "I am so glad you are safe."

Emerson gave them both a big bear hug.

All of them planted themselves in the living room, each with a sheet of paper and a pen.

Emerson took charge. "Okay, let's begin."

"Olivia, when was the last time you saw Alicia?" Reese asked.

"I saw her at the Grace Center hair salon. Let me think for a minute. You and Emerson arrived on Tuesday. I think it was the week before you arrived, sis. Pretty sure it was the Tuesday before."

"That was over a week ago," Peter hung his head, placing his hands over his face.

"Peter, somehow you have to get it out of your head that Alicia is your daughter," Emerson said. "Think of this as another special ops task. Think man think!"

"She is probably dead already," Peter ran his fingers through his thick hair. "And it's my fault." His hands shook.

"Damn it, Peter!" Olivia jumped all over him. "Knock it off. You don't have a body. Do you? Do you?" She repeated. "I'm guessing she didn't go out with her friends until the weekend, am I right? Isn't that when the kids go out these days? On Saturday nights."

Emerson squeezed Reese's hand. "She's right. It's likely only been a few days. When did you get the anonymous phone call about that she had gone missing?"

"Saturday night about 3 am. So, it was technically Sunday

morning." Peter sat up straight. "When did your mom start talking about her being taken?"

"That's the odd part," Olivia said. "She has been saying this stuff for at least a month now."

"This is just a theory," Reese said. "What if she believes it was Alicia because she overheard someone's conversation? How many clients does Alicia have in the facility besides mom, Liv?"

"I have never heard of her doing anyone's hair there, except for Mom, of course."

"Olivia," Peter asked, "were you ever working with your clients in the salon at the same time Alicia was doing your mom's hair?"

"Yes, of course. I split my time between my salon and the one at Grace Center. More so because I can keep a closer eye on my parents by being there. Mostly for Dad's sanity right now."

"I need you to write down your clients' names and contact info. Please. And anything you know about each of them. I'm guessing that's almost everything about their lives, knowing how much people tell their stylists."

"Yep, you can say that again. I hear more than any bartender or psychiatrist."

"While you do that, Emerson, can I borrow you? I want to visit the Vermont State LEOs. I need to know more details about the BOLO they issued when the 911 call came in. They just can't know who I am. Not yet anyway. Understand?"

"Absolutely." Emerson gave Peter's shoulder a strong squeeze. "We can leave first thing in the morning. It's getting late. PD is only about a mile from here. Reese, are you okay to handle the home front? I think we can get more info if Peter and I show up as a duo."

"Yes, I will check all doors and windows this time, sweetheart. No one is getting in here alive. So, you better call before you come waltzing in the door."

"Yeah," Olivia said. "I don't want my sister shooting the man of her dreams. And I don't want her to attack Sherlock here."

Peter locked eyes with Olivia. Hearing her call him that name again gave him a shiver…or was it butterflies?

# CHAPTER 20

Alicia wanted to kill him, but she remembered the lessons her dad taught her. Keep calm and keep talking to your captor as though he is human.

"I forgive you. It was a mistake. Why hurt me anymore by leaving me here alone? Why not help me?"

He paced the room silently, intertwining his fingers, then cracking his knuckles.

"Do you want me to die?" She asked. "Because if that were true, I think you would have done it by now."

He knew she was right.

"Tell me about your wife. Do you have children together? Please talk to me. Maybe I can help you."

"No one can help me," he replied. "I've already hurt too many people."

"Meaning what?"

"I've done things to people who lied to me and hurt me."

"That's what we humans do, right? We hurt the ones we love the most. Your wife must have loved you at some point, right? Why else would she marry you?"

It's not love that excites me, he thought. It's power. "I remember my father told me when my mom disappeared that a woman should always obey her husband."

"Did your father hurt your mother? Tell me what happened."

Mom deserved what she got, he thought.

"Why did you remove my clothes when I was under sedation?"

"I just enjoyed looking at how beautiful you are, and it reminded me of how my wife looked."

A sudden bolt of pain rushed down Alicia's legs like an electric current. "Oh my god, my legs! The pain is unbearable." Her heart rate was climbing. "I can't breathe. Help me! Please help me!"

He ran to her side. "If I help you, will you allow me to make love to you?"

"Yes, yes!" she cried. "Anything you want, just make the pain go away. I can't breathe."

He pushed the medication through the IV behind her. She closed her eyes, praying the dosage wasn't strong enough to knock her out. Quickly, the pain began to subside. She soothed herself by moaning, then pretending to drift off to sleep. She knew if she was going to survive at all, she would have to do as he asked.

He unhooked the straps that held her down. Then positioned her to accommodate his wishes. He moved her thighs apart, stroking her gently to lubricate her. Kissing her breasts, hoping that when she woke, she would know how gentle he could be.

He climbed on top of her and unzipped his trousers. He shimmied his pants and briefs down his thighs admiring himself as he exposed his manhood. This is my greatest source of power, he thought. He was startled when her hand suddenly clenched his penis with her the bandaged hand. His head snapped back as she yanked his hair with her other free hand. What the hell is happening? She must like it rough.

Using every ounce of strength she had, Alicia rolled over on her side, dumping him on the floor. She grabbed his tie before he fell. Pulling tighter and tighter. His pants wrapped around his feet as he slid side to side trying to regain his footing. His mouth gaped open trying to suck any trickle of air as he tried to loosen her grip. Both hands holding onto that tie trying to break it free from his neck. He could feel his body weakening. His vision was fading.

"Die, you fucking piece of shit. Die!" Alicia pulled tighter until his body slumped and his hands fell away from his neck.

Alicia was weak and nauseous. She threw up on his face, still not letting go of his tie. The pain returned quickly to her legs and feet.

For the first time since her captivity, she was able to look at the end of the table and was confused. "You didn't cut off my legs?" She raised her bandaged hand, "I'll bet I still have my fingers too!"

The pain and whatever drug he gave her was overpowering. Very weak, she vomited again. She fell backward on the table, losing consciousness. Losing her grip on his tie.

# CHAPTER 21

"Can I ask you a question, Pete, before we get to the police department?"

"Depends."

Emerson laughed. "Depends on what? Whether I decide to toss your ass out of the car or not. Smart ass. Seriously. How is it that no one will listen to you about your wife's accident? You're not just an off-the-street guy who is grieving the loss of his wife. Something is seriously wrong with that picture."

"There certainly is something wrong. Either I pissed off someone, or there's a group that doesn't want me interfering with their business."

"I'm guessing a combination of both. You said there was nothing left of her but ashes. Were the ashes taken to the labs for DNA testing? You're sure it's her?"

"Yes. It's her." He hung his head.

"Did they offer you any of her ashes from the accident? You know, like cremains, from a funeral home."

"Yes. It's a nightmare to do it once, but to have it done twice will probably haunt me forever. I need her to rest. So, I can rest.

I'm not sending her to another lab. That's what you're thinking, right?"

"It was just a suggestion." Emerson began to fidget behind the wheel. "I'm sorry I brought it up."

"I had them sent to a funeral home where we used to live. Our daughter wanted a service for her. So, we did. It was just the two of us. Judy didn't have any family left. Losing her so suddenly shocked me, and I don't think I'll ever find peace of mind, my friend."

"I can't imagine what you are going through, although I came very close."

"What the hell happened? Oh, never mind. I remember Reese's car exploded on your last case, right?"

"Yes, right after a good friend pulled her out of the car. He saw a red light flashing under her wheel. Thanks to him, I still have the love of my life. We're friends with a few FBI agents. Carly Brennen used to work in our precinct in South Dakota. She's in the New York City field office now. Maybe they could help without interfering with your work.

"Oh, I don't know about that."

"One more thing before we head into the police department," said Emerson, now being a little cautious with this question. "What's your wife's maiden name?"

"Maxwell, Judith Maxwell. Why?"

"I was just curious. You said she always used her maiden name because of your job. Did she have any enemies? Anyone who had an issue with her? Maybe a coworker?"

"I've been racking my brain for two years trying to figure out who would want to hurt her."

HER NAME IS EVE

"And what did you come up with?"

"What do you mean?"

"I'm not stupid, I know you have an idea. You just didn't stop living when she died. You must know something."

Peter shook his head. Thoughts running through his head. Do I want to trust my gut with this guy?

"C'mon, Pete. If you think you can do this on your own, then tell me now. Trust is a big issue I understand. Say the word, and I'll stay the hell out of it."

Pulling into the parking lot of the Vermont State Police, Peter turned toward Emerson. "I need your help to prove there was a large sum of money involved in her death."

Emerson reached out his hand. Peter shook it.

# CHAPTER 22

Emerson and Peter approached the dispatcher at the front desk of the Vermont State Police Department.

"Detective Emerson Lake," he flipped his gold badge on the desk. "This is Peter Andora. We understand there is a BOLO out for a missing young lady. Alicia Holmes. Can you tell us some details? Where she went missing? What time of day was it when the 911 call came in? Who reported her missing?"

The dispatcher took a closer look at the badge. "Detective Lake, is it? You're a long way from South Dakota. What's the deal? Do you know this young woman?"

"Not personally. My fiancé's sister, who lives here in Manchester, employed her. Olivia Clayton. We came to visit her and found out Alicia was missing. I'm investigating her disappearance."

"And your fiancé's name?"

"Detective Reese Clayton."

"Really? I knew her from high school. How is she doing? Gosh, it seems so long ago."

"It was. We are not getting any younger, and every time we

try to plan our wedding, something comes up. I'll tell her you were asking for her. What's your name?"

"Dispatcher George Reagan." He shook Emerson's hand. He reached for Peter's. "You a local?"

"No, I'm not. I'm his best man, though."

George nodded. "I'll see what we have for you, detective."

He took forever, or at least it seemed like it, to pull the info from the computer. "Here it is. The call came in at 3 a.m. according to the national database. From South Londonderry, about 10 miles from here. No name, burner phone. The message conveyed that someone had taken Alicia, her friend, from Kyle's Tavern and she did not return. The caller expressed concern for Alicia, stating that a well-dressed man led her out of the bar. The caller also said Alicia seemed unsteady on her feet but was only drinking club soda all night. Claims they tried to call her a few times but went straight to voice mail. That's all we have on the case so far."

Emerson asked, "Did anyone inform Alicia's relatives?"

"No. So far, we couldn't find anyone connected to her."

"Thanks for your help. We'll be in touch, and I'll let Reese know you're the dispatcher here. I'm sure she'll want to stop in to say hello. Here's my card. If you hear anything else, please call me day or night. Oh, one more thing. Can I get a printout of that?"

"Of course."

Peter didn't say a word on the ride back to Olivia's house.

Emerson threw the car in park, "Look, Pete, snap out of it. When it's your own family, you just want to kick the shit out of whoever did this. I get it. But right now, I think Alicia has to come first, don't you? I promise I will help you find out what happened to both your wife and daughter.

Peter didn't say a word. He just nodded as he opened the car door.

"Wait, Peter, Jesus. Are you crazy? I wouldn't go near the front door without calling first. Reese will shoot first and take names later."

"That's right, I forgot about that." He hopped back in the passenger seat. "I think I need a drink, a strong one." Tears welled up in his eyes. "First my wife and now my baby."

Peter's anger did not surprise Emerson or the tears that he tried to hide unsuccessfully.

"I guess you're not the hard ass, I thought you were," Emerson elbowed him in the arm, trying to make light of the situation before entering the house.

"See what I'm like when I get my hands on whoever is doing this to my family?"

Emerson picked up his phone to call Reese and saw her text. *We're headed to Grace Center. I'll text you when we're on our way home.* "We're safe to go in. The girls are at the nursing home."

Emerson texted her back. *Peter and I are heading to Londonderry to check out something and then grab a bite. See you shortly. LUV you.*

# CHAPTER 23

Reese feared there could be more hidden cameras in the house. It was an uneasy feeling, so she and Olivia decided to have lunch and visit their parents. Before they left, Reese secretly placed a large metal pot of water in the fridge right in front of the camera.

Arriving at Grace Center, Reese asked Olivia. "What do you think? Mom or Dad first?"

"I say, Mom. I can usually rely on leaving with a better attitude with Dad."

Reese chuckled. "I hear you loud and clear, sis. Mom it is."

When they arrived at Eve's room, they were surprised to see her sitting on the bed and Dad in the recliner. "Are you okay, Mom? What's wrong?" Olivia was concerned. Eve stared vacantly at the wall; her face contorted as if she were ready to bawl.

"Mom, do you know who I am?" Reese placed her hand on her frail shoulder.

"My daughter Reese."

Olivia carefully sat at the foot of her mom's bed. "And who

am I?"

Eve never broke her gaze at the wall. "My daughter Olivia. Why the stupid questions?"

"Is there something you want to say to us, Mom?" Olivia asked.

"I'd like to go home now."

"Why?" Reese asked. "Don't you like it here? This is your new home, remember?"

"No!" she exclaimed firmly, brushing Reese's hand away from her shoulder "This is not my home, and I don't want to die here."

"Mom! That's an awful thing to say." Olivia wanted to suddenly cry. "Why do you think you're going to die? Do you feel sick?"

"No! Damn it. But I will die if he finds me."

Reese and Olivia were stunned. Olivia tilted her head toward the door. Reese shook her head no to her sister.

"Mom, do you know who is trying to hurt you?"

Eve finally broke her eyes away from the wall and faced Olivia. "You know."

"Mom, look at me." She pulled Eve's shoulders toward her. "Mom, who is it you think I know?"

Eve scowled at Olivia. "I want to go now." She stood up and headed out to the hall.

"Olivia, we'll be right back." Reese followed Eve into the hall. Olivia followed a few feet behind. "Mom, tell me who Olivia knows that's trying to hurt you. Please tell me."

"He took her. I know he did. Why won't you believe me?"

"Because I need a name or a description, something to help

me find out who is trying to hurt you."

"Doctor."

"Doctor? Is it a doctor who's trying to hurt you? Mom, does he have another name?"

"Levis."

"Mom, was he wearing jeans?" Olivia had to ask. "Is that what you're trying to tell us?"

"Let's go." Eve continued pacing the halls. Never saying another word. After about 10 minutes, she re-entered her room. Standing still.

"Dad, are you up for keeping a close eye on Mom for us?" Reese asked.

"Yes," he said, "I've got this end."

They both helped Mom get into the chair next to her husband, watching as she grabbed his hand, gently intertwining her fingers with his.

# CHAPTER 24

Emerson and Peter arrived at Kyles Tavern in Londonderry, just as the lunch crowd was piling in for beer and free pickled eggs.

"Geez, that's shit I would never try," Emerson wrinkled his nose at the oversized mayonnaise jar sitting on the bar. Eggs bobbing up and down in a nasty yellow liquid. "Who the hell ever thought of that idea, especially with beer?"

"It's not bad," Peter laughed. "Not that I want it every day, but I have tried it."

"Better you than me, pal. I have to say," Emerson looked around, "it's pretty damn clean for a bar. Even the table linens are clean. Although the bar is full, not the tables." Emerson noticed.

"Yeah, I expected a lot less. From a local bar."

"A pretty good size stage for bands, too. At least your daughter wasn't hanging out in a dive."

A server came out from a back room, nice looking, not a kid, maybe mid to late thirties.

"Hi guys, this table by the window, okay?"

"Perfect," Peter replied.

"My name is Liz. Can I get you something to drink?" She handed them both a menu.

"I'll have a Bud, Liz." Emerson made eye contact with the young woman.

"I'll have the same," Peter said.

"Would either of you like a free pickled egg to start?"

"Not today," Emerson shook his head. "We're both riding in the same car."

She laughed at the remark. "I get it. Be right back with your drinks."

"Where do we start?" Peter asked.

"I think we start a conversation with the server."

Peter nodded.

Liz brought them their lunch, which they both seemed to enjoy without saying so.

"What's for dessert?" Peter asked while Liz cleared their plates. "I have a sweet tooth."

"Seriously?" She smiled. "You're not from around here, are you? It's fall in Vermont. Apple pie. Homemade apple pie, of course."

"Ooh," Emerson rubbing his hands together. "I'll have that."

"Make it two. With vanilla ice cream, please."

"You got it. And I'm guessing you'll have the same?" She nodded toward Emerson. "Coffee for you both?"

"Absolutely!" Emerson could never pass up a la mode.

When she returned, Peter asked, "So, how long have you worked here?"

"Since I was in my teens," she answered. "And that was too long ago to say."

"Do you mind if we pick your brain a little?" Emerson asked. "If you have time."

"What do you want to know?"

"I'm sure you know about the girl who went missing after leaving this establishment last week."

"Her boss is frantic, that no one has heard from her," Peter said. "We were hoping you might know something that could help us."

She wrinkled her brow. "We already told the police everything we know. Are you guys cops?"

"No. My fiancé's sister, Olivia, is her boss. They are hairstylists. We came here from South Dakota to make wedding plans with family, and Olivia was planning to have Alicia do a trial run of hair and makeup on my fiancé while we were in town. Now she's missing. And we're all worried about her. Looks like we hit a dead end, Peter. Oh, I'm sorry, my name is Emerson Lake, and this is my best man, Peter Andora. Thank you for your time, Liz."

"Yes, good food, and even better service," Peter winked. "Can we get the bill, please?"

"Separate checks?"

"One is fine," Emerson said. "I guess I have to treat him nice if he is my best man."

Liz walked away to retrieve the tab. When she returned, she ripped the check from her pad and smiled. "Have a great day and thank you for stopping in." She laid the check on the table and slid an additional piece of paper underneath.

# CHAPTER 25

Her entire body ached. The drugs were starting to wear off. What did he do to me now? She was groggy but found the strength to lift her head. She couldn't see him anywhere. Where did he go? She glanced down at the table and realized she was still naked.

"Oh my god! Did you rape me?"

Silence.

"I know you're here. You're a piece of shit!" She banged her fists on the table and realized she wasn't restrained. What the hell? He didn't secure the straps. She lifted herself onto her elbows to see where her abductor was hiding but couldn't see him anywhere. She leaned over the side of the table and saw his lifeless body on the floor. His face was blue, eyes still open and bulging. The tie was still around his neck.

"I hope you're dead, you sick bastard." Droplets of spittle spewed from her mouth in his direction. Panic hit her like a ton of bricks. "How do I get out of here?"

She moved her legs a little to see if it might be possible to stand, getting them to the edge of the slab. The opposite side to avoid disturbing the body. The pain was excruciating. Carefully, she eased her feet downward toward the floor. Her hands slipped and her legs could not hold her weight. She fell screaming in pain.

"You fuck, you lousy fuck, you broke my knees." She started to cry. Not sure if it was due to the pain or fear. How could she escape? She wanted to scream for help, but what if he wasn't dead and woke up? She took a deep breath. I have to get out of here. She looked around the room and couldn't see a door or window. Rolling over on her stomach, she tried inching herself toward the head of the slab to get a fresh look. Still crying, she kept pulling herself forward with her hands, now becoming raw and bloodied from the concrete floor. She ripped away the bandage that covered three of her fingers. She was right. He didn't amputate her fingers, but he had pulled out three of her nails. Now angry that she removed the only protection from the concrete, she stopped crying and said a brief prayer for help. But no one came.

"Think! Think! What would Dad do?"

She strained to pull herself to a sitting position. Her breasts were bloody and raw from pulling herself across the floor. Forget trying to scoot on her naked ass. She couldn't imagine the damage the concrete would do down there. She glanced around in the dim light and caught a glimmer of hope. She saw a door. Ok, no stairs. That's a relief. I'm not in a basement, but I need to get to that door. A wave of pain flooded over her body. It made her dizzy and weak. She could feel herself losing consciousness again. No, this can't be happening again. As her body slumped over, she saw a silhouette of a woman in the doorway.

"Mom? Mom, help me, please." She reached her hand out toward the vision as everything went black.

# CHAPTER 26

Emerson put the piece of paper in his wallet with his change after leaving Liz a generous tip.

"What was that?" Peter asked.

"Let's go. Now!" Emerson whispered.

Once out of the area, Emerson pulled off the road.

"What's going on?"

Emerson reached for his wallet, looking around to see if they were being followed. "She wrote something on a piece of paper." He unfolded the sheet. "It's a name. Dr. Levy."

"What the hell? She knows something about Alicia's disappearance. Turn around. We need to find out more."

"Peter, snap the fuck out of it. Use your fucking head, man. I know it's your kid, but you have to think like the federal agent you are if you want to find your daughter. This woman just gave us the biggest lead we have."

Peter ran his fingers through his hair. "Your FBI contact. Call her and see what she has on this guy. He must live or work somewhere between Manchester and Londonderry. I'm guessing he is the one that took her."

"You don't have your connections?"

"I do, but if I call them, I'll be asked to step away from this case because it involves my daughter. Fuck that."

"I'm guessing the same. Peter, call Olivia and Reese to check on them. Don't say anything about this to them. I'll call Carly Brennan."

The call from Emerson's former cohort, FBI specialist Carly Brennen, came back in minutes. "What'd you find?"

"First, there is a guy named Dr. Jonathan Levy. His practice has been closed for a few months. Lives just outside Londonderry. About twenty minutes from where you are now."

"How do you do this so fast, my friend?"

"I've told you before, it's best not to ask."

"Thanks, Carly. We're on our way. Send me the address."

"Hold your horses, Lake, there's more. Vermont State Police are on the scene as we speak."

"What? Why are they at his house?"

Looks like a neighbor called 911 to check the welfare of his wife after they heard screams. "Lake, the chatter, it's a homicide investigation. The victim is Janice Levy, the doctor's wife. State and local LEOs are on site."

"Send the address," Emerson ordered.

# CHAPTER 27

Emerson's phone rang. It was Reese.

"What did you find in Londonderry?" she asked.

"We got a lead on a guy named Dr. Levy. I had to involve Carly once again to track him down. We're in route to the scene now."

"What do you mean scene?"

Emerson gave her the rundown of the details he had so far.

"What scene?" Olivia heard bits and pieces of the conversation.

Reese and Emerson put their phones on speaker.

"Your Mom is no doubt right about this lunatic. Olivia, is Janice Levy a client of yours?" Peter asked.

"Yes, but she's not a resident at Grace Center. She's younger and only goes to Grace Care at my request when mom is having a bad day. Normally, she comes to my salon. Why? How did you get that name?"

"Cancel her next appointment. They found her dead with a pillow over her face."

Oliva gasped in horror. "I recently told Janice to leave that bastard." Her mind started to spin. "Mom was getting her hair done that same day. She was sitting in Alicia's chair listening to our whole conversation. She kept saying, bad man."

The memories of that day crashed over Olivia in waves. "That was the same day Mom escaped out the back door. Alicia ran after her at the same time Janice was leaving the salon. Janice's husband was picking her up. I thought nothing of it when Alicia went after Mom. She was always wandering away from her. Only this time, she made it out the door."

Reese was puzzled. "Ok, but what does any of that have to do with Alicia's disappearance and Mom claiming to know who took her?"

"When Alicia and Janice got to the parking lot that day, Mom was talking to Dr. Levy. She was telling him to his face that he was a bad man. I bet it started an argument between him and Janice. Maybe Janice told him I suggested she leave him. Maybe he got angry, and he mistakenly assumed Alicia was his wife's stylist instead of me. What have I done?"

Reese helped Olivia to sit down and got her a cup of tea. Allowing her to cry it out. "It's not your fault."

Peter and Emerson reached the address of Dr. Levy, discovering the entire home surrounded by yellow tape and law everywhere.

"Boy, that's a lot of power right there," Peter said. "Especially for such a small town."

"Probably because it is a small town."

They approached a female trooper as they got to the tape. "You can't come any further." She put her hand up to stop them. "There will be a statement later today."

Emerson flashed his badge quickly. "This might have something to do with a case we're working on. Who's in charge here?"

"Let me get the captain," she turned and used the radio on her shoulder to get a message to the house. Soon after, a Vermont State Police captain sauntered up to Emerson and Peter.

"You sure are a long way from home, detective," taking a close look at Emerson's badge. "What's your connection to this case?"

"Captain," Emerson paused. "I'm sorry I didn't get your name."

"Connelly. Captain Shawn Connelly."

"Captain Connelly, we believe the husband of your victim may be responsible for the disappearance of a young hairstylist from Manchester. Dr Levy was reportedly seen leaving a bar with her in Londonderry last Saturday around 3 a.m. We had lunch at that same bar today. Asked a few questions. The server slipped me this piece of paper with our check."

"Can I see that piece of paper, detective?"

He showed it without letting it out of his hand.

"That still doesn't tell me your connection to this case and why you're here."

"The young girl missing is Alicia Holmes."

"I am well aware of her name," the captain was annoyed with this distraction.

"Sir," Peter took a step toward the captain. He wanted to punch him in the face. "She's, my daughter. You must have seen the BOLO. They're sent out nationwide."

"I did see the BOLO; I was merely asking what your connection was to the case. So cut the attitude."

Emerson put his hand on Peter's chest and pushed him back. "Before everyone gets their feathers ruffled, can we take a breath?

We're hoping to find this young girl alive, captain. You'd feel the same way if it were your kid. We believe that Dr. Levy," Emerson continued, "thinks Mr. Andora's daughter, told his wife to leave him because he was allegedly abusing her. The problem is," Peter continued, "he has the wrong hairdresser. Olivia Clayton is Janice Levy's stylist, not Alicia."

"And you know this how?"

"Because Olivia is my fiancée's sister. Olivia told us she advised Janice Levy to leave her husband."

"Why are you in town, detective?"

"To plan our wedding. My fiancée is from Vermont."

"And you, Andora, what's your connection to the detectives? Are you a cop? I see you didn't show me a badge." Peter looked at Emerson for help, but Emerson just shrugged his shoulders.

"Not exactly, Sir. However, I am on your side. I just can't say anymore. At least not yet."

"Let's say I trust the detective, the one with the credentials. You, Mr. Andora, I understand your predicament. This is your child. We are here to help. I expect your full cooperation even though you cannot say which branch you work for at this time. Please understand I have a job to do as well. Respect is key here. Welcome to Vermont." After shaking their hands, he led them into the house. "It's not a pretty sight, detectives, and I'm calling you both 'detective' until further notice."

"Mind if we have a look around, captain?" Emerson asked. The stench was expected, and Emerson and Peter were prepared by carrying and using a small plastic container containing a menthol-smelling rub for under their noses. "It never gets easy to see something as horrific as this."

"Do not interfere with my staff. Remember this is a Vermont State Police case. Just let me know what you find. Remember, this is a courtesy to fellow law troopers. Got it?"

"Of course, captain."

The beating of Janice Levy had resulted in severe wounds, including bruising on her thighs, ankles, and breasts. Forensics was there and knew she was most likely raped even before pulling the fluid from her body. Her husband's fingerprints were everywhere, but of course, they would be. It was his home, his wife.

Emerson and Peter walked around the house. "Would you happen to have any extra rubber gloves?" Peter asked a trooper.

"Sure." The trooper offered them two pairs.

Peter and Emerson looked for any evidence that Alicia had been in the house.

"Geez, that's a lot of books," Peter said as they entered the den. He spun around in awe of the built-in bookcases surrounding the room. "How the hell do you read that much? I see a lot of medical journals and shit like that, but who reads that many history and romance novels?" Peter removed some of the books, looking for a secret entrance to another room.

Emerson laughed at him. "You are a Sherlock Holmes type. Seriously, you're looking for an escape room?"

"Yeah, well, it's not unheard of, my friend."

The den wasn't turning up any clues, so they moved on to a nearby bathroom. "I'm sure someone drugged my daughter, Emerson. Wobbling while only drinking club soda, just makes no sense. Peter opened the medicine cabinet. I bet the prick has Rohypnol in here, better known as roofies."

"I know what a roofie is, my friend. I'll take the linen closet."

"Take out all the sheets and towels. Everything in there."

"A little bossy, you sound like Reese." Emerson thought a joke might ease the tension.

"Maybe." Finding out the doctor's wife was dead made Peter feel discouraged, and he thought it was unlikely that Alicia would still be alive. He slammed the cabinet door shut. "I can't see anything of value in this house to help find Alicia, detective. Can you?"

"I want to ask the captain if he has any leads on the missing person's report. Then, we probably should go."

"Agreed, I'll meet you outside."

Instead of waiting, Peter went to the neighbor's house without Emerson to question the person who called the police.

"Hi, my name is Peter Andora. I'm with the team investigating a crime next door. Are you the one who called it in?"

The woman at the door was well into her eighties, maybe even nineties. Peter noticed the house was old but well-maintained and quite sure she wasn't the person who took such good care of the landscaping.

"Well, now won't you come in and have a cup of tea, Peter? Just call me Stella."

"I would love that, but I would like to ask you a couple of questions if you don't mind?"

"Of course, young man. C'mon in. How can I help?"

Peter thought it was a well-cared-for home inside as well considering her age. Maybe she has help, he thought.

"Do you know the doctor that lives next door?"

"Why yes, I do. Lovely man, always willing to help me."

"How so?"

"He mows my lawn, gets me groceries, takes in my garbage cans. Things like that. Exceptionally good to me."

"That's Nice, Stella. When was the last time you saw him?"

"Oh, I think it was yesterday. Maybe the day before. My memory isn't what it used to be."

"You are doing fine, Stella. You told the police you heard screams coming from the doctor's house?"

# CHAPTER 28

Breathe. She said to herself. Fill your lungs with air. Deep breaths. Let it out like you're blowing up a balloon. She tried to remember the instructions from a meditation class she took. Keep breathing. It will help ease the pain that you feel, not only in your body but also in your mind.

"I can survive. I can do this." Alicia placed her arms out ahead of her torn, battered, naked body. "I can do this."

It looks like a door, but what if it's not? Stop it. Breathe. One arm at a time pulls me forward. Stop. Breathe. Pull me forward. She screamed as her broken knees scraped the rough cement floor. Screaming again and again, but she kept going.

"Just a few more feet. I can see it," she sobbed uncontrollably. "I can see it."

She took a deep breath. Her throat was dry as desert air and felt like sandpaper. I have to wait until my mouth can be wet again. She wiped her tears and tried to lick them off the back of her filthy hand. She tried to breathe through her nose, not her mouth. Yes, that's it. She could feel her tongue getting moist. Swallow. Her breasts and arms were raw from the concrete floor.

I have to keep moving. I have to get to that door. You can do it. She kept telling herself.

# CHAPTER 29

Peter's phone rang, causing Stella to jump off her seat. "What was that?"

"It's just my phone. Are you okay Stella?"

She clutched her sweater and nodded her head.

"I have to take this call, Stella. Will you be all right while I step outside?"

She nodded again.

Peter answered the call.

"Where the hell are you?" Emerson asked.

"I'm in the house to the left of you. Get over here now!"

Lake ran over to meet him on the front stoop. Peter returned to Stella's home. "It's only me Stella, are you doing, okay? I brought my friend with me; his fiancé lives nearby. Is it okay if we invite him to have tea with us?"

"Why yes, of course? I'll put more water in the teakettle on the stove."

"It's a pleasure to meet you, Stella," Lake said, massaging the top of her hand as he held it. "Thank you for inviting me to have tea with you and Peter. Is it okay if I ask you a couple of questions, Stella? I'm a detective investigating the crime that took place at your neighbor's home."

"Oh my, a real detective?"

"Yes, ma'am, and so is my fiancé Reese Clayton."

"I think I may know her from the library in Manchester. But oh, that was a long time ago. She was just a little girl back then. I worked there before my husband..." the tea kettle's whistle screamed and, once again, startled Stella.

"I'll get it," Peter patted Stella's shoulder. "Do you want me to pour you more, Stella?"

"No," she said. "I have enough."

Peter returned from the kitchen when suddenly something caught his attention. He stood perfectly still. "Lake, did you hear," he stopped mid-sentence.

"Yes, I heard it," he raised his eyebrow at Peter.

"Oh, that's just the teakettle whistling again," Stella said.

Suddenly a high-pitched shriek pierced the air. Stella gasped clutching her hands close to her chest. "There it is again. Is she still alive?"

The hair on Peter's neck stood on end as he glanced at Emerson and then down at the teakettle he was holding in his hand.

# CHAPTER 30

Peter set the tea kettle on the dining room table. He knelt in front of Stella's chair. "Stella, do you have a basement in this house? It's a lovely home."

Emerson waited patiently for the answer.

"Well, I guess you would call it a basement. I don't have a way into it from up here, but that's where the doctor keeps my garbage cans and my lawnmower. It's noisy when he starts it up down there."

"Do you mind if we look?" Peter asked. Now fearing the worst. "Well, I guess that would be all right. But why?"

Emerson patted Stella's shoulder. "We just want to make sure the doctor left everything in place before he went to work. Would you like Peter and I to take your garbage cans out of the basement and place them by the curb?"

"That would be very nice, thank you."

"Miss Stella, do you have any children in the area?" Emerson asked.

"I have a great-grandson that comes to check on me every other day or so. Why?"

"Nothing important. Just making sure you have some help with the day-to-day stuff. I have someone looking in on my dad when I'm not around."

"Peter, your friend here is so sweet and kind. My husband was like that," she smiled.

"Yes, he is Stella," Peter nodded.

"We will be back. Make sure you lock the door behind us," Emerson instructed as he pulled the door shut.

# CHAPTER 31

Emerson signaled the female state trooper who was standing by the yellow tape. They met between the two homes. "Tell your captain we may have something. We need to get into this lady's basement."

"Got it," she radioed the message to her colleagues at the doctor's house.

Peter saw the captain running toward the house. Stopping him before he entered the home.

"What's going on? What's the big emergency, detective?"

Emerson noted the tinge of sarcasm. "Captain, we spoke with Stella, the owner of this house."

"I know who she is. She's the one who called 911 about the screams next door. We already interviewed her."

"Sir," Peter said, "I don't mean any disrespect. She is older and the screams she heard may have come from her basement. We need to get in there right now. Stella says the doctor leaves the mower and garbage cans in there and helps her take care of the place."

"Let's go take a look." Captain Connelly remarked. "No stone unturned."

The men walked to the rear of the house. "Well, there's the mower under the deck."

Peter tugged on the metal padlock. "I'm guessing the doctor has the key."

The captain radioed for backup. "Bring the equipment to open this basement door."

"In these old homes, these basements were used as shelters from severe storms," the captain said. "Most homes in this part of town have them."

A trooper arrived with the equipment. "Thank you, trooper. We'll make quick work of this." The captain clamped the cutters onto the padlock and squeezed. The metal snapped easily.

The captain made his way down the cement steps first, gun drawn. Peter, right behind him.

"Fuck, it's a storm door," the captain said.

Peter put his ear to the door, banging on it. "Alicia? It's Dad. Can you hear me?" He kept banging on it till his hands were raw, yelling as loud as he could. "Alicia, Dad is here, honey! Captain, we have to get in there. Now!"

"I am in charge here, Agent Andora." The captain grabbed Peter by the shoulder. "Now step out of the way, or I'll have my trooper's remove you from this scene."

Emerson saw the fury in Peter's eyes and stepped between the men.

"Step away, damn it," the captain repeated.

"Knock it off, buddy," Emerson tried to calm Peter down. "This is not our jurisdiction. Give the captain a break. He's trying to help us."

Peter nodded his head, walking back up the steps, sitting down on a woodpile, looking straight down, and mumbling. Think, damn it, think. He picked up his phone and made a call, not wanting to, but it was his only solution. Before dialing the last digit, Peter hung up.

"Emerson, look!" Peter yelled. In front of them was a group of heavily armed police with a battering ram.

"Holy shit!" Emerson said. "Guess these guys know what they're doing."

Peter jumped off the woodpile, sending the logs rolling off the stack. Then, he headed back toward the scene. "I'm going to see if I can help."

"Oh shit, I'm coming with you, just in case the captain wants to take a shot at you or something."

The captain saw Peter and waved to him to come down the steps.

"What have you got, sir?"

He handed Peter a device. "Put it up to your ear and place this end on the door. Can you hear anything?"

Peter did what he was told and leaned in close to the door. "Yes, I can! I hear moaning, maybe crying sounds."

"Okay," the captain said. "I heard it too. Now, get out of the way."

"Captain, sir. If I may?"

"What the hell now, Andora? You're beginning to piss me off."

"The sounds are close to the door. If we use the battering ram to knock down the door, it might land on top of her. What if we drill through the lock first, see if that works?"

"Good thinking. Better yet," he yelled to one of his men,

"grab that power saw."

In a matter of minutes, the saw had done its job. The hole remained where the lock had been. And the door easily pushed in.

As the door swung open, daylight flooded the dank, dark room revealing the naked body of a woman face down.

Peter rushed to her side and collapsed to his knees. "Alicia?"

The only sound was a gravelly voice. "Dad?"

The young woman lay on her stomach, her face battered and bruised. Her naked body was bloody, including her fingertips from clawing her way toward the door. She was almost unrecognizable, except to her dad.

Peter grabbed his phone. "I need a medivac chopper now! I'll drop a pin for this address."

"Peter," Emerson put his hand on his shoulder, "the ambulance is already on its way."

"No offense to the medical facilities in Vermont, but I need to get her to a Level 1 trauma center. She's going to need more than medical attention. Captain, I think you already know what I'm talking about. Am I right?"

"Yes, Mr. Andora, I understand. We will take care of the scene here. Glad to be of help." They shook hands, before hearing the whir of the chopper blades.

The chopper began to land in the middle of the road. Its roaring blades generating powerful gusts of wind, causing the remaining leaves on the trees to cascade down in a flurry. Troopers led the medics into the basement, where they prepared Alicia Holmes for her transport.

As the medical chopper blades began spinning again. Peter whispered to his daughter. "Everything is going to be fine." He turned to Emerson "I will be back in a few days to help sort out the rest. In the meantime, take care of your family and tell Olivia, *Sherlock* says thanks and see all of you soon. I'm still your best man, right?" He punched Emerson in the arm and jumped on board the chopper sitting at his daughter's side.

Alicia lay on the stretcher, receiving IV fluids and feeling the pain rush through her body as the paramedics on board applied temporary splints to both of her broken knees.

"Alicia. I'm right here. Love you so much. I'm sorry you had to go through this."

She began feeling the effects of the drugs relieving some of her pain. "Dad, I'm so happy to see you." Tears rolled down her cheeks. "I killed him, Dad. I killed him."

Peter took out his phone and sent a message to Emerson. *Your wife-killer is still inside the basement. Dead.*

The chopper arrived at Albany International, where a private jet was waiting to take them to a hospital in D.C.

"Olivia's mom was right. Son of a bitch, she was right all along." Peter mumbled to himself.

"Sir?" the medic on board asked. "What was that? I am not sure what you mean."

"Sorry, I was thinking out loud."

Alicia, spooked by the medic's white coat screamed, "No! No! I killed you. Stay away from me."

Peter placed a calming hand on his daughter's shoulder. "Alicia, sweetheart, daddy is right here. No one will hurt you ever again, I promise. Can you give her something to calm her down?"

"Sir, I'm not sure that's a good idea. The mild sedative isn't working, but who knows what kind of drugs her abductor gave her. We need to do bloodwork on her first."

Alicia went wild, swinging at the medic. "Stay away!" Peter tried to hold her down. Tried to calm her. "Alicia, it's okay."

"No," she sat up as far as she could. "It's not okay. You fucking piece of shit," she screamed at the medic. "You tried to rape me!" Her heart rate spiked, and she slumped back on the pillow. The machines she was hooked to beeped wildly as she lost consciousness.

"Open the IV feeds as far as they go. Push the fluid." the medic yelled orders. "Shit, she is going into cardiac arrest. Grab the paddles. Clear!"

# CHAPTER 32

Captain Connelly and his team spread out over the basement looking for the man, finding him on the floor next to the table.

"Lake," the captain said, "over here."

Emerson saw Captain Connelly taking the pulse of a man on the concrete floor. "I can't believe she got away from him. He's a big guy for such a small young woman to overtake him. I hope to God, he didn't rape her."

"Me too! That's some serious shit to get over. Why do you suppose the asshole would be wearing a tie in the first place."

"Probably, status. He wanted her to feel inferior. So much for that."

"What an idiot. I'm going to go check on Stella, captain. She was unnerved by all that is going on."

Emerson knocked on Stella's door. "Stella, it's me, Detective Lake."

She didn't respond.

"Stella, it's okay to open the door now. You're safe."

His fears grew stronger with every second. "Stella, please open the door." Making a bold move, he tried the doorknob. It turned. Cautiously, not wanting to frighten her, he peeked in. "Stella? Stella?" There, slumped over the sofa. Stella.

Emerson yelled out the door to the paramedics still on scene. Ambulance lights are still flashing. "I need help here, now!" Not getting an answer, Emerson dialed 911. He explained there was an ambulance at the residence, but no one could hear him.

The dispatcher radioed the call. "They are on their way up to you now, sir."

Emerson left the front door open while he went back and tried to revive Stella with CPR.

"We got it from here, detective." Sweat was pouring from Emerson's forehead. "Go into the kitchen and get a glass of water, detective. You look like shit. I don't want you both in my ambulance. And while you're at it, breathe. I know your fiancé and don't want her pissed at me if you croak."

"How do you know who I am?"

"Detective, you are hard to miss in this small town. Everyone is talking about the big wedding event. Olivia has been bragging about the two of you before you even arrived in town."

"Really?" Emerson thought, well that's interesting coming from Olivia, and here we thought she was mad at us.

Emerson followed the paramedics to the nearest hospital. He wanted someone there if Stella survived. He called Reese and filled her and Olivia in on the events that took place in the past few hours.

"We found Alicia."

"Is she alive?" Olivia and Reese asked at the same time.

"Yes, she is alive. But physically and mentally, she will have a long road ahead of her."

"Thank God," Olivia said.

"Emerson, where are you now."

"I'm at the hospital with a woman named Stella who, whether she knows it or not, is a huge part of the reason we found Alicia. I'm going to stay with her until we can find her great-grandson. In the meantime, stay put and keep the doors locked."

"Where did they take Alicia?" Olivia was concerned for her.

"Don't know. Peter had a medivac helicopter at the scene in minutes and a medivac jet waiting in Albany to fly her to a D.C. hospital."

"Will he be back?" Reese asked, after seeing the look on her sister's face.

"He will, just not right now. His daughter comes first."

"Did you find Dr. Levy?"

"Yes, he's dead. He killed his wife first and was probably going to kill Alicia too, but Alicia killed him first."

Olivia gasped for air. Realizing it should have been her that was abducted, not Alicia. "How is she ever going to get over having to kill someone?"

"Olivia, sit down. Take some deep breaths, sis. I know this is hard for you." Reese held her hand, it was ice cold.

"I can't believe it." She was shaking like a leaf. Reese grabbed the crocheted throw from the sofa and covered her with it."

"You can't believe what?" Emerson asked.

"Mom," she held onto Reese's arm. "Mom was right all along."

"It appears that she was," Emerson said.

"I may never forgive myself for what happened to Alicia. It should have been me, not her." Olivia began to cry like never before. "How will Peter or Alicia ever forgive me? I'm sorry. I'm sorry."

"Emerson, I have to go and help my sister. I love you."

"Reese, pack up your sister and take her to our hotel. I think it's safer than Olivia's house right now."

"I agree, hon. Will do. Call me with updates on this. Love you."

"Love you too. The doctor is coming out now. Gotta go."

"How is she doing doctor? I'm Detective Emerson Lake. I'm the one who found her and started CPR."

"We've got her stabilized, detective. Her great-grandson is on his way."

"What was it?" Emerson asked. "Her pulse was next to none. And she was nonresponsive. Do you think she just forgot to order medication from the pharmacy? She is quite old. I looked in the medicine cabinets and refrigerator and saw nothing."

"No, her great-grandson either picks them up at the pharmacy or has them delivered to her home. Stella is well known in this hospital; she used to volunteer a while back. Just got too much for her. All her doctors are here, in this hospital or have ties to it. We have all her records. She takes heart medications for bradycardia. Perhaps she forgot to take them. Skipping doses could cause heart failure. My guess is that she was just overwhelmed by all the commotion going on around her home."

"When will the great-grandson be here, doctor? Did he say? I'd like to speak to him before I head out."

"He said five or ten minutes."

Emerson waited. Foot tapping on the floor. I'm going to kill this kid if he took his grandma's meds to sell on the street.

"Are you Detective Lake?"

"I am, Father. How can I help you?"

"I'm Father Gregory. You're the one who saved my great grandmother's life?"

"Oh, Father, pardon me, you were not what I was expecting for Stella's great-grandson. Um, I mean, I was expecting, well I don't know what I was expecting." Emerson blushed for probably the first time in his life. "Nice to meet you, Father." Lake gave the man a firm handshake.

"Thank you. You have questions for me?"

"I was just wondering where your grandma was hiding her medications."

"I believe she keeps them next to her bed, in her nightstand. Why?"

"Of course, the only place I didn't look."

"Here's my card, Father. Captain Connelly will explain everything to you. Please call me day or night about how your grandma is doing."

"I will, and Detective Lake," he placed a gentle hand on Emerson's arm, "God bless you for helping my grandmother."

Emerson nodded and smiled, as he left the building, feeling a bit ashamed. That's what I get for assuming the worst in the younger generation.

# CHAPTER 33

Emerson had an uneasy feeling as he exited the hospital. Something just didn't add up. He dialed Reese.

"What's up?" she said.

"Will you two be all right if I swing back to the crime scene?"

"Sure. What's going on? Why are you doing that?"

"Just a feeling, I guess."

"Gut speaking to you again, sweetheart?"

He smiled. "Maybe? Or just indigestion. I'll talk to you soon."

He dialed his pal, Carly Brennen, at the FBI.

"What now, Lake? I have another career, you know."

"Sorry, my friend. That Dr. Levy we spoke about. Do you know how long ago his practice closed?"

"Hang on a minute. Looks like he retired from his practice in 2001."

"Will you send me a photo of him? And find out if he had any kids."

"Emerson, I want to help you, but I can't delve into this right now. I'm going to give your name to a friend. Her name is Macy. Her name will appear on your phone. I'll send her your request. That's the best I can do. I have to go, my friend." She hung up the phone.

Emerson arrived back at the crime scene. "Hi captain."

"What can I do for you, detective? I'm a little busy here."

"I'm well aware of that sir. Is the body still here?"

"Yes, but not for long. Why?"

"I have some information I'd like to share with you. But first I need to see the doctor's body."

"Make it quick, detective."

"Will do, captain."

They walked down the steps to the basement, crawling with forensics and State Police searching for clues. Making their way to the body. The bright lights brought in by the forensics team were blinding.

"What have you got?"

"Did you ever get the feeling, captain, that something just isn't right?"

"Not since I moved here, but yes, many times working in a bigger city. Why?"

"Do you mind if I take a photo, captain?"

"Only if you share whatever you think you've found."

Emerson's phone vibrated. The screen said, Macy.

"Hopefully, I have some answers for you after this call."

He tapped the screen. "Detective Lake here."

The voice almost sounded robotic, like Siri's. "I sent you the info you requested."

# CHAPTER 34

"Captain, do you have a positive ID on this guy? Fingerprints?"

"Yes, Dr. Jonathan Levy."

"Are you sure?" The words came out of Emerson's mouth before he could stop himself.

The captain stepped close to Emerson's face. "Of course, we did a fingerprint match. Are you trying to say I don't know my job, detective? Get out of my crime scene before I have you thrown out or worse!"

"Captain, I'm not trying to insult you. My FBI resources provided me with a photo of Dr. Levy." He handed the phone to Captain Connelly. "See for yourself."

He took the phone from Emerson. "This is an accurate picture of Dr. Jonathan Levy. The deceased. What am I missing, detective? Why are you questioning the fingerprints?"

"Captain, my fiancé Reese and I have run into this guy twice since we've been in Vermont. Once at the Grace Center hair salon and the other time, he was inside Reese's sister's home. Alone. He addressed both of us by name and introduced himself as Craig Stockton."

"You're sure it was this guy?" The captain pointed to the corpse on the floor.

"I'm positive."

"Well, I don't know who Craig Stockton is or why the doctor gave you a false name, but this man right here on the ground is 100% Dr. Levy. Fingerprints don't lie."

"I agree, captain, but here's where it gets really puzzling. You might not know Craig Stockton, but I know someone who does."

"Who?"

"Reese's sister, Olivia. Her boyfriend is Craig Stockton. How would the doctor know to use Olivia's boyfriend's name? No way that was just a coincidence. And why did he break into Olivia's home? Something doesn't add up."

The captain raised an eyebrow. "Well, this case just got a little more complex, didn't it? Looks like we could use each other's help. Let me finish up here. I'll meet you back at the station. Say 4 p.m.?"

Emerson agreed and headed back to the hotel. He stepped into the elevator and once the doors shut, he closed his eyes and let out a deep sigh. I wish this was just a romantic trip for two, he thought. Just me and Reese, alone. No family drama. No work shit. Just Reese and I enjoying the Vermont scenery. Or maybe not even leaving the hotel room. He smiled at the thought of them making love all day. The elevator suddenly made a ding sound as it reached the floor, rousing Emerson from his daydream.

"Well now," he swung the room door open. "Two beautiful women just waiting to greet me. How lucky am I?"

Reese put both arms around his neck and kissed him passionately. "Are you okay, sweetheart? We've been worried about you." He wrapped his arms around her tiny waist, holding her tightly. "I love you, Reese." He kissed her gently but wanted to take her now.

"Hey you two, get a room. Oops, sorry, I guess this is your room."

"Oh, dear sweet Olivia," Emerson released Reese for a moment. "Come here, kiss me."

Olivia popped off the bed and gave him a peck on the cheek.

"Hey, the cheek? Really?" Emerson gave her his best sad face. "I love my sister and know she can also kick my ass."

Reese smiled, squeezing Emerson's hand. "Okay. What have you got so far?"

"Nothing good. I'm meeting with the police captain later. In the meantime, Olivia, I need to speak with you. Seriously, and I expect honest answers. We have a situation. Sit down and take your time answering."

"Okay, you're kind of scaring me. What the hell is going on now?" She sat down on the small sofa.

"What do you know about your gentleman friend, Craig Stockton? Where did you meet and how long have you been seeing each other? The photo on your mantle, you believe to be Craig Stockton?"

"Jesus Emerson, don't treat my sister like a criminal." Reese was appalled and smacked him on the arm.

"I'm not treating her like that," he rubbed his stinging arm. "I just need some answers. Olivia, how long have you known Craig?"

"About two years. Why?"

"How serious are you about him?"

"I guess pretty serious. There's been no talk of a ring or any-thing like that, not to say I wouldn't say yes if he did ask."

"Are there any other men in your life that know you are dating Craig?"

"I don't know the answer to that question, Emerson. Why?"

"Do you know this man?" Emerson held up his phone so Olivia could see the photo of Dr. Levy. "This is the guy we saw at the Grace Center salon and in your house. He told Reese and me his name was Craig Stockton. Your boyfriend."

Olivia quickly stood up; her legs buckled. Reese and Emerson caught her under each arm before she fell to the floor. They eased her gently onto the sofa, her eyes fixated on the image in front of her.

"Liv," Reese asked. "Who is this guy? How did he get into your house?"

"I don't know."

# CHAPTER 35

Reese's phone rang. "It's Grace Center."

"Hello. Reese Clayton." There was silence on the other end. "Hello, this is Reese Clayton." Click.

"Whoever it was just hung up." She redialed the number. "We're sorry. The number you have reached is no longer in service. Please hang up and try again."

"Olivia, pull yourself together," said Reese. "We're going to the nursing facility. I don't know who or what that was, but I'm about to find out."

"Reese, can you handle this? I have to meet with the captain."

Reese nodded.

"You and your sister take the stretch. I'll use the rental. Keep me posted."

Reese got behind the wheel of the limo, Olivia next to her. "Liv, I'm sorry all of this is happening I was hoping this trip would be all about reconnecting with my sister."

"I know that now. I was already overwhelmed handling Mom and Dad on my own. Now all of this? It's just too much." She buried her head in her hands and sobbed.

Reese put her hand on Olivia's shoulder to console her. "I know this is a lot to handle and now some strange asshole is using your boyfriend's name and breaking into your house."

"Reese," she wiped her nose on her sweater. "I know the strange asshole that broke into my house. I know the guy in the photo."

Reese jerked the car onto the shoulder of the road and slammed on the brakes. "What? Who is it?" "My gynecologist. Dr. Steven Morton. I went to see him less than a year ago. Reese, I thought I was pregnant."

"Oh, wow, Liv. Did Craig know this?"

"Yes, he told me to go see this doctor. Said he knew him. One of his investment clients."

Reese swallowed hard, trying not to cry.

"So, I went to see him. His office was in Londonderry. I only saw him once. Don't judge me, Reese. I'm almost at my breaking point."

"Not judging you at all, sweetheart." Reese tucked a stray hair behind Olivia's ear. "I'm worried sick about you. So, I'm guessing you weren't pregnant?"

"No, but the doctor asked a lot of questions. I didn't think anything of it at the time."

"And you told him what, honey?"

"Just where I worked, what I did for a living. You know, just conversation starters." Her heart sank knowing it was her that was meant to be in that basement.

"And Craig sent you there, so Dr. Morton, aka Dr. Jonathan Levy, knew Craig. That's how he knew all about Emerson and me. Am I correct? Come here," she leaned over the seat after releasing her seat belt. "Hug me. I love you, sis, and I promise we will sort this out."

"I never actually said to leave him. I just suggested to her she has other options. She is not the only one who has told me their horror stories that no one wants to hear, but they feel they can trust the hairstylist. I think it may have something to do with not being judged by friends or family."

Something enthralled Reese, listening to her stories. "Olivia, have I ever told you how proud of you I am?"

"For what, having a client murdered because she wanted to leave her husband?"

"That's not true. She died because her husband is a cold-blooded killer."

They continued the few hundred feet to the parking lot of Grace Center.

"Liv, go into the bathroom and see if you can splash some cold water on your face. We don't want Dad to worry about you."

Olivia freshened up and then headed to Eve's room. "Hi, girls. Happy to see you both."

"Dad," Reese said, kissing him on the cheek. "Did you try to call me from here?"

"No, but I think your mother tried a few times. She was angry again. Said you are never there when she needs you and has been walking the halls ever since."

"Dad, I asked you to not leave her side."

Anger hit him quickly. "I have to eat and take a piss, you know. I've had it, taking orders from you girls. I'm your father and I demand a little respect from you both. Now, in case you want a report from me, I am headed to my wing. I am having my lunch, dinner, whatever the fuck it is, and then I'm going to bed." He turned away.

"Dad," Reese put her arm around his shoulders. "I'm sorry Dad. We love you. Thank you for taking care of Mom."

"Can we have a kiss goodnight?" Olivia asked. "Please?"

His heart took over. "Make it quick," he announced. "Love you too." He left to go to his apartment.

"I don't know what to say, Olivia."

"Me either. That's the worst I have ever seen him. She must have been a handful today."

After searching the halls and peeking into other rooms, they found her sitting on the floor near a window, hunched over, rocking back and forth. Her arms wrapped around herself.

"Mom, are you okay?" They both kneeled beside her. "We're here now. Can Reese and I help you back to your room, Mom?"

"Find him. I know he took her. I know it."

"Mom, listen to me, please," Reese said. "We found Alicia. She is okay. You saved her life, Mom. That doctor won't ever hurt anyone again."

Eve stopped rocking and sat motionless for a moment. "We have to go now." She stood and the feces from her overflowing diaper began running down her legs into her sneakers.

"Oh my god, Mom. Don't move." It sickened Reese to see her mom soiled and dirty like an infant. "Olivia, you take Mom to her room and get her cleaned up. I'm going to pay the head nurse a little visit. This is ridiculous. There is no reason for her to be sitting in, her own, well you know."

"You mean shit?" Eve replied.

"Now, Mom, that's not nice." Reese stifled a laugh. But it was true. Both girls shrugged their shoulders as they went in separate directions.

Olivia yelled to her sister. "I told you, there is no rhyme or reason."

"I hear you, sis."

Reese reached the desk but saw no one. Then she noticed the phone was off the hook. Peeking over the top of the high counter of the nurse's station, she saw a leg. She ran around to the other side only to see a woman in scrubs lying on the floor, her body pushed halfway under the desk. The phone cord was wrapped around her neck.

Reese yelled for help from a nurse down the hall. Grabbed her cell and dialed 911. While checking for a pulse, she ordered what nursing staff were available, not many, to check all the rooms on the floor. Bathrooms as well. "Make sure all the patients are in their own rooms. Tell them to stay put and close their doors. None of them need to see this."

Paramedics arrived within minutes, and the police were right behind them. It was too late. The nurse was already dead.

Reese sat in the corner of the open-air nurses' station watching the medics trying to revive her. She tried her best to pull herself together. She saw Olivia and her mom standing in the hall next to her mother's room. What else do you know, Mom?

# CHAPTER 36

Emerson saw Reese talking to the State Police. He approached them both. Showing his badge to the young trooper.

"Are you okay, Reese?" He asked.

"Yes, I'm just giving this young man my statement. I'm sorry sir, I didn't get your name."

"Trooper Matthews," he replied.

"This is my fiancée, Detective Emerson Lake."

Emerson offering his hand to shake, the trooper doing the same.

Emerson took a step back, knowing this was her statement to give, so he let Reese handle the situation.

"Thank you. If you think of anything else, you know how to reach us I assume. We will be in touch later for your written statement."

Reese shook his hand and nodded. "Trooper Matthews, it was a pleasure to meet you."

"You as well, Detective Clayton."

"What else could happen on this trip, Reese?" Emerson asked.

"I sure as hell don't have a clue. Do you think I'm too old to run away from home?"

He kissed her hand. "As long as you take me with you."

# CHAPTER 37

"Detective Lake," a recognizable voice yelled to him "A word, please."

"Captain Connelly, this is my fiancé, Reese Clayton."

"I'm aware of that, detective. I doubt you would be kissing her hand if you weren't attached in some way. What are you doing at my crime scene? Again."

"Captain, I can explain," Reese said. "This is the nursing facility where my mother lives. She insisted her stylist was in trouble and taken away by a doctor. How she pieced that altogether is a miracle. The brain is a complicated machine, I guess."

"I know all those details, detective, but what happened here and how are you connected to this murder?"

"Just lucky I guess," Emerson joked.

Captain Connelly folded his arms across his chest, clearly not amused.

"Forgive my fiancée," Reese said. "Sometimes he cracks jokes in uncomfortable situations."

"Yes, I can see that. Not his best quality. Somehow everywhere you guys show up I have another dead body to deal with."

"Captain, you called that young girl a murderer. It's fucking survival." Emerson said.

"That's not up to me."

"We know, captain," Reese said. "We have no idea what's going on. We thought this case would be closed once we found Alicia."

"Where is your friend, Peter?"

"I'm sure he's in D.C. somewhere at a secure hospital with his daughter. Isn't that what any of us would do for our kids?" Emerson asked.

Reese pulled on Emerson's coat sleeve. "Can we go check on Mom, Dad, and my sister now?" Not wanting a problem with the local authorities.

"Wait just a minute. Captain, can you get the film from the cameras inside and outside of this place?" Emerson asked.

"I know little about South Dakota, detective, but around here, everything is as modern as it comes. We are looking at it as we speak from our precinct. Are you done questioning our abilities?"

"I apologize, sir. I didn't mean to sound obnoxious. We're just trying to help."

He looked at Reese and back again at Emerson. "Look, as much as it pains me to admit, my team is short-staffed, and this situation is quickly getting out of control. We could use your help but, if I let you assist, I need to be kept in the loop on everything. No secrets, you understand?" pointing, his thick, weathered finger, a stern command.

"Of course," Reese said. "Anything you need, we can handle it."

"Ok. Take statements from the staff. We need to know who saw what and where. Timeframes. Everything we can get."

"We're on it." Reese said.

"Thank you, detectives. Lake, I think it would be a good idea to contact Mr. Andora and let him know the latest developments. There is more to this than we thought."

"I agree, captain. I'm on it." Emerson saluted.

Captain Connelly shook his head and turned to leave, then stopped. "Oh, one more thing. I received word from the hospital that Stella has passed away."

"Oh no," Emerson said. "That's too bad. She seemed like a gracious lady. Her great-grandson must be devastated."

"He is. Nice kid. Well, mid to late twenties is still a kid to me. He has had a few issues with the law."

"Meaning?"

"Nothing major. He was always in trouble, not heavy stuff, but more annoying. Fights in bars, speeding. He worked at a local burger joint for a while. At the request of the courts, he got community service. His mother lives in California and his stepdad goes back and forth from Cali to New York for work. Don't know what happened to his real father, why he left his mother and all. None of my business. I have to say the kid did take good care of his great grandma."

"What's his name?"

"Gregory Collins." Stella is his paternal great grandma.

"Well, it's nice to see he turned his life around. Do you know the name of the church where he is the priest? I'd like to send them a donation in her name."

"I think someone misinformed you, detective."

"Meaning?"

"Meaning, her great-grandson is anything but a priest."

# CHAPTER 38

Though it felt like hours, Peter knew the hospital was the safest place for his daughter. He glanced at his phone every few minutes to see if there was any word from his sources about this character that ruined his only child's life. A name appeared on an incoming call.

"Andora here. What's up Lake? I didn't expect to hear from you so soon."

"First, how is your daughter?"

"Still waiting to hear. Have you got something for me?"

"Thought you would like to know, Stella passed away at the hospital."

"Oh, no! The poor thing. All that commotion was a bit much for her, detective. You could see how nervous she was every time she heard the whistle of the teakettle. I think she knew something was wrong but was just too frightened to say so."

"Here's another piece of the puzzle."

"What now?" Peter asked.

"When I first brought her to the hospital, I waited around to talk to her great-grandson and was surprised to see a young priest walk up to me."

"So?"

He said to me, "You're the gentleman that saved my grand-mother. I'm Father Gregory."

"Shit, who the hell was he?"

"Connelly said he was her great-grandson, and definitely not a priest."

"In trouble a few times, but the captain said he was always good to his great grandma. So, I'm not sure what to think yet."

"Do you think he may have killed Stella to shut her up?"

"Nothing concrete right now. They're going to do an autopsy on her, but I will stay in touch with you. Oh, one other thing."

"What's that? You're like a walking newspaper, my friend."

"Dr. Levy had an alias. Olivia figured it out when I showed her a photo. Turns out Dr. Levy is also Dr. Steven Morton. OB/GYN."

"What the hell? Is he Olivia's OB/GYN?"

"Well, not exactly. From what Reese told me, Olivia thought she might be pregnant, and her boyfriend Craig recommended this guy. I guess she never said anything to Reese before because she didn't want her to think less of her."

"Jesus, it's the 21st century, Lake. Who cares about that stuff? Shit happens in life. You deal with it."

"I know she doesn't have a clue that Reese told me. And I'm guessing by the way she looked at you, she wouldn't want you to know either."

"Well, I found myself a little enamored by her as well. Even though it's been two years since Judith passed, I need to find the truth about what happened to her before I start a new relationship. If I start a new relationship. I'm not sure it's safe for anyone to be in my life right now."

"I understand, buddy. We will find out what happened to Judith. We promise. Reese and I will also do everything in our power to help sort this out."

"Gotta go, Lake. The nurse just gave me the sign that the doctor is ready to talk to me about Alicia. Call you later."

# CHAPTER 39

As Reese was taking statements from staff and residents, she noticed a gentleman sitting on an old wooden rocker. Looked as though it may have been an antique, built just for him.

"Hello sir." she said politely. "My name is Detective Clayton. What's yours?"

"Does it matter?" he asked. "What do you want?"

"I would just like to talk to you and maybe ask you a few questions. First, I would love to know your name. I told you mine. Reese Clayton."

He looked at her with tears in his eyes. Removing his glasses to wipe them with a tissue and then blotting his eyes. "Reese?" he questioned her. "It can't be." He perked right up. "The last time I saw you," he put his hands through his now gray hair, "was when you were in my ninth-grade English class. What are you doing here?"

"Visiting my mom and dad. Mr. Horton?" She knelt next to his chair. "Oh, my goodness, now I remember you."

"Well, I'm happy somebody remembers me."

"What are you doing here? You look perfectly fine to me."

"I'm just waiting for an apartment on the other side. None available, right now anyway. My kids are all off doing their own thing in different states. Haven't seen them in a few years. I can't take care of a house of my own anymore. So, I just sit, read, and think about when I used to teach. What can I do for you?"

"I'm sure a place will open up soon and then maybe you can spend some time with my dad."

"I suppose so. That's what that nice young priest said to me just before you came in."

"Mr. Horton, do you know this priest?"

"No, the first time I ever saw him here. Nice young man. Why?"

"How long ago do you think you saw him, Mr. Horton?"

"Maybe two or three minutes."

"I'll be right back, my friend."

She ran to find the captain. "Our murderer may still be in the building. A young priest just left Mr. Horton's room."

"Shit." He urgently radioed his troopers at the exits.

One of them radioed back, "It's too late. We just let him go, captain."

"What part of lockdown don't you understand?" The captain was furious.

"He said he had to perform the last rites on someone at another hospital. He's a priest. What was I supposed to do? Say no."

"You are to follow my orders," his face was beet red. "Do you understand me?"

"Yes sir."

"Pull the video footage. We need to ID this guy and see if we can get a plate number to put out a BOLO."

# CHAPTER 40

Peter stood in front of the doctor, anxiously waiting for his update.

"Mr. Andora, your daughter has been through a lot. She has two broken knees and one broken finger. We can fix those. Her bloodwork came back. We assume she was drugged."

"Are any of them addictive?"

"Unfortunately, Mr. Andora, toxicology reports usually take anywhere from four to six weeks to come back. I'm sorry, but there is nothing I can do about that. I'm afraid it will take a very long time for her to recover from the aftereffects if they are addictive. She is a strong woman. She freed herself from this guy, but a long recovery is most likely. My suggestion is to let her recover after the surgeries right here. Then begin our addiction program. And the psychological aspects of her recovery could also take time."

"Doc, when we found her, she was naked and the prick that did this to her was partially disrobed. His pants were around his ankles." Peter fought back the tears of fear. "Doc. Did he rape her?"

"No, there is no sign of sexual abuse. Not to say he wouldn't have. She was naked."

"I know. Thank you, doctor."

"She is brave to have even attempted to overtake him like that. I'm guessing you gave her some of your field training over the years?"

Peter smiled. "I'm just glad she listened well. Thank you, doctor. When may I see her?"

"You can see her now for a few minutes and then we will prepare her for surgery." He entered her room with a smile on his face but could not stop the tears that followed.

"Hi, sweetheart, you look like you went a few rounds with Ali." Peter couldn't believe how swollen her face was, the cuts on her lips. Her beautiful hair was shaved to military length, for a man. But she was alive and that is all that mattered to him.

"Is he dead, Dad?" She tried to sit up but was still weak.

"Yes honey, he is indeed. You handled yourself perfectly." The doctor stood in the doorway nodding his agreement.

"I killed him," she cried. "I didn't mean to kill him. He told me he cut off my legs. Did he do that, dad? Did that monster cut off my legs? Dad, I can't feel my legs."

"Alicia," he held her head close to his shoulder, kissing the top of her shaven hair. "You have both of your legs, sweetie, you're just numb from the injuries to your knees. The doctor is going to fix it. You'll be walking again in no time."

"Dad, he was going to rape," the lump in her throat prevented her from finishing the frightening thought.

"No Alicia, listen to me. He did not rape you. You did all the right things to save yourself. I'm proud of you."

"I tried. I tried. I tried." She swung her arms at her father. "Get him off of me!"

"Mr. Andora, it's time for you to leave. We will let you know when she comes out of surgery."

The doctor put a firm hand on Peter's shoulder. "She has the best team caring for her."

Peter kissed his little girl on the forehead. "I love you, Alicia. I'm right here." She was already asleep.

He went into the men's room and cried his heart out, knowing this was his fault, vowing to get out of his chosen career. He slammed his fist against the wall of the stall, cracking the panel.

# CHAPTER 41

Reese called her sister's phone. "Hey, are you and Mom, okay?"

"Yes, but now I'm worried about Dad. Do you think I should go get him?"

"Yes, but not alone. Take Mom with you and stay on the phone with me all the while you're gone. Keep a close eye on her. I think she knows something else that just hasn't come out of her mouth yet. Wait, I better check with the captain. I don't want my name on his shit list."

The captain agreed to send one of his men with her. And said when she was ready to return her mom to her wing, Reese would be the one to escort them back. "I'm not running an escort service here, Clayton."

"I understand, sir."

"It's all set, Olivia. An escort will be there in a minute. Make sure it's a trooper before you open that door."

"Do I get to wear a badge if I do this? Honestly, I'm not an idiot Reese," said Olivia.

"No! But I could easily take you over my knee if you're not careful. I am the oldest, you know? And the smartest."

"You're also a pain in my ass, sis, but so glad I have you with me. Anything on Peter and Alicia yet?"

"Yes, I spoke with Emerson a little while ago. They are taking her into surgery for double knee replacement."

"Do you think I should call him, sis? You know, just to let him know I'm worried about her, and him, of course?"

"I hear you, but I would wait until I see Emerson to find out what he wants us to do."

"We're here at Dad's apartment," Olivia said. "Hi Dad." She hugged him as she entered the apartment. "Reese wants to see you." Olivia thanked the trooper before closing the door behind her.

"Is she playing cop again?"

"I can hear you, dad." She could also hear a knock on the door. "Olivia," she yelled, "don't answer it. Lock it up now! I'm on my way."

"I've had just about enough of this cloak-and-dagger shit, you two. The lady at the door is my cleaner. Now, get the hell away from the door." He took Eve's hand. "You know I would never let anyone hurt you, right?"

"Dad, she doesn't understand you. She has Alzheimer's."

"I am not an idiot, Reese. I'm still your father, and the two of you are making her worse. As her husband, I say what's best for my wife. And right now, you, Olivia, need to look through the peephole and confirm that it's my cleaning person. And you, Reese, need to take a breath. Olivia, you can stay here with me if you wish while the young lady cleans my apartment, or you can leave. It's up to you."

Olivia had not seen her father act like this in many years. It reminded her of when they were teens. Looking through the peephole, she knew the cleaning person and let her into the room.

"I'm sorry," Olivia said, "for taking so long to answer the door."

"No worries, I get it. There is a lot of stuff going on in this building right now. The place is crawling with police. I'll just tidy up and be on my way. Is there anything special you want done, Mr. Clayton?"

"No, just change my sheets and replace the towels today. Next time I'll have you vacuum the rugs. Thank you, Sara."

"No problem, Mr. Clayton."

Eve wandered around the apartment, not having a clue what was happening. She walked up behind Warren, grabbing him around the back of his waist. "I love you, honey," she said to the surprise of everyone.

Warren held her arms, his back still facing her. "I love you too, Eve." A rare tear fell to his cheek.

"I'm sorry, Dad," Reese said through the telephone.

"Me too, Dad," Olivia said. "May we stay and visit with you for a while? Mom seems pretty calm right now."

"Sure."

The cleaner finished her job and left the apartment with a few extra bucks in her uniform, placed there by Olivia.

"I'm going to hang up for now," Reese said. "Olivia. I think you have this under control. Call me when you're ready for me to escort you back to Mom's room."

"Will do."

Reese headed back to where she had left off.

"Mr. Horton, I'm sorry for leaving so quickly. May we talk about what happened with the priest who was here with you a short while ago?"

"Not much to say. He just came in and said hello and asked if I needed any help from God today. Asked if I needed to pray with him. I said it couldn't hurt. We bowed our heads, he took my hands, and we said the Lord's prayer, then he left."

"Mr. Horton, this may sound strange, and I'm sorry to have to ask, but did he touch anything in the room when he was here?"

"No, just the footboard at the end of the bed when he was leaning on it. Oh, I get it, that Covid thing, right? There is only one chair in here, and that's my rocker. I made it myself you know. I took an after-hours shop class when I was teaching. Made it for my wife a long time ago. She sat in it a lot when she became ill. Before she passed away."

Reese hated to leave him again. "Mr. Horton, may I ask you a favor? Are you able to take a walk with me?"

"Of course, that would be nice."

She helped him up and walked out the door with him, making a stop in front of Captain Connelly. "Captain, we need fingerprints from the Mr. Horton's footboard."

He nodded his head to her. "Mr. Horton," the captain shook his hand. "How are you today? Taking a stroll with our detective here, I see."

"Yes, I am. She was one of my students, back when I was teaching. She is pretty easy on the eyes too!"

"Mr. Horton!" Reese gave him the side eye. "Behave yourself, I'm engaged." She winked.

"Oh, I agree with you," the captain said. "Enjoy your walk. I'll take care of the matter, detective. I'll text you."

# CHAPTER 42

Emerson saw Reese as she walked the halls of Grace Center with her new friend.

"Emerson, I want you to meet someone. This is my ninth-grade English teacher, Mr. Horton. He's staying in this wing until there is an apartment for him where Dad is staying. Mr. Horton, this is my future husband, Emerson Lake."

"How do you do, sir?" Emerson shook his hand.

"I'm well, but if I were you, I would kiss this young lady hello. If you don't, I might just have to give you a run for your money, young man."

"I hear that Mr. Horton." He leaned in to kiss his future bride.

"That's better. One never knows how many more chances you get in life to give those kisses and hugs."

"I know what you mean, sir. Reese, I think Mr. Horton just taught me how to love you. Should I pay attention to him?"

"If you don't, I have a backup man right here on my arm. Isn't that right, Mr. Horton?"

"If only!" he laughed.

Reese pulled out her phone and sent a text to Emerson.

*The priest was in Mr. Horton's room. Forensics is checking for prints; can you see if they're done?*

Emerson's phone pinged. He looked at the screen. "Sorry, hon. I have to go, but I'll see you in a few," He leaned in and gave Reese another kiss. "Mr. Horton, it was a pleasure, and hope to see you soon as well. Take care of my girl."

# CHAPTER 43

One of Peter's close friends and former colleague sent him a message on the BOLO for the priest.

*The vehicle the priest was last seen driving was registered to a brokerage firm in New York City. Stockton and Associates. It has not been reported missing. No signs of the priest yet.*

Holy shit, he thought, does this have something to do with my wife, Judith? He dialed Lake's number.

"Lake, I need your help. Once Alicia comes out of surgery and is stable, can you meet with me? Perhaps halfway between where I am and Vermont?"

"It would help pal if I had a clue where halfway is. You didn't tell me where you were taking your daughter."

"I could use both yours and Reese's help right now, but I don't want Olivia alone."

"Okay," he said, "but what's going on?"

"I'll send you details when I'm ready to leave the hospital. Make sure you clear it with Reese. Explain why I need her there to protect Olivia. And Emerson, I owe you."

"Damn straight you do. I expect a huge bachelor party."

# CHAPTER 44

Captain Connelly gathered his men and women and the two detectives in the lobby of the Grace Center facility. "I believe we have every nook and cranny checked out on both sides of the building. I will leave my men outside every exterior entryway. No one gets in or out without proper identification."

"Captain, we need to let you know my sister has a connection to Dr. Levy," Reese confessed.

"And what might that connection be, detective? I thought we agreed no secrets."

"We did. I apologize. On the suggestion of her boyfriend, my sister recently had an appointment with Dr. Levy."

"Dr. Levy wasn't practicing anymore."

"We believe he opened a new practice in Londonderry under an alias. Dr. Steven Morton. No one knew him there."

"And what's her boyfriend's name?"

"Craig Stockton, Sir. What now, captain?"

"Thanks for the update, Detective Clayton. Let's put a pin in that for a moment. I need to get downstairs for the press conference."

"Captain," Reese said. "The media must know by now that we found a woman dead. How are you going to explain that?"

"I'll let you know when I get outside. Are you coming?"

They stepped outside. A podium stood on the sidewalk. Microphones perched on top. A small crowd of reporters anxiously awaited their arrival, practically salivating. Reese and Emerson flanked either side of the captain.

"Earlier today, the body of a 67-year-old nurse was discovered at her desk. The cause of death is yet to be determined."

Before he could continue with his prepared statement, a reporter shouted, "Captain, do you suspect foul play?"

"We will have a statement once a cause of death is determined."

"Reese, Reese Clayton, or should I say Detective Reese Clayton."

She turned to see the prom queen, now a reporter for the local newspaper.

"I remember you from high school. What's your reason for being here?"

"Not that it is any of your business, but I'm in town looking for a wedding dress. And visiting a relative."

The captain could see this was going to quickly go off the rails and decided to end things. "No further questions." He and Reese walked away, Emerson trailing behind.

"What the hell was that?" Emerson asked her. "Why so rude to her?"

"She was one of those I'm-better-than-you types in school."

"Oh. So, I guess I'm not marrying the popular girl."

"Nope, guess it's your loss, detective."

"Not a loss, sweetheart. I was just joking."

"I know you were."

She walked back into the building, where Mr. Horton waited for her.

"Sir," she said to him. "How would you like to meet my parents again after all these years? I could take you to the other wing. My dad will be delighted to see someone other than his two daughters for a change of pace. My sister Olivia is with him now and Mr. Horton, please don't be alarmed by my mother. She is liable to say anything. She is a resident here, on this side of the building, living with Alzheimer's."

"I understand Reese. Completely. Your Dad could probably benefit from some male bonding. I think they call it that now."

Emerson and Reese laughed.

"How long were you a teacher?" Emerson asked.

"Over 50 years. I retired a while back, when my wife was ill. Now, I'm kind of lost. Without her, I have nothing to do. Our children do not seem concerned about dear old dad."

"I'm sorry for your loss, Mr. Horton. Reese and I are both sorry."

"I think you are old enough to call me by my first name, don't you?"

Reese chuckled. "I don't think I ever knew what your first name was."

"Arthur," he said. "Simple as that."

"Okay," Emerson said. "Arthur, it is."

# CHAPTER 45

Peter abruptly snapped out of his nap on the hospital waiting room sofa when he heard his name.

"Mr. Andora?"

"Yes," he answered still half asleep.

"The surgeries were successful. I'm afraid her healing process will mainly be psychological at this point. Our goal is to see how she handles the therapy without drugs."

"My daughter is stronger than you know. She saved herself from that freak that abducted her. By herself. She is resilient."

"That she is, Mr. Andora, but I know of no woman who has been through this kind of trauma that has had a simple time letting go. No matter what you may have taught her in the past. And she remembered it well. Narcotics are involved here."

"Oh crap," Peter rubbed his chin anxiously. "That's another whole ballgame. It's like alcoholics once you come off the need for it. You spend the rest of your life fighting to be free of it."

"You're absolutely right, and we don't know how much and how often he pumped this stuff into her system. We found traces of a truth serum in her blood. Sodium thiopental. That is a huge worry for you. I do not know what your job entails, but I'm guessing it is top secret. If your daughter knew any heavy details, I would be concerned."

"That fucking piece of shit is dead. She took care of that."

"Yes, but who did he tell anything to? Do you know what I mean? He may not be the only piece of shit, as you call him, involved."

"When can I see her again?"

"You can go in now, but just remember the frail state she's in."

He tapped gently on the door before opening and peeking his head in. "Can I come in?"

"Hi Dad, they say I'm going to live, but it sure doesn't feel like it."

"I'll bet, baby girl. The pain must be excruciating."

"It is, and they tell me I can't have anything for the pain."

"Listen to me, Alicia. If you can stand it, try not to ask for anything for the pain. I know it's difficult. That guy drugged you with stuff that is addicting. Some stuff showed on your bloodwork, but the toxicology report won't be back for a while."

"I remember something, Dad."

"What's that, sweetheart?"

"I remembered you telling me to keep him talking."

"That's a good thing, honey. You remembered that from so long ago."

"I must have said it out loud though, Dad," she started to cry, "because he asked what else my daddy told me. And he asked who you were? I think I told him to fuck off or something. He slapped me, then knocked me out with his fist. Dad, I don't know if I said anything else or not. I hurt so much. How am I going to do this?"

"I know you can."

"Dad, can you sing to me? Don't leave me, please. I'm so scared and I hurt. I keep seeing his eyes bulging from their sockets. Can you stay in the room with me? Please?"

"I'm right here. No one will ever hurt you again. Now deep cleansing breaths, in and out." He hummed a tune as he watched her bandaged chest as it went up and down. The tune he wanted to sing to her during the father-daughter dance at her wedding one day. She stopped crying and fell asleep. All he could do was watch and wonder what torture that freak had placed upon his only child. He leaned over and fluttered his eyelashes on her cheek. "I love you, my little butterfly."

He needed Emerson. That would be his next call. He couldn't leave Alicia alone, at least not for a few days, maybe weeks. Time was running out.

Think, damn it, think. I can feel it. Judith's death was not an accident.

# CHAPTER 46

Emerson felt the buzz of his cell phone on his chest, pulling it from the inside pocket of his jacket, hoping it was good news about Alicia.

"Lake here. Hang on for a minute. I was just about to go into the hotel. Let me find someplace private." He went back to the gazebo. No one was there.

"What's going on, my friend?"

"Can you do some digging for me from where you are in Vermont? Maybe your contact at the bureau?"

"I can try, but wouldn't it be easier for you to reach her, instead of the cloak-and-dagger way?"

"I found out the priest was driving a vehicle owned by a brokerage firm in New York City."

"Oh shit, buddy, I don't like where this is going."

"It gets pretty complicated, I know. But hear me out."

"Go on," Emerson grabbed a small spiral notepad from his jacket pocket and a pen. "Okay, what do you need from me, and where am I meeting you?"

"I can't leave Emerson. Alicia needs me. I need someone I can trust to look into my theories. Right now, that's you and Reese. Please, I'm asking for your help."

"Of course, but what can we do that you can't from D.C.?"

"I need boots on the ground in Vermont."

"Okay, we'll do whatever we can. So, you said Judith worked for a firm in New York City. I thought you said you and your wife moved to South Dakota?"

"We did, but she worked remotely. All the accounts are on a computer. Not much need for her presence at the stock exchange."

"What if a client wanted to meet with her in person? Wouldn't that be a problem?" Emerson asked.

"Never would happen. My wife wasn't high enough up the chain to do that. I doubt the clients knew she was the brains of this company. She knew how to build those portfolios. She also knew it was a red flag when the funds in those portfolios skyrocketed for no good reason. I think that's why someone murdered her and made it look like an accident. Remember the heist from your dad's gallery? The one I had to recover?"

"Yeah," Emerson replied.

"That item along with the documents for it, was sold to a foreign country for unthinkable sums of money. It was Judith's files that tipped off the bureau about who the item was sold to. It means Judith was likely always in danger because of what she knew. These people are ruthless. Not to mention, I didn't just go ask for the document back, you know?"

"I figured that."

"I may have pissed off some very bad people retrieving that piece of work. Even though she didn't go by Andora, she went by her maiden name Maxwell, people saw us together a lot. She could have been targeted because of what I did too."

"So, she was being investigated as well, because it was her client?"

"I don't like to think of it that way, but yes. It's protocol. They knew she wasn't at fault here."

"This is so fucked up Peter, but I'll try to help as much as I can. I'm sure Reese will want in on this too. Give me a list of what we are looking for. Must be something serious for them to be investigating her."

"I will need a list of her clients. Do you even have a clue who she worked for at this firm?"

"The bureau seized her computer to confirm the names and location of the document and Artifact. The FBI handles most of what is happening inside our borders, and the CIA works outside. And the NSA National Security Agency handles our national security. Because of my military background, they sent me to retrieve the item. Once in a while, we work together with law enforcement on complex issues ranging from counterintelligence to counterterrorism."

Emerson was regretting his decision to get involved with this at all.

"And your wife thought it was fine that you went after the item?"

"She never knew it was me. We agreed when we first got married, no tell, no worry."

"Yikes! Reese would probably shoot me if I kept that to myself."

"I'm sure my wife would have felt the same way."

"She was a smart woman, though. She would have known she wasn't the only one monitoring this portfolio. She would have covered her ass."

"What you're trying to tell me is she kept a copy of her computer files somewhere?"

"I would bet my life on it. I just didn't think about it until now."

"So, you think Reese and I should fly back to South Dakota to your house and search for this?"

"Jesus no. My wife would never keep anything like that there. I want you to go to my daughter's apartment. I'll bet she hid it there."

"How would you know that, or even think she would do that?"

"Judith had a red briefcase for her client files, contacts, etc. Something she could refer to if needed. After the bureau seized her computer, she went to visit Alicia. She was upset that she might have to go to trial and thought a trip to see our daughter would be an excellent distraction. It was only a long weekend. I remember she had the briefcase with her when she left and a small carry-on. When she got back, no red briefcase. The next day, I was called out on the case of the missing items and when I returned about a week later, someone discovered her car at the bottom of the cliff."

Emerson could hear Peter's voice crack. "Give me Alicia's address."

"I'll give you the address, but I'm sure the police have been all over it by now. After she killed that asshole that abducted her. What I need you to do is go talk to Captain Connelly. See if they found the briefcase. If it was there, tell him he needs to contact the FBI. That red bag has a lot of information that can prove who killed my wife. I'm sure of it."

"You don't think the captain will give it to you?"

"I highly doubt it. Especially if it contains confidential information and names of her clients with their financial info on the stock exchange."

"Okay, I'll see what I can do. And if they did not find it, you want me to go to her apartment and look for it myself, correct?"

"Yes, with or without the captain. That's your call. I'll text you the lock code for her apartment. And address. One more thing, my friend."

"What's that?"

"She has a bookcase. Do you understand? A rather large one."

# CHAPTER 47

Reese and Olivia felt comfortable having a police presence at Grace Center and decided to take a break and go out for lunch.

"Lunch at Chez Dubois? How does that sound, sis?" Olivia asked.

"Pretty damn good to me. Are we dressed right?"

"Awe who gives a crap. What are they going to do, toss us out?"

"Exactly," Reese laughed. "Our money is still green like anyone else's. Although I will use my credit card," she snickered. "If they don't accept us, I'll put the owner in a headlock."

They laughed at the thought of that visual. Finally, it felt like they were kids again, always looking for trouble and usually finding it.

Olivia kept laughing as she reminisced about Dad's fights with neighbors and teachers. "I convinced him we were good girls who would never misbehave."

"Well, not sure we convinced him, but he fought for us. Mom knew we were trouble from the get-go."

"What the fuck happened to us, Reese?"

"Life happened, that's what."

"I guess."

Arriving at the restaurant, Reese elbowed her sister. "Oh, sis, I would refrain from using the word fuck in here. You know, because I'm a little too old to kick the shit out of a bald guy with a white towel over his arm."

Olivia snorted, which made them both laugh even harder. "I think I may have peed myself a little."

"You know they make things to put in your underwear for that?"

"Stop it," Olivia was in stitches. "Well, you should know, you're older than me."

"Yeah, and I've been told I walk around with a stick up my ass, too. That's probably why my bladder is in place."

Escorted to a nice table with white linen and crystal-clear glasses on top. A young woman poured from the Saratoga water bottles to fill their glasses. Announcing their waitperson would be right with them. Olivia looked at Reese. "Sis, I love this place. Beautiful."

A gentleman approached the table, bald, with a white linen towel over his arm. Oliva shot Reese a knowing glance, nearly choking on her water over their shared inside joke.

"Are you all right, miss?" he asked. "Is there something wrong with the water?"

"I'm fine, thank you." Olivia dabbed the white linen napkin to her lips. "It just went down wrong."

"I can't take you anywhere." Reese shook her head.

"And I am going to chew with my mouth open, just to embarrass the shit out of you, Reese Clayton."

"I miss you, sis, and I miss this." Reese placed her hand on her sister's arm.

"Me too. Thank you for coming here to help me for a bit."

"Actually, I came here so you could help me."

"With what?"

"Pick out my wedding dress."

"Oh my God, are you serious?"

"I am profoundly serious; I thought we could also look for your dress too. That's if you want to be my maid of honor. I want to ask Dad to come with us too!"

Olivia jumped out of her chair and grabbed Reese as she stood up. They hugged, cried, and laughed.

The whole lunch crowd applauded. "Oh shit," Olivia said. "They think we just got engaged. How could they not, with that 100-watt light bulb you have on your finger?"

Reese smiled as she waved around her diamond ring.

Their waitperson waved his white towel around his naked head. "She said yes," he yelled. The crowd continued clapping and yelling with delight.

Reese whispered to Olivia. "I'm not kissing you on the lips. I don't give a crap what they want us to do."

"Awe come on, sis. Where's your sense of humor?"

"Strapped to the inside of my thigh," she gave the crowd a quick smile and nod. "Let's eat. I'm starving."

# CHAPTER 48

Emerson sent a text to Reese. *Need to speak with you. Call me back.*

"Shit, I forgot they were going to the nursing facility."

His phone rang seconds later. "What's up?"

"Where are you?"

"Took my sister to lunch. Why?"

"I need to talk to you privately."

"Okay, I'll drop Olivia off at the nursing home and meet you at the hotel in half an hour. Love you."

He waited patiently, trying to relax for a few minutes. He heard the whir of the door lock releasing as Reese entered the room.

"What's going on? Why the secrecy?"

He explained the phone call from Peter. "What do you think we should do?"

"I'd like to say let's hop a plane back home and forget about all of this, but that's not gonna happen. We told him we would help him find out who killed his wife. Or determine if it was truly an accident. I say let's cover our asses. Let's have the captain go with us to Alicia's apartment."

"Okay, I'll call him now and see if he has time to see us."

Emerson dialed the station and was connected immediately.

"Captain, we would like to see you as soon as possible. We have new information."

"You can come over now. I just have to make a few phone calls first."

"No problem."

They drove over to the station. Emerson feeling anxious. Fidgeting with his fingers on the steering wheel. Reese noticed but decided to let it go for now. They entered the trooper barracks and were greeted by the desk sergeant.

"We're here to see the captain," Emerson said politely.

"If you can wait a few minutes, he will be right with you."

"Thank you, trooper."

"How do we always get into these situations, Emerson?"

Emerson rubbed his forehead. "Well, it sure as hell isn't luck. I'll tell you that."

The captain greeted them and escorted them to his office.

"Have a seat," he motioned to the empty chairs in front of his desk. "What can I do for you, detectives?"

"Have you searched Alicia Holmes's apartment yet?"

"Yes, but we didn't get much evidence. We just checked Dr. Levy's fingerprints. Why?"

"Peter Andora asked me to confirm if you found anything unusual in Alicia's apartment."

"Such as?"

"A red briefcase, sir. The red briefcase contains information that could prove that his wife's car accident may not have been an accident at all. And if you didn't find it, Peter asked us to search again. He even gave me the apartment keypad code. He really needs that briefcase found and sent to the FBI."

"What did his wife do for a living, Lake, work for the FBI?"

"No captain, she was an investment manager for a firm in New York. He believes she stumbled across some illegal financial activity. We're not talking about your average white-collar crimes. No, this involves priceless information, being sold on the black market to international adversaries. The Feds seized her computer, but Peter said his wife was a very savvy woman and likely hid copies of her files in Alicia's apartment."

"Your friend Peter is involved in some serious shit. Let's go, you two."

The captain followed Reese and Emerson to Alicia's apartment building. They entered carefully, just in case. No problems there.

"Where do we start, captain?" Reese asked.

"You take the bathroom," he answered.

"I'll take the living room," Emerson said.

"I guess that leaves the bedroom for me," the captain said. "Just for shits and giggles, I'm going to check her freezer. People have hidden money in the freezer. Why not a file?"

Emerson saw the bookcase that lined the whole back wall of Alicia's living room. "Son of a bitch, that's a lot of books." He removed one book at a time, shaking each vigorously to dislodge a hidden document."

After 20 minutes, the captain joined Lake in the living room. "Nothing in the kitchen. I'll start at the other end of the bookshelves."

They removed the books one by one. Bookmarks and pieces

of notepaper with chapter numbers on them fluttered to the floor. "Wow, apparently she was an avid reader," the captain said.

"More so than you would think," Reese appeared from the main bathroom. "Come, look at this."

In the walk-in closet was a wall of shelves layered with books. Emerson knew immediately what he was looking for. He started tossing books on the floor, on the ottoman, and on the dressing table.

"Emerson!" Reese jumped back as a hardcover nearly missed her foot. "What the hell?"

He continued frantically tossing books everywhere until he came across a book that didn't move. "I'm looking for this." He reached toward the back of the bookcase wall and pulled the book forward. They all heard the click. The heavy wall emitted a groan as it slid open to reveal a room.

"Holy shit." The captain was in total awe of what he just witnessed.

"That's it," Emerson said. "Captain, do you see this?"

"I sure as hell do, detective."

"And right there is a red briefcase."

Captain Connelly put on a fresh pair of rubber gloves before removing the case. "Son of a bitch, I didn't know anyone had panic rooms these days."

"Me either," Reese agreed. "How do you suppose she did that?"

"I'm guessing she didn't," Emerson replied. "This looks like the job of a dad who was hell-bent on protecting his daughter."

"Emerson, do you see a key for the briefcase anywhere?" Reese asked.

"I suspect Peter's wife did not leave one behind. Probably didn't want it opened by her daughter," the captain said.

"Or anyone else for that matter," Emerson shook his head. "I sure as hell hope the Feds can find the answers Peter is looking for."

# CHAPTER 49

"Dad, are you still here?"

"Yes," Peter said. "I'm right here. Can I get you something, maybe a drink of water?"

"Only if it has a quart of scotch to go in it. I hurt all over Dad. Why can't they give me something for the pain?"

"You drink scotch?"

"I was just being a smart ass. I drink club soda if I'm out but mostly water. Have you ever seen me drink, Dad?"

"No, I have not. And I don't believe we need to add that to your liquid consumption, at least not for a while."

"How about never?"

He smiled at her. "That's my girl. Sweetheart, can you remember anything about how this happened to you? Or aren't you ready to talk about it?"

"If I could remember anything, I'd tell you, Dad. One minute I was laughing with some friends, listening to music at a bar, and the next thing I knew I was on a slab."

"Do you remember the bar?"

"Kyle's." A look of panic flashed across her eyes. "Dad, you have to help me find Liz. You need to make sure she is okay, Dad. Please!" Her arms grabbed at him, tearing at his shirt.

"Alicia, calm down. Relax, take some deep breaths."

"No, no, get away from me. I need to go find her." Trying to get up, yet unable.

The shrill beeping of the monitors spurred a rapid response from the hospital staff who swiftly entered her room with a crash cart. "Sir, I'm afraid you will have to leave."

"That's my daughter. I need to stay with her."

"Get out of the way!" a nurse yelled.

He backed away from the bed and headed out to the waiting room. "Please God don't...."

After what felt like forever, the team filed out of the room. Peter jumped to his feet. "How is she? Can I see my little girl?"

"Her doctor wants to speak to you first. She will be right out."

Peter wrung his hands and paced. All he could do was wait and pray it wasn't bad news.

His phone vibrated, snapping him to attention. "Lake, I have to call you back."

Emerson pulled the phone from his ear and looked at the screen. "Huh, that can't be good. He just hung up on me. Something must be wrong with Alicia."

"I don't like the sound of that," Reese said.

"Well, what now captain?" Emerson asked.

"We wait. Let's get something to eat. I know a great place for lunch. Not fancy, but good, clean food."

"What about this briefcase?" Reese said.

"That stays right with us until we hear from your best man, detectives. Follow me to the restaurant."

Reese and Emerson followed Captain Connelly for about a mile before they noticed his car drifting out of control.

"Reese," Emerson yelled, "call him. Find out what's wrong."

His phone barely rang before they heard the captain shouting. "I have no brakes!"

"Hold on, Reese," Emerson sped up, pulling alongside Captain Connelly's cruiser. "I'm going to pull in front of you!" he yelled out the window. "When I hit the brakes, you know what to do. We'll be fine."

The captain nodded, gripping the wheel tight. "Hurry! There is a hairpin turn. Large drop-off on the right side of the road."

Emerson could see the turn up ahead. Getting closer and closer by the second. "Ready Reese? Brace yourself!"

She pulled her seatbelt taught as Emerson hit the gas, pulled in front of the captain's cruiser, and violently hit the brakes.

# CHAPTER 50

"Mr. Andora, I'm Dr. Shirley Stone. Psychiatrist for the hospital. Your daughter has been through some major trauma. She needs round-the-clock nursing care. We can provide that for her. We cannot have her getting upset right now. Please understand with all the drugs in her system. She needs quiet. I'm asking you to leave until we have her system flushed out of these mind-altering drugs."

"Dr. Stone, my daughter, can have round-the-clock care. I will be happy to pay for that. But as far as me leaving her? No way in hell. So, either you treat her with me here, by her side, or I will find somewhere else to take her. Now, what happened to her in there? She just started freaking out."

"She has severe anxiety, Mr. Andora."

"Excuse me, doctor, but wouldn't you have it too if you went through what she did? I mean no disrespect, but I am at the end of my rope. I lost my wife, and now this is happening to my daughter. Now, get the hell out of my way. My child needs me."

The doctor stepped closer to his face and stared him directly in the eye. "Whether you believe me or not, I am trying to help her too!"

"Really, how? By making her talk about what happened to her? That's what I'm here for. I'm her father. She doesn't need you to rehash this nightmare. She needs a person who loves her and cares for her. That's me. So, like I said the first time, either I am with her at all times, or you are not here at all."

"Well, I never."

"I'm guessing you never did either." Peter firmly nudged her out of his way.

# CHAPTER 51

"Dad, I'm sorry," Alicia said. "I didn't mean to make you worry. I have to tell you something that I should have told you a long time ago."

"Alicia, you don't have to tell me anything that you don't want to. I'm your father and whatever it is you have to say, we will work through it together."

"Dad, please listen to me before I have another episode."

"Okay, I'm listening." He placed his hand gently on her arm.

"I met someone, a special someone. About a year ago. We became close, Dad. I didn't want you to know because I was afraid you would want to do a background check and all that shit."

"You're probably right, sweetheart."

"That night, at Kyle's I was supposed to meet my special someone for a late dinner. I had visions of an engagement ring and the love of my life getting down on one knee to propose."

"Really, that serious? Good for you Alicia. Can I contact him for you? I promise no behind-your-back stuff. Can't wait to meet the love of your life. I'm so happy for you. Shit, he must be in a panic right now. Wondering why you didn't show up for dinner."

"Dad, that's why I need to find Liz. She works at Kyle's."

"You mean the server, Liz?"

"Yes Dad, I love her." Alicia visibly began to shake.

"Sweetheart, I love her too! She is the reason I found you. My friend and I went to Kyle's to ask questions, and she secretly slipped us a note with a tip about the man who took you. I'm so proud of you for telling me this." Peter leaned in and gave Alicia a gentle squeeze. "Did you think I would care if you were in love with another woman?"

Alicia's tremors subsided as she relaxed in her dad's warm embrace.

"And do you know what, my little butterfly? I'm thrilled about the opportunity to walk you down the aisle."

"Love you, Dad. I'm going to work really hard to heal."

"I know you will. Now, you get some sleep, and I'll have my friend contact Liz to let her know we have you safe and sound."

"Who is your friend, Dad?"

"I believe you may already know the family. He's a detective. His fiancé is Detective Reese Clayton. Olivia's sister." He looked down. Alicia was smiling, her eyes closed. "Love you, baby girl."

# CHAPTER 52

The captain braced for impact, fearing the worst, both hands clenching the steering wheel like his life depended on it.

He slammed into the rear of Emerson's vehicle with alarming speed. The sounds of crunching metal reverberated throughout the cabin. The force of impact propelled him forward. The deployed airbags encasing him in a protective barrier.

Emerson and Reese took a moment to gather their wits once they came to a halt.

"Reese, are you okay?" Emerson hit her seat belt release button to free her from her constraints.

"I'm fine."

They both got out and ran to the captain's car. Reese tapped on the driver's window "Captain, are you okay?" He was slumped over.

Emerson inhaled deeply, "Reese, I smell smoke. We have to get him out of there." He grabbed a wrench and sharp razor-type knife out of the toolbox in the back of his car and smashed the side window. Then reached to open the door from the inside. "Reese," Emerson yelled, "the briefcase. Do you see it?"

"Not yet. Engine smoke is filling the cabin. We need to get him out, Emerson, now!"

Emerson took the knife and inserted it under the captain's seatbelt that was bolted to the floor. With a swift slice, the captain was free. Emerson pulled the captain onto the ground and jumped back into the car to search for the briefcase. Flames erupted around him. The smoke burned his throat and made it difficult to see. There! The briefcase was still intact on the floor of the back seat. He grabbed it and flung it onto the ground.

Reese grabbed the captain's collar dragging him as far away from the vehicle as she could.

Emerson followed gagging from the fumes. "Is he still breathing?" he asked.

"Yes, I already dialed 911. I think he's just knocked out. They are on their way."

"Reese, I'll tend to him. You put the briefcase in our car."

"I'm going to move our car away from here," she said. "We don't need ours going up in smoke too."

"That must be some kind of vehicle. Not even a fucking dent." Emerson shook his head in disbelief. "Just some paint chipped off."

"It seems our SUV limo is built like a tank."

EMTs, state police and fire vehicles arrived, sirens blaring.

"We got this, sir," the EMT motioned Emerson to step away and applied an oxygen mask over the captain's mouth and nose. Reese and Emerson gave State Police the account of what took place on the road, while fire trucks tried to douse the flames shooting skyward from the captain's car.

"Your vehicle is undamaged?" State Trooper Matthews asked.

"It is, just paint damage," Emerson said.

"Really? Mind if I have a look?"

"Not at all."

The trooper walked around the SUV, then opened the door to look inside.

# CHAPTER 53

"Captain Connelly how are you feeling?" the EMT asked.

"I've been better," he rubbed the back of his neck. "I feel like I was dragged through a knothole ass-backwards."

"I don't understand," the EMT raised his eyebrow.

"Never mind. You're too young to know what I mean."

"Well, between the impact of the accident and being dragged across the pavement, it's no wonder you feel banged up. How's your breathing? Any better?"

"Yes, I'll be fine. I feel like I can taste burnt leather. Must be from the melted seats, I guess."

"We're going to take you to the hospital, get you checked out and get those abrasions bandaged."

"Where are the detectives that saved me?"

"They are talking with the police."

"I need to speak to them and Trooper Matthews before you haul me off."

"Well, what do we have here?" Trooper Matthews pulled a briefcase from the SUV. "I need to see your identification. Both of you."

Reese and Emerson looked at each other, confused. "You know damn well who we are," Reese said. "We've been introduced. We saw you at Grace Center, Dr Levy's home, and at the station."

"What the hell is your problem, man?" Emerson was getting pissed.

"The problem is, we don't know anything about either one of you. You claim you are detectives. This briefcase smells like it came out of a fire. I'm guessing from our captain's car. That's theft."

"Give me a break! It did come out of your captain's car." Emerson was furious. "Did you expect I would leave it in there to burn?"

"What's so important in this charred bag that you had to save it?"

"I'll answer that," the captain said as they wheeled him on the stretcher toward the SUV. "Matthews, give the bag to the detectives. Now! Then, I want you to go with the tow truck."

Trooper Matthews reluctantly handed over the briefcase. And walked away. You assholes. You have no idea who you are dealing with, he thought.

The captain turned his attention back to Reese and Emerson. "When we were in Alicia's apartment, I'm guessing someone tampered with my brake lines."

"I'm guessing the same, captain," Reese replied. "Don't be too hard on your young Trooper Matthews, captain. He will learn like the rest of us did."

"Yeah, with my foot up his ass. Thanks for saving my life, you two."

"We will contact the bureau and deliver the briefcase to them personally. Are you all right, captain?" Emerson asked.

"Yes, but I wanted to go to the FBI headquarters. That would have been a trip."

"We will let you know how it goes, captain," Reese said. "Take care of yourself." Reese patted his arm as the electronic lift raised the stretcher into the ambulance.

Trooper Matthews watched as everyone left the scene, then followed the tow truck closely as it carried the police vehicle toward the state police garage. They would inspect the wrecked vehicle for unknown prints and examine the brake line to see if someone tampered with it.

As the tow truck headed down the hill and into the hairpin turn, Trooper Matthews sped up alongside it and inched closer and closer.

"What the fuck are you doing?" the tow truck driver yelled. He tried to desperately steer the truck away from the edge, but there was no stopping its momentum. The combined weight of the tow truck and the captain's damaged vehicle careened off the road, hurtling down the embankment.

Trooper Matthews brought his vehicle to an abrupt stop. He jumped out of his vehicle and watched as the tow truck and police vehicle plummeted down to the ravine and explode.

He ran back to his cruiser and threw it in neutral. He placed his hands on the trunk and shoved with all his might until the vehicle gained speed, eventually dropping out of sight over the edge of the cliff. Trooper Matthews disappeared.

# CHAPTER 54

The detectives arrived back at their hotel, exhausted emotionally and physically.

"Reese this could have gone bad in a heartbeat."

"I know. What the hell is that vehicle made of?"

"Whatever it's made of, I don't think we were supposed to find that out."

"Emerson, you make the call. Let the Feds know what is going on. I'm going to Grace Center to check in with Olivia and give her a hand with mom and dad for about an hour. I'll be back before we have to deliver the briefcase."

"Okay." Emerson kissed her gently on the lips. "Before you go, my love, I need you. We are alone for the first time since we got here from South Dakota."

"I hear you, and I feel the same way. Meet you in the shower in one minute. We both smell like smoke. Call the FBI, tell them we have a (need) to fill before we meet with them."

She walked away, playfully pulling her sweater over her head, and then tossing it on the sofa. "Well, are you coming or not, detective?"

"Yes, ma'am."

As they finished making love, or as Reese called it, a necessary turn of events, Emerson's phone rang.

"Lake here."

The voice was familiar, but he could not quite place it. "Listen carefully," the male voice demanded. "I want that brief-case, and I want it now. I will meet you at Kyle's Tavern in one hour. The clock is ticking."

"Who the fuck do you think you are talking to, a third grader? I'm not giving you a damn thing. Who is this?"

"Oh, I think you will do as I say, detective. I have an acquaintance of yours right here with me. I believe you know her. Isn't that right, Liz?"

# CHAPTER 55

"We need to contact Peter immediately, Emerson."

"I'm on it. I'll put it on speaker."

Peter answered on the first ring. "Hey Lake, sorry I hung up on you earlier. Things were a bit tense here."

"We completely understand. How's Alicia?"

"She is a strong woman. She told me just now that she is going to push herself to get better. I believe her. She also told me something else. She's in love, Emerson. With the woman from the restaurant, Liz. Alicia thought Liz was going to pop the question that night she was taken."

Reese inhaled sharply holding her hand to her chest. "Could this get any more complicated?"

"Why?" Peter asked. "What's going on? Did you find what you were looking for, detectives?"

"We did. But there is more, a lot more."

Emerson filled Peter in on the captain's accident and their theory that someone may be after them because they found the briefcase.

"Holy shit! You need to get that briefcase to the FBI right away."

"We were about to make contact when we got a disturbing call." Emerson said.

"Disturbing, how? Who was it?"

"The voice was familiar, but we don't know who it was. Buddy, Liz is in trouble. The caller is holding her hostage in exchange for the briefcase."

"No! Damn it, what the fuck is going on? Listen to me, both of you. I am going to call the number I gave you and have my contact meet you at Kyle's Tavern. Reese, keep the briefcase with you. Do not, under any circumstances, let it out of your sight. Do you understand?"

"Yes, I understand. How will we know who we're supposed to meet and hand off the goods to?"

"I'm going to call you back in 5 minutes with details. In the meantime, start heading to Kyle's. I'm sending help. As soon as you can, put Liz in the chopper. Our guys will take it from there. Tell her Alicia needs her."

The line went dead. Emerson and Reese left the hotel as they were instructed.

"Emerson, how the hell are we supposed to get Liz out unharmed?"

"I'm going to take a wild guess here, sweetheart, and say it won't be us getting her out."

"That's what I'm afraid of. Heavily armed troops and a hostage that doesn't know what's going on. Someone is bound to get killed in this extreme situation. I'm hoping this guy doesn't go off the deep end when he hears the chopper."

"Emerson, pullover. Right here, stop the car."

"Reese, at a computer store? What the hell are you doing?"

Reese jumped out and ran to the store entrance. Please have what I need, she thought to herself.

Emerson's phone vibrated. Unknown number. "Where are you, detective?" The familiar voice seemed edgy. "Time is running out for Liz."

"We are on the way. I had to put air in my tire." It was the first excuse he could think of. "We were in an accident, must have pinched the air valve. It will only take a minute. We're close, I swear."

"You have an extra five minutes, detective, and then I kill her." The line went dead.

Reese ran back to the car with her arms filled. "Open the back of this thing."

She scrambled to place a pile of papers from the store's trash bin into a new red briefcase, locking it up tight. She took the original case and shoved it into the spare tire well. She hopped into the front seat, putting the key in her bra.

"Hurry, Emerson! I think we should do this our way."

"I hope you know what you're doing, sweetheart."

When they arrived at Kyle's, they both leapt from the car. Reese with the fake briefcase in hand.

"Reese, leave the case in the car."

She wasn't sure why but tossed it in the back seat.

They entered Kyle's cautiously, heads on a swivel, guns now drawn. "Hello? Anyone here?" Emerson asked.

No answer.

"Fuck, where the hell is he?"

Reese tried. "Hello, it's Detectives Reese Clayton and

Emerson Lake. Can you hear me? We need to see Liz."

"Reese," Emerson whispered, "listen."

Reese strained. The silence in the restaurant was deafening.

"It's the chopper."

Reese could now hear the whir of the blades in the distance.

"We need to find Liz. Where the hell would he take her?"

The chopper landed at the back of the restaurant. Emerson crawled on his hands and knees, staying low, away from the windows. Reese made her way toward the kitchen, also staying low to the floor. She heard a sound near the walk-in freezer. She heard it again. Looking around, she carefully pulled the handle to open the freezer.

There sat Liz. Someone tied and gagged her. Bruised, but not hurt. Reese held her finger to her mouth as a signal for her to be quiet.

Suddenly, a man in uniform barged through the kitchen door with a machine gun. "Hold it right there!"

Reese and Emerson stood, announcing their names, and carefully presenting their shields. They pointed to the young woman tied up on the floor of the freezer.

"We have the guy. He thought he could run into the field in the back and get away. What a fucking moron. Can you guys handle this? Nodding toward the girl tied up on the floor."

"Yes of course, lieutenant," Reese responded.

He nodded. "We are taking him with us."

"Got it. Thanks for the help." Emerson shook his hand.

Emerson waited until they left, before untying Liz. He could hear the whiz of the blades as they fired up the bird.

"Are you all, right?" Emerson pulled the rag out of Liz's

mouth.

"Just scared." Tears were falling down her face.

"Come on, we need to get you cleaned up before we send you to D.C. to see Alicia," Emerson said.

"She's okay, detective?" Liz asked.

"Been through a lot, no doubt about that. But in time, she will recover. She's at a hospital with her dad." Reese held Liz's hand that was shaking from fear and the cold walk-in freezer. "I'm sure Alicia can barely wait to see you." Reese hugged her.

"Come on," Emerson said. "We are taking you to our hotel until we can make travel arrangements for you to go to D.C."

"D.C.?" Liz asked. "I have to go home first. I have an engagement ring to give her. It doesn't look like that one on your finger, though."

"Liz don't do that. It makes no difference in the size or the look, it comes from your heart." Emerson held her hand. "Now, let's get you ready for your trip."

"My house first though, okay?"

"You got it."

Emerson messaged Peter while the girls went into Liz's house. He also sent a photo he captured on his phone of the lieutenant who put the perp on the chopper before it took off. The perp he never saw.

Peter called back immediately. "Emerson, who in the hell is this guy you sent me a photo of? That is not the person I asked to be sent there to help. What about Liz? Is she okay?"

"Beats the shit out of me, pal. I was hoping you knew. Yes, Liz is fine. She knows she's going to go see Alicia. We just made a stop at her house to pick up a certain gift for your daughter."

"The guy in the chopper never mentioned the hostage?" He asked.

"He saw her tied up and asked if we could handle the situation. We said of course. But when we got back in the car, the first thing we noticed was the red briefcase was gone."

"Are you fucking kidding me? Now we'll never prove Judith was murdered."

"Now don't get your panties in a knot, Sherlock. My beautiful fiancé is also extremely smart. Just before we arrived at Kyle's, she planted a fake case in the car."

"So, where is the real one?"

"Hang on," Emerson walked to the back of the car and opened the spare tire hatch. "I'll call you back."

# CHAPTER 56

She dialed Peter's cell; she just couldn't wait any longer to hear his voice and find out about Alicia in his own words. What she did not expect was for him to answer so quickly, if at all.

"Olivia!" his voice sounded panicked. "Are you okay?"

"Yes, I'm fine. I just wanted to see how Alicia is doing." She paused for a second. "Truth, I just wanted to hear your voice."

"Liv, I'm so glad to hear your voice too! I'm sorry I haven't called to check on you."

"No worries. I know you're busy with your daughter and trying to figure stuff out. Please tell her I'm sorry for all that she went through. Peter, if you need anything, please call me. Anytime, day or night. I'm here for you."

"Thank you. When I return, whenever that may be, would you like to have dinner with me? You know, like a date?"

Olivia, ready to fall over at the invite, was speechless for a second.

"If not, that's okay. I understand. I know you have a boyfriend."

"You think you know everything, Sherlock? I do not have a boyfriend. I'm done with that guy. If I ever see him again, which I highly doubt, he will get a piece of my mind and not a piece of ass."

"I'm sorry, Miss Clayton. Is that a, yes?"

"It is indeed. I don't care if it's a hot dog and fries."

"I think I can do better than that. Thanks for thinking of us, Olivia. I appreciate the call and the humor. Can't wait to see you again."

"I have to help my dad with some paperwork now. I hope to see you soon. Oh, and Sherlock, keep your head up. Things will work out eventually. I'm sending you an advanced hug; you know, for the hot dog."

"Right, back at you Liv. Talk soon." As he hung up the phone, a feeling came over him he had not felt since his wife passed. Snap out of it, soldier, you have work to do he told himself.

Oliva made sure her mom was clean, her hair combed, and dressed nicely before going to visit Dad.

"Are you feeling okay today, Mom?"

She didn't answer as usual.

"Well, what do you say we go for a walk? Possibly go visit Dad for a while?"

"Let's go." That is all Eve said as she headed for the door.

"Wait a second, Mom. We need to have someone go with us."

She was already walking out the door before Olivia could stop her.

"Mom, stop."

"Going somewhere?" The voice echoed through the halls.

"I'm sorry, trooper. My mother doesn't understand any of this. She just likes to walk. We need an escort to the assisted living side to visit my dad."

"I'll take care of it, miss."

He spoke into his shoulder radio while Olivia walked at a fast pace to reach her mother.

When they arrived at Warren's apartment, Olivia thanked the trooper and knocked on her father's door. "That's odd. I just spoke with him about 15 minutes ago."

"Try it again," the trooper said.

She knocked. No answer.

"Do you have a key, miss?"

"No, I don't. It's not my dad that needs watching, it's my mom."

As she turned to look at her mother, she was already heading down the hall toward the front door of the building.

"Try calling him."

Olivia and the trooper started walking in Eve's direction trying to catch her before she escaped.

Olivia dialed. "No answer. Something is wrong."

"Mom, damn it. Stop!" Olivia grabbed her mother by the elbow.

"Let me go! This is the way he went."

"Oh, for Jesus's sake, mom. What the heck are you talking about?"

"He went this way."

"Who went this way?" Olivia asked. Frustrated.

"That guy. I know he took her."

"Mom, I don't have time for your ranting. Trooper, help me get her back to my dad's apartment, please."

They each took an arm and guided her back. Still, there was no answer when she knocked on the door. "I have to get in there, officer."

The trooper got the manager to come with a master key to the apartment door.

"Oh no, Daddy!"

Warren lay hunched over the dining room table. His papers lay strewn across the floor.

"I'll take Mrs. Clayton back to her room, trooper." The manager took Eve's hand. "If that's okay?"

They both completely ignored him. The trooper checked for a pulse and then called for an ambulance. Lowering Warren gently down onto the floor.

Olivia pushed the trooper away from him. "I'll do this, Dad!" The tears flowed. Frantically, she began chest compressions. "Daddy please don't leave me."

# CHAPTER 57

*I need to speak with you Now!* Emerson hit send on his phone.

Reese pulled the car over and picked up her phone. "What's wrong?"

"Did you tell me you put the briefcase in the back of the SUV under the spare tire?"

"I did."

"It's gone."

"No, it's not. Oh, ye of little faith, my love. Pick up the rug where the spare tire is."

"I did that. It's just the tire."

"Pick up the spare. Underneath it is another rug."

"Are you kidding me? How the hell did you know that?"

"I'd like to say I'm smarter than you, but seriously, I was thinking, this is like a freaking James Bond kind of vehicle. I just picked up the tire a little and saw another rug under it. Lifted it and tossed the briefcase in."

"Son of a bitch, it's there."

"Gotta go, I'm getting a call from Olivia. Love ya!"

Emerson dialed Peter back.

"What happened? Why did you hang up?"

"Peter, I have it. My beautiful fiancé hid the real case a little too well."

"So, you, have it?"

"Yes, now what the fuck do I do with it?"

"I'll let you know as soon as I can, pal. Where is Liz?"

"I've got to drop. I'm getting a call from Reese."

Emerson accepted the incoming call. "What's up?"

"They took my dad to the hospital. It appears he had a mild heart attack. Olivia went with him. I'm staying with Mom until I hear from her. Geez Emerson," her voice cracked. "Are we ever going to have a normal life?"

"Reese, sweetheart, I'm on my way. Where is Liz?"

"She is with me. I didn't want to leave her alone. She's actually been a big help to me."

"That's great. I'll be there soon. I want you to know that I love you, Reese Clayton."

"Emerson Lake, I love you too."

Liz sat next to Reese's mom, gently stroking Eve's hair. "Detective Clayton, are you okay?"

"Yes, I'm fine," Reese took a deep breath and pulled herself together.

"What's the plan for me to go to D.C.? I'm not trying to rush you at all. I'm grateful for all you have done for me and Alicia. Just eager to see her."

"Not sure yet. Alicia's dad is making the arrangements. I would feel the same way, Liz. Do you mind if I ask you a few questions?"

"Go ahead. What do you need to know?"

"Did you see Dr. Levy take Alicia from the restaurant that night?"

Liz looked at Reese. Puzzled by the question. "Why?"

"You tipped Peter and Emerson off about Dr. Levy. I was wondering, if you saw him take Alicia, why didn't you yell for help or try to stop him yourself?"

# CHAPTER 58

Emerson's phone buzzed. Captain Shawn Connelly's name appeared on the screen.

"Captain Connelly, are you out of the hospital already? Didn't they like you enough to help with your wounds?"

"Smart ass South Dakota riffraff. Seriously, yes, I'm fine. I'm headed back to the station with a badly bruised ego. I wanted to call you myself and tell you that my squad car didn't make it to the garage for inspection. Neither did the tow truck nor the driver."

"What? Where are they?"

"The report says the tow truck went off the road on that hairpin turn. The truck and my car exploded. The driver is dead."

"Holy shit!"

"That's not all, Lake. Trooper Matthews is missing. His cruiser was also found at the bottom of the cliff."

# CHAPTER 59

Emerson was greeted by local law enforcement at the Grace Center entrance. Asked for ID and the usual questions. They gave him the okay to go inside. He was surprised they didn't ask for his firearm.

He arrived at Eve's room to find Reese standing in front of Liz with her arms folded. "I'm here, ladies."

Reese's expression softened. She greeted him with a hug and a quick kiss.

"What's going on? The tension in here, you could cut with a knife."

"I was just asking our friend Liz here a few questions about the night Alicia disappeared."

"And?"

"I just wanted to know why she didn't stop Dr. Levy from taking Alicia from the bar that night?"

"That is a great question. And your answer, Liz?"

"It's not what you're thinking."

"Why don't you enlighten us then," Reese refolded her arms.

"When I came out of the kitchen that night, I saw Dr. Levy

and Alicia getting cozy at the bar. I didn't know what to think. I felt hurt. I never thought for a minute she would cheat on me, especially with a man. I was still really upset."

"Then what happened?" Reese asked.

"I returned to the kitchen to get another order. When I came out, he was leading her out the door, and she was close to him. Her head was leaning on his shoulder, his arm around her waist. I went to the restroom and cried. Even thought about tossing the ring down the drain. I also thought about shooting that bastard. When I came out, a mutual friend of ours told me Levy must have put something in her drink. Said she was wobbly. Alicia does not drink, detectives. That's when I called the police."

"Why didn't you tell them that Alicia was your girlfriend?"

"Seriously, detective? I know things have changed a lot for the gay community, but my boss does not approve of this at all. He made that clear by the way he talked about queer people with his friends. I needed the job. Alicia and I kept it quiet. That is, until she told her dad, I guess."

"Reese, are you through questioning our friend here?"

"Yes, I'm sorry I made you feel uncomfortable, Liz, but I had to hear it from you."

"I understand."

"Now, what have you heard about your dad, Reese?"

"Olivia said they are keeping him for observation and to run some tests before they release him. Probably will change his meds. She will stay with him for a while. Said she will call before she leaves the hospital."

"Okay, that sounds positive. Glad to hear it. I know this is out of left field, but do you still have FBI Agent Wells's number on your phone?"

"You mean the good-looking agent who tried his best to steal me away from you when he helped us catch that serial killer in South Dakota? That Agent Wells?" She squinted her eyes and then winked at him.

She picked up her phone and scrolled. "Yes, I have it."

"Good. I'll ask you later why you still have it." He nudged Reese in the arm and gave Liz a little wink.

Liz smiled and gave him the thumbs-up. "You guys are too funny. I guess I need to lighten up a bit about being in love."

"Exactly!" Reese and Emerson said at the same time.

"Now let's see about getting you to D.C." Emerson said.

"I'm leaving for a bit, Mom." Reese rubbed her mother's back. "Will you be, okay?"

"Why don't I stay with her till you get back?" Liz offered.

Reese looked at Emerson for approval. He shrugged.

"Are you sure you want to do this, Liz?"

"Of course. It's the least I could do after all you've done for Alicia and me. Besides, my grandma had dementia, and I guess that's pretty close to the same thing. Eve seems to like me."

"That's true. This is the quietest I've seen her since we arrived, Emerson. Didn't even dawn on me how calm she has been having Liz play with her hair."

Emerson nodded to Reese.

"All right, then we'll be back in about an hour. Remember, she likes to walk a lot. Up and down the halls. Are you comfortable accompanying her?"

"Of course. Go, make my travel arrangements, please."

Reese hugged her mom and then Liz. "Thank you, my friend,

187

for doing this."

"I'm headed to the hospital. I need to make sure Dad is all right. Emerson, call me later."

"Will do." He kissed her, hugged her, and asked, "Will you ever marry me?"

"You can't say we haven't tried, my love. But yes, of course, I'll marry you."

# CHAPTER 60

"Captain Connelly, please. This is Detective Emerson Lake."

The dispatcher put him straight through.

"What did you find out, captain?"

"Not much yet, Lake. The medical examiner says it could take days or weeks to come up with answers to the whole mess. And Trooper Matthews is still missing. His body hasn't turned up at the morgue, so I'm guessing he's still alive. But now, I have to consider him a suspect. What about the two of you? Have you found anything yet?"

"I believe we have found a reliable person to hold the briefcase, captain. He's an agent with the FBI. His name is Mike Wells. We worked with him on an escaped serial killer case in South Dakota. He saved my lady from being blown up in her car."

"I remember that case. It was all over the news and, of course, our wire. By the way, how is your captain doing? I heard she left her position?"

"We're not sure if she will return or not. Terrible about what happened. It affected all of us in the department."

"So, how do we do this? Should I contact Wells, or do you want to do this?"

"I'll see if he's in the New York office first. If he is, I can set up a meeting."

"Will Mr. Andora be comfortable with this, detective?"

"Right now, captain, I don't care if he's comfortable. I should be on a beach somewhere. That would make me comfortable."

# CHAPTER 61

"Amazing," he said. "I never in a million years expected to hear your beautiful voice again, detective. How are you?"

"Awe, I'm flattered, Wells, but this is Emerson you're talking to, not my bride-to-be."

"Ah, bride-to-be. You mean I still have a chance with her," Wells laughed. "I knew she was too much for you to handle. What's up Lake? You must be calling for a better reason than me busting your balls."

"You would be right. We need a favor."

"I'll try. What's this about?"

Emerson explained they were on Alicia's case. "Mike, do you know an agent named Peter Andora?"

"How the hell do you know him, Lake? No one outside the bureau is supposed to know his real name. What the fuck is going on?"

"Alicia is Peter's daughter. She's being treated somewhere in a D.C. hospital. He asked for our help. He won't leave her side."

"I wouldn't either. So, someone abducted her?"

"That's what I'm trying to tell you. Yes, she is the one. She went by the last name Holmes, not Andora."

"Why didn't Peter tell us? Lake, we have an entire team investigating his wife's death."

"Well, so are we, my friend. He thinks she was murdered for something she uncovered at her brokerage firm."

"Lake, we have already confiscated her computer."

"I know, but she had copies of her records and other key documents. Stashed them, in case if she needed to defend herself in court."

"And I'm guessing you're telling me this because you have them?"

"Yes, but the only people we know we can trust are you and your recruit Carly, of course, but this might be too deep for her to help."

"Do you want me to meet you at your precinct?"

"No, Reese and I are in Vermont."

"Vermont? Why Vermont?"

"Long story. Are you in the New York office?"

"Yes, so that will make things easy. Send me the address where you're staying. I'll be there in a couple of hours."

"Thanks Mike. Oh, and agent, call if you get lost."

"Yeah, I'll do that. Right after I call your girlfriend first. Smart ass! See you shortly, my friend."

# CHAPTER 62

"Peter, it's Reese. We have some news for you. Good news, but still need your permission to move forward. We have a friend in the FBI who wants to help you. We need to know if you trust us to do this for you."

"Who is this friend, and what exactly are you trusting him to do?"

"We've worked with him before. He saved my life. We want to give him the briefcase."

"What? I don't know Reese."

"Listen Peter, we trust him with our lives. He told Emerson they've been hitting a brick wall with what they have on Judith's case. There is nothing so far to convince them your wife's demise was not an accident. If they could get a look at that red bag of hers it could prove otherwise."

"I know, but trust is something I'm having a problem with lately."

"Do you trust us?"

"I do, but you aren't the ones I work for. Someone at my job has thrown a monkey wrench into the wheel of justice. I just can't pinpoint who it could be or if there is more than one."

"Peter, may I ask you a question? I want an honest answer."

"I'll answer. Honestly? That's a maybe."

"Why did you tell us your real last name? We were told no one was supposed to know your true identity."

"No one was supposed to know, Reese. But I no longer give a rat's ass. I'm done hiding in filthy places all over the world. I'm done with the cloak-and-dagger shit. I'm tired of killing people who are trying to infiltrate our country. While knowing if something went wrong, it would be my fault. Ever hear of the saying Reese, shit flows downhill? I'm through with being a deep agent. As soon as I find out who is responsible for killing my wife, they're dead. I will be free to fish and swim all summer and I don't know about winter yet. Spend some time with my daughter and her betrothed."

"I hear you, believe me, I get wanting to run away from our jobs. It's not easy. The point is you trusted us then. Can't you trust us now? We also want our friend to arrange for Liz to get to D.C. safely."

"You're asking an awful lot from me Reese. If I agree, can you and Emerson do one more thing for me?"

"We'll try our best."

"Would one of you be willing to travel with Liz to D.C.?"

# CHAPTER 63

Craig Stockton stood in front of the floor-to-ceiling windows, staring down at the streets below his sixteen story Manhattan office, waiting on word from a young man. If anything goes wrong, he thought, all of this is gone. "I need to see Olivia. She always makes me feel better."

His secretary gave a knock on his door. "Mr. Stockton, sir. Your next client is here."

"Show him in. See you tomorrow. Have a great evening."

"Thank you, Mr. Stockton. I'll see you in the morning."

The young man sat in a chair in front of the mahogany desk. A chair fit for royalty. Plush white silk fabric. The overstuffed back with wings and an armrest so wide and comfortable it made you want to take a nap.

"I'd like to see my portfolio." The young man's body snuggled into the embrace of the opulent chair, a symbol of the lifestyle he hoped to have one day soon. "I hope my portfolio is as large as this desk."

"Oh, you won't be disappointed." Craig Stockton opened the file on his desk and slid it across the desk. "By the way, is everything done on your end that I requested?"

The young man cocked his head slightly. "Hey man, you hired me to  do your dirty work. And in return, you were supposed to make me rich so I could retire from this god-awful job. I held up my end of the bargain."

"Good. Now let's see what I have for you. The companies that I have invested with for years have always been good to me. They are doing well for you too." He spun the folder around so the young man could see a long list of investments. However, there were no totals indicated. "What do you say we go out on the veranda and have a glass of champagne? Dom Perignon?"

They walked out into the evening sky; the breeze was strong at that height.

"Have a seat. Let's talk. When did you decide you wanted to work in law enforcement?"

"I didn't. It was my old man. That was his dream, not mine. I want out of it as soon as I see how my money is doing with your firm."

"Look," Craig said. "The market is a hit-or-miss investment. You know that. You're not a stupid kid."

"No, I am not. And I'm hoping what I just did for you was not a mistake. One that will cost me my job and land me in a prison cell. I would like to withdraw the amount that's in my account now. We part ways and never see each other again."

"Look, that's not possible until the market reopens on Monday."

"And then on Monday, I'm guessing my investments take an incredible hit. Am I right? You are fucking me over, aren't you?"

"The market is a tricky business. It has its ups and downs. I think it's time for you to leave, kid."

Trooper Jared Allen Matthews stood and pulled out his weapon. "Give me my fucking money," shoving Stockton toward the glass doors.

"Who the fuck do you think you're talking to?" Craig Stockton punched him in the face, landing the young trooper over the table, the champagne landing on the plush rug against the wrought-iron railing.

Never once losing his grip on the gun, "I'm your worst nightmare," he said, blood dripping down his lip.

The gun fired.

# CHAPTER 64

"Agent Wells, so nice to see you again, my friend." Emerson opted for the man-hug instead of a handshake. "How was your flight? Sorry, Reese isn't here right now. She's at the nursing home with her mom."

"That's okay. At some point, I'll see her. I hope you are ready when she flies into my arms, Lake."

"I'm not worried. Sit. Let me get you a drink."

"How about a cup of coffee?"

"Sounds good. Now, how is your partner Agent Olden these days?"

"He's good, taking a vacation with his family. About time."

"I get it. Us too, but as you can see, that isn't working out so well."

Emerson filled Mike Wells in on all the details of how they met Peter and everything else that had led them up to retrieving the red briefcase.

"That is fucking weird. What are the odds of something like this happening?"

"Beats the shit out of me. This briefcase needs to be in the

198

right hands, and those hands belong to you, my friend. We hope anyway. We also could use your help to get Peter's daughter's fiancé into a D.C. trauma Center where she was admitted. She was kidnapped too. Until we know who is behind all of this, we'd like her to have an escort for her safety."

"I think we can arrange that. Now, back to this briefcase. Before we open it, we need someone here with us, someone to verify what it is we find or don't find. I'm letting you choose."

"Captain Shawn Connelly, Vermont State Police."

"Okay you contact him. I'll get everything ready to record the event."

Emerson made the arrangements. "He's on his way. I better get Reese in the loop." He pulled out his smartphone and tapped away.

*At the hotel with Mike. Going to ask Captain Connelly to be a witness. Can you stay occupied for a short while until we're done?*

Three pulsating dots appeared on his screen.

*I somehow doubt it will be a short while, but yes. Peter asked if one of us could accompany Liz to D.C. I have to stay here with my family. Can you go?*

Emerson responded.

*I'll speak to him later about that. I love you, sweetheart. BTW... Wells says hello.*

*No attempts at wooing me away from you, babe? I'm disappointed.*

Emerson chuckled to himself.

*Oh, believe me, he still has his mind set on getting you! I'll talk to you soon!*

There was a knock at the door.

"Captain Connelly, c'mon in. I'd like you to meet a friend of mine. FBI Agent Michael Wells."

"Looks like you had a run-in with a train, captain," Wells said as he shook the captain's hand.

"Feels like it too! Nice to meet you, agent. Shall we get started?"

Mike Wells hit "record." For documentation purposes, he stated the date, time, location, who was present, and the reason for this meeting.

"Do either of you have a key to this briefcase?"

"No, I do not," Captain Connelly responded.

Emerson stated the same.

With no key, they had to force it open. Using a pocket-knife and small hammer, they MacGyvered the case open in under five minutes. Mike Wells removed a pile of folders, each containing files and documents on clients of Judith Andora. Handing some to Emerson and the captain, while keeping the rest for himself to review.

"What exactly are we looking for?" the captain asked.

"Any transactions involving large amounts of funds being transferred between the United States and foreign adversaries."

"How large are we talking, agent? Everything I'm looking at seems large to me. I can't imagine having this much money bankrolled."

"I understand," Wells said. "For the average person, investing in the stock market through their 401K is a way to secure a comfortable retirement lifestyle. The rest of these investors are already multi-millionaires, and all they want is power."

Lake raised his hand. "I may have found something."

The captain's phone buzzed. He answered abruptly. "I told you I did not want to be disturbed unless it was an emergency." He listened intently for several minutes and then disconnected the call. "It seems like I might have something as well, gentlemen."

"What is it?" Mike asked.

"That phone call was from my station. It appears we have another body, Detective Lake."

"You're kidding? Who is it?"

"One of my own. My missing trooper. Jared Matthews."

"Oh shit!" Emerson was stunned. "Where was he found? Do they know what happened?"

"Wait," Wells raised his hand. "Don't say another word. Let me shut off the recording."

"No," Captain Connelly said, "leave it on."

"What's going on?" Emerson was confused.

"It appears, and I'm using that word lightly, that he fell off the 16th floor balcony of an office building in Manhattan."

"What?" Lake gripped the files in hands. Squeezing them in disbelief.

"How did they know he fell from the 16th floor?" Wells asked.

"NYPD did a search of the building and discovered the trooper's service weapon on the balcony. From what they just told me, it sounds like it was brutal. His body hit a parked car before smashing to the sidewalk."

"Oh, shit." Emerson winced at the thought. "Manhattan? What the hell was he doing there?"

"I don't know, but that's not all. NYPD says Trooper Matthew's weapon had been fired recently."

"Did they find the bullet? Or was your trooper shot with his own gun?" Wells asked.

"Neither, but they found blood droplets on the veranda."

# CHAPTER 65

"Okay," Wells said. "Let's back up a minute. What the hell does any of this have to do with Judith Andora's death?"

"My future sister-in-law, Olivia Clayton, is dating this guy."

"Which guy?"

"Craig Stockton."

"So, you feel there is some connection to Judith's death and this Stockton guy?"

"I would bet my life on it, Michael Wells." Emerson handed him the wrinkled folder that he had clung to since the conversation began. He held back one sheet of paper. He looked directly into the camera that was still videotaping "I found a note attached to this folder that we found in the briefcase. It reads:

*To Whom It May Concern:*
*My name is Judith Maxwell.*
     *I am an Investment Manager with C.A. Stockton and Associates in Manhattan.*
     *I need you to know the truth and since I likely can't speak*

203

*for myself, I hid this briefcase so it could do the talking for me. In it are copies of suspicious transactions I discovered in portfolios that indicate they were assigned to me. You will find copies of stolen items that were sold to unreliable overseas corporations for exorbitant amounts of money. These were NOT my clients. I never met with them. I did not form nor encourage any of these transactions.*

*When I flagged the activity, I received a note stating that if I leaked any information to the authorities, there would be deadly consequences to me and my family. You'll also find the note in the case. In order to protect my husband and daughter, I kept the secret. But I was never safe. I knew it wouldn't be long before the Securities and Exchange Commission discovered what I already knew. Brokers are not allowed to make transactions like this, only Investment Managers, and with my name falsely listed on these portfolios, I knew I would be the scapegoat and go to prison.*

*Please, if anything happens to me or my family, the Securities and Exchange Commission needs to investigate Mr. Craig Stockton. So does the FBI, CIA, Secret Service, or all of the above. He is trading with overseas accounts, using fake documents. These people are looking to gain access to real estate and financial wealth in our country. This could turn into a money laundering scheme with a much higher terrorist threat to the U.S.*

*I made a video of myself. Look in the lower, right-hand back corner of the case, under the fabric. My testimony, if needed.*

*Last but not least. If you're reading this note, it probably means I'm dead. Please share these final messages with my family.*

*Peter,*

*I love you. Always have, always will. Release me and find new happiness. I'm sure you will do as I ask of you. One more thing, Sherlock, give up that damn job!*

*Alicia,*

*You are the heartstrings of my very soul. I love you so much. If you need me, I will answer in a manner that only you, my beautiful, kind daughter, can feel.*

*Thank you,*

*Judith Maxwell-Andora*

"I'm turning off the video and audio equipment now. I believe we have all we need." With that, Emerson clicked off the power.

"Gentlemen." Agent Well's stated, "I'll make sure the contents of this red briefcase get into the proper hands."

"Thank you, agent, for your help." The captain extended his hand.

"Oh, we are not through yet, captain. Are you hungry?"

"I am now."

"Emerson, contact Reese. See if she's available for dinner. Tell her I'd like her to bring Liz too. Bags packed. I'm escorting her to D.C. I need to have a conversation with Peter."

"Yes, that's fine, but we'll need a place for Liz to stay that's secure," Emerson responded.

"We have accommodations in the guest wing of the hospital. She will have 24/7 security. Or, if she wishes, we can add another bed to Alicia's room."

"Agent Wells, will you keep us informed as your case progresses?" Captain Connelly asked. "I still need to investigate what happened to my trooper and why he was at C.A. Stockton and Associates. It doesn't look good. The press will have questions."

Wells began collecting the papers and putting them back into the red briefcase. "Captain, because someone possibly murdered your trooper, that, as you know, is a capital offense. You know what you have to do. I'm sure the NYPD will help wherever needed, but if you confirm Trooper Matthews was working with Craig Stockton, I will need all the information you have on him. Here is my card with private contact phone info. As for the press, keep it simple. Confirm his off-duty death and confirm it is being investigated. Other than that, no comment."

# CHAPTER 66

Emerson wrote as fast as he could on a pad of paper. "Wait till Peter hears this."

"I'm not sure if we should let Peter know until we are sure we have this guy," Wells said.

"I suppose you're right." Emerson put the pad on the table.

"Hey, you mentioned the helicopter pilot that picked up Liz's captor was not the person Peter was expecting to make the grab."

"Yeah, strange. I did get a picture of him. It's not very clear since I was holding my phone at my side, but we could run it to see who he is or if he's in the system."

"Good idea," the captain said, more engaged with the FBI than he ever thought possible. He had always thought the feds were all full of themselves, but this experience made him realize not all of them are like that. They probably think the same about small town LEOs.

"Send me the photo, Lake," said Wells, picking up his cell phone. "I'll get it to Carly and tell her to put a rush on it."

"Got it. Yeah, I'm afraid Carly will tell me to go to hell if I ask her for anything else in her lifetime."

"I doubt that would happen, Lake."

"May I say something here?" Captain Connelly asked.

"Have at it, captain."

"Agent Wells, people are dropping like flies around here, and it seems they all have a powerful connection to this one case. So much so that we have round-the-clock security at the Grace Center facility."

"Yes, Emerson filled me in on the murdered nurse and the young man portraying a priest. I'm guessing the connection is this Stockton character. This guy could lose billions of dollars, and his life, if things go wrong with his overseas dealings. The people we are talking about will not just give him a slap on the wrist if things go sideways and he knows it."

"We need to find out whose blood is on that Manhattan veranda. If it's Craig Stockton's, we may have him by the balls. It might take some time before the medical examiner knows if the trooper took a shot at Stockton before going over the railing. Ballistics will have all of that."

"I hate to say this, captain, but it is also possible your trooper is involved with all of this. Or should I say, was involved."

"I agree with you, agent, but I need to find out for sure. If that's the case, why did he want to become a cop in the first place?"

"Maybe the money?" Agent Wells speculated. "It's possible he was investing with Stockton. When we get into those files, we'll know for sure why he was there. I can't imagine he found Craig Stockton on his own. Are we done here? Because I could eat a horse right now." This time, Mike Wells reached for Captain Connelly's hand. "Thank You captain for all your help in this matter. Hopefully, we can have a good outcome in this case."

"Anytime, Agent Wells, anytime."

"Lake, did you hear from Reese?" Wells asked.

"Yes, we are going to meet all three of them here at the hotel in the dining room. Reese's sister Olivia will be joining us as well. They have a nice menu."

"How nice?"

"Oh, you know, beef tongue, octopus soup, pickled eggs. The usual stuff."

"You're still an ass, Lake." Wells shook his head and headed for the door. "Captain, how the hell have you put up with him?"

"Just fucking lucky, I guess." The door clicked behind them as they headed to the restaurant.

Reese, Liz, and Olivia walked into the lobby to see their dinner partners already having a drink at the bar. Michael Wells's face lit up when his eyes fell upon Reese.

"Michael, I am so excited to see you again," Reese met him halfway and gave him a big hug.

"I told you Lake, huh, I knew it all along," Wells gave Emerson a wink as he grabbed Reese around the waist. "I missed you, Reese, and that beautiful face of yours."

Reese pulled away a bit. "How have you been and how is Agent Olden these days?"

"He's fine." His arms released her from the embrace. "And I'm better now that I'm looking at you."

"Stop it." She backed away and grabbed Emerson. Kissing him hello.

"Agent Wells, I would like you to meet Liz...." Reese cocked her head. "Liz, we don't know your last name. How stupid is that?"

Wells offered his hand. "Mike Wells FBI. Pleased to meet you, Ms. Carter."

"Seriously, you already know her?" Emerson was impressed.

"You're not the only one connected to Carly." I contacted Peter for information on Liz, and all he had was her last name from Alicia. The rest is from Carly.

Captain Connelly shook his head. "Can we eat, please? The shenanigans here are making me hungry. And a wee bit thirsty."

All agreed as they took their seats.

"May I?" Mike pulled a chair out for Liz and waved his hand toward the seat.

"Of course. Thank you."

They ordered their meals before discussing what was next. Olivia, taking all of it in, just nodded her head as they introduced Mike Wells. All the while thinking, wow, my sister is important.

"First," Mike said, "thank you, Liz, for helping to find Alicia. I'm sure you are eager to see her. Are you comfortable with me escorting you to the D.C. hospital?"

"If the detectives are saying you are the good guy, yes, I am, sir."

"We will leave after dinner, drive to Albany International, and then board one of our planes. We'll arrive in D.C. in no time at all. Once there, our agents will meet and drive us to the hospital. Do you have questions?"

"Actually, yes, I do. Why was Dr. Levy not put in jail when he lost his medical practice? Why was he allowed to reopen somewhere else? Olivia told me that's what happened. Could it be deep pockets? It just pisses me off." Liz slammed her fork to the table.

Shocked at how upset she was, Mike Wells responded, "I don't know how that happened. I really don't know anything about his case. I'm here because of the death of your fiancé's mother. A case that is long overdue to be solved. Alicia's dad and I work for the FBI, and I have been on the team looking into her untimely death for two years. We now have the answers, at least some of them. When I bring you to see Alicia, I am hoping Peter will find some sort of peace in his life after all this time."

"I would certainly hope so, Agent Wells. Alicia has never been whole after losing her mom."

"From what I know about Peter, he has not been whole either," Olivia interjected.

"I'm thrilled to meet Mr. Andora." Liz's expression seemed to lighten. "I hope he sees how much I love his daughter."

"He already knows, Liz." Reese gave her a pat on the hand.

"Okay, Agent Wells, I'm in if you are. But if something goes wrong, I'm calling Reese. She knows how to handle you."

Mike nearly choked on his mashed potatoes, trying not to spit them out. "Deal. You are one tough cookie, young lady. Ever thought of joining the bureau?"

"Not in this lifetime."

"Then why did you get a degree in criminal justice?" Mike asked.

"How do you know that?" She raised an eyebrow.

He cocked his head. "Ms. Carter, how can you ask that question? Do you think for one moment I would allow you on my aircraft, yet alone into D.C., without checking you out?"

"Ah, right, forgot you have resources. I am a lesbian Mr. Wells and although we've come a long way, we still battle for our rights every day in the LGBTQIA + community. I got that degree because I wanted to know everything I could about those rights."

"Then why not use that degree to fight for those rights?" Reese asked. "Why be a server at a bar when you could be an attorney fighting legal battles by belonging to a different bar."

Mike Wells handed her his card. "When you are ready, Liz, call me and I will lead you in the right direction to become an attorney or an advocate for civil rights." His phone buzzed. "Excuse me, I have to take this call, be right back."

"We have your back, Liz," Reese said. "All of us at this table do."

Mike Wells returned to the table, carefully sending a text to Emerson.

*That chopper did not belong to us. No I.D. on the pilot either. Could have been anyone. We'll probably never know. Possibly one of Stockton's cronies.*

Emerson saw the text and slipped his phone back into his pocket.

"Now can I have dessert?" Captain Connelly asked. "I rarely get to eat in a place like this."

"Me neither," Liz said. "I'll have the biggest dessert they have."

"Before dessert," Liz said, "I have one more question. Reese... Emerson...is it possible for one of you to travel with us? I'm still nervous about traveling with someone I barely know."

"Emerson, you'd have to make the trip," Reese said. "I can't leave my sister with Mom and Dad right now, sweetheart. So, you go and hurry back."

"Will do."

They all enjoyed their delicious desserts and paid the bill. As they were all leaving the table, Emerson caught a brief glimpse of someone passing by the window. The face was somehow familiar.

"Something wrong, honey?" Reese asked as they walked toward the lobby. "Everything okay?"

"No, it's not. I just hate to leave you alone to handle things while I'm gone."

Everyone smiled at how sweet it was that he was worried about Reese.

Emerson pulled Reese toward him into a tight hug and quietly whispered in her ear. "I just caught a glimpse of a guy with blonde hair staring at us through the restaurant windows. I couldn't quite see his face, but I got an eerie feeling. Please be careful and keep your eyes peeled." He released his grip slightly and kissed her passionately. "I love you. Be back by tomorrow night. I hope anyway. I'll call when I'm on my way."

"We will be fine," she reassured him. "Love you too." She leaned closer and whispered. "Did you set the date yet?" Her eyes beamed.

"Yes, I did. When I return from D.C., I'll meet you at the courthouse."

"I think that's a splendid plan, detective. It's perfect." Her eyes welled up with tears. She kissed him again. "Now go, before I cry."

Reese gave Liz a warm hug. "I wish you all the happiness in the world, young lady. My best to you and Alicia."

"Thank you, detective, and I will think seriously about my career choices, promise."

"Michael, take care of my man or I'll shoot your ass."

"I will, the lucky bastard." Michael reached out his hand to shake hers.

"Seriously?" Reese gave him a quick hug.

"Captain, if you are ever in need of anything, anything at all, you now know how to reach me." Mike said.

"You as well, Agent Wells. It's been a pleasure. Sort of."

They all laughed and went their separate ways.

Olivia grabbed Emerson, pulled him aside, and whispered something in his ear.

He smiled at her, giving her a big hug.

As Liz and Olivia headed for the elevator, Reese pulled Emerson back. "What was that all about?"

"She thanked me for bringing you back into her life." He then handed Reese a handkerchief from his sports coat pocket.

# CHAPTER 67

"How the hell did you get shot, Stockton? And by whom?"

"Don't know. I was walking on the street and saw a bunch of guys roughing up a young woman. She was yelling and fighting back, but you know damn well she didn't have a chance in hell of getting away from them. I just said, hey, get the fuck off of her, and one of them took a shot at me. Can you fix me up, Doc? I've got a serious meeting in a few hours. There is no way I can hand it off either. You have my word that I will be back later this afternoon, so you can check on me."

"I'm warning you; this is going to hurt like hell. Do you want me to give you something for the pain? It's going to cloud your thinking for a few hours. Not sure if you will handle the meeting in a drugged state. What do you think? The choice is yours."

"No drugs, Doc."

"Okay, I'll just numb the area with lidocaine, but you are not driving back to your office. I will call you a cab. Be back here before closing. Got it?"

"I got it. Just get on with it."

The Manhattan physician removed the bullet and placed it

on a metal tray with all the bloody gauze. He stitched Craig Stockton's shoulder wound. "You are one lucky bastard. You need to be in a hospital getting IV antibiotics."

"Can't right now. I changed my mind, give me something for the pain."

"Whatever I give you will not help much at all. The bullet missed your carotid artery by only a couple of inches. I need to send you to the hospital."

"I said no. Now help me up before I kick your ass."

"Okay, okay. Calm down. No hospitals. Sit tight, I'll get you something for the pain."

The doctor left the room, mumbling, "I'm not losing my license to anybody. I don't care if he was my investment broker or not."

Approaching the nurse at the desk, "Have an ambulance pick up, Mr. Stockton. Send him to NY Presbyterian Hospital." He then handed her his report.

"Yes, doctor. Right away."

"After you make the call, collect the bullet and bloody gauze from the exam room. We need to send it to the FBI forensics lab immediately."

The doctor walked back to the exam room only to find the door ajar. "Craig?"

The room was empty.

# CHAPTER 68

Reese and Olivia arrived at Grace Center. "Mr. Horton, what are you doing out here? It's cold out."

"I was just getting some fresh air and thinking. I need to speak with you, Reese, when you get a moment."

"Okay, but first I want to check on Mom. Olivia, can you stay with Mr. Horton?"

"Actually Mr. Horton, I think you should go inside now." Olivia laced her arm under his to help him up. "I don't want you getting chilled out here."

"Okay." He nodded his head and held onto Olivia for support.

"Go ahead, Reese. We'll meet you inside," Olivia said.

Reese searched the hallways. You must be roaming around here somewhere, Mom.

The door to Eve's room was closed. "Huh, that's unusual. Where is everybody?"

No nurses anywhere. She glanced over the desk, just in case. Nothing.

Reese cautiously opened the door.

"Oh My God! Mom, are you okay? Come out of there. Let

me help you, Mom. It's me, Reese."

Eve was crouched in the corner of her room, alongside her dresser. Tears ran down her contorted cheeks, a perplexed knot of confusion. Shaking with fear. "He's here. He's going to kill me. I think he killed Warren. I can't find Warren."

"Mom, come sit with me on the bed, sweetheart. Dad will be back shortly. He had a doctor's appointment today." Reese lied.

"Oh, that's right." Eve said as she tried to get up from the floor.

"Let me help you, Mom."

"We can change your clothes if that's all right with you. Make you look pretty for Dad."

What am I going to do? Reese wondered. Who knows how long she has been sitting here? Reese found a washcloth in the bathroom and wiped the tears from her Mom's face and then her own.

There was a knock at the door, just as she got her mom to sit on the bed.

"Detective, it's me, Captain Connelly."

"Come on in. Where is everyone?"

"There's a problem."

"What kind of problem?"

"Word got out that the nurse was murdered. Relatives started taking their families out of the facility. Nurses walked out. Only a few remain. For now, at least."

"Oh shit. What are we going to do now?"

"The higher-ups are on my ass for not securing the building without drawing attention to the homicide. Her family let that cat out of the bag."

"When you have a police presence, it's difficult to not draw attention."

"Exactly. I assume even families who never visited their loved ones were involved too."

Reese felt like crawling under a rock somewhere, knowing she was one of those relatives who never visited.

"Are you okay, detective?"

"I'm fine." I'll never let Olivia handle our parents alone again, she thought.

Eve sat very still on the bed, waiting for the captain to leave.

"I just heard that all patients are being transported to a different facility for their safety. There are only a few patients left anyway."

"That will not be good, captain," she whispered. "People living with Alzheimer's do not do well with change. They become more confused and more difficult to handle."

"Luckily, there are only five with that diagnosis, including your mother. The other facility is in Burlington though."

"No, absolutely not! That's too far away from Olivia." Reese shook her head. "What about the assisted living side where my dad lives?"

"Arrangements are being made for them at other locations, temporarily, of course. Just till we find this guy."

"I will arrange for my sister to house both of them under special nursing care at my expense until this is over. Dad is being released today."

"Are you sure, Reese?"

"It's fine. We'll manage."

The captain left and when Reese turned around, she saw

her mom sound asleep under the covers. Good time to see my teacher, she thought.

She made her way to Mr. Horton's room where he and Olivia were waiting. "What's wrong, Mr. Horton? You seem very sad today."

"Reese, I have something to tell you. I need to tell someone. Might as well be you. I can't live with myself if I don't."

"Mr. Horton, you can tell me anything."

"Remember when you came into my room and asked about the young priest?"

"Yes. What about him?"

"I saw a guy beating on the nurse behind the desk."

"The priest?"

"No, it wasn't the priest. The man beating the nurse kept saying, where is she? I didn't hear who he was asking about. I yelled at him to stop. He looked up at me with fury in his eyes. It was right at that moment that the priest came around the corner. The guy ran. The priest told me to go into my room, and that's when he asked if I needed to talk to God."

"Mr. Horton, do you think you can describe the guy assaulting the nurse? Maybe recognize him in a photo?"

"What struck me was his blonde hair."

# CHAPTER 69

Mike and Emerson boarded the agency plane with Liz.

"Holy shit," Liz's head spun around not knowing where to look first. "Is this a plane or a chalet with wings?"

Emerson laughed. "You wouldn't expect anything different from our government, would you?"

"I guess not. But it seems a little over the top. To think my hard-earned tax dollars pays for this thing."

"When you have to fly high-ranking officials around the world, comfort is a necessity. Here, this is what's available right now," Emerson motioned her to a seat. "Buckle up, Liz. You are on your way to see Alicia. She handled her attacker with the grit of a Marine. Whatever her father taught her over the years was certainly useful."

"Do you know if the guy...," she hung her head. "Was she abused in another way?"

"No, she was not raped, if that's what you're asking. Came damn close. He might have had she not dumped his naked ass on the floor!"

"That's my girl." Liz pumped her fist.

"But you should know Liz, he did administer some heavy narcotics. It may take Alicia a very long time to recover from that. The hospital thinks she should stay there and work with their addiction specialists to safely help her through withdrawal and recovery."

"Makes sense." Liz looked out the window as the plane started to taxi down the runway.

The plane landed, and a car was waiting to transport them to the hospital. Liz was not sure what to think of all the upper-echelon treatment she was getting.

Once they arrived at the hospital, Liz took a deep breath as they entered.

"Peter Andora, I would like you to meet Liz Carter," Emerson said. "Your daughter's betrothed."

"It's a pleasure to meet you properly, Liz," Peter said. He extended his hand, then stopped. You're about to be my daughter-in-law. "Come here," he grabbed Liz by the shoulders and pulled her close. "I need a hug. I don't know how to thank you for saving my daughter's life."

Not accustomed to parental affection, Liz held back a little, not wanting to seem over-excited. "Thank you, sir. Um, when can I see her?"

"Did they prepare you for what you are about to see?"

"As best we could, Peter." Mike replied.

Peter opened the door to Alicia's room. Liz gasped at the sight of the woman she loved. "Alicia, my love, my rock, I'm here, sweetheart." She slowly walked to the bedside, not wanting to scare her. "Alicia?" she repeated. "I'm here for you, honey. I've always been here for you." She gently kissed her forehead. "I'm here to help you, my only love. I'm sorry I didn't find you. I tried. I will always love you, Alicia Holmes. Always." The tears and the rasp in her throat were something she couldn't stop. She kissed her forehead again, watching as Alicia stirred, turning her head toward Liz. Her eyes were still closed.

Liz opened the purse that was slung over her neck and shoulder. Everyone in the room waited for that ring. The one that Alicia was hoping to see on the night of her abduction. It didn't matter if it was big or small.

Although they were men, Peter and Emerson had tears in their eyes.

First, Liz pulled out a tissue. "I'm sorry you had to go through this." She gently wiped her own eyes and placed it back in the purse. Her hand rummaged around in the bag.

Everyone in the room was waiting with anticipation.

Liz pulled her hand slowly from the satchel, only she wasn't holding the ring. It was a gun.

# CHAPTER 70

"Liz, no!" Emerson yelled before Peter even saw the gun.

Peter grabbed her arm, trying to pull her away from his daughter. The gun went off, hitting the left side of Alicia's head. Blood splattered on the pillow. And the wall behind her.

Agent Wells tossed Liz to the floor, wrestling for the gun that was now aimed at her own temple. "No!" he shrieked as she pulled the trigger.

The room flooded with staff and troopers. Guns drawn. While Peter lay across the limp body of his baby girl.

"Mr. Andora, please! Let us help your daughter," the doctor pleaded.

It took two doctors and Emerson to pull Peter away. His face wrought with anger, he moved toward Liz, blood spilling from her head onto the white tile floor. "Why? Why?" He kicked her in the side as she lay dead on the floor. "You piece of shit! Why?"

"Get her into the O.R. stat!" The doctor continued yelling orders at the staff.

Blood seeping through his shirt, Wells grabbed Peter, pushing him against the wall. "Fucking pull yourself together! Think like an agent. Why would she try to kill your daughter and herself? Did Alicia ever say her girlfriend had any mental issues?"

Peter's chest heaved. His heart raced. "No, all she ever said was we need to find her. She loved this girl. She killed my baby."

"You don't know that yet. Snap out of it."

"It's too late."

# CHAPTER 71

"Reese?"

She could tell this was not a good call. "What's wrong, hon?"

"It's Liz. She's dead. Shot herself in the head after attempting to murder Alicia."

"What?" Reese stumbled back and eased herself onto Eve's bed. "Emerson, what about Peter?"

"He's not good at all. Alicia is in the O.R. now. Reese, we made a mistake. None of us thought to do a search of Liz before boarding the plane. Something is so wrong with this whole thing, Reese. I just can't put my finger on it. How am I going to help Peter?"

"I'm not sure you can, Emerson. What does Michael have to say about all this?"

"He's trying to get Peter to think like an agent, not a father."

"Good luck with that."

"I know. I won't be back soon. Sorry about our plans, Reese."

"Me too, but I haven't had time to think about that either." She briefed him on her conversation with Mr. Horton and her father's release from the hospital. "Emerson let's just hope for a

good outcome for Peter and his daughter. I will handle everything here. I love you. Call when you hear about Alicia."

"I will."

"Emerson, wait. Search Liz's luggage. It might give us a clue.
It seems like she had this planned all along."

"Good idea. I feel like an idiot. She had all of us wrapped
around her little finger. One thing doesn't add up though. If
Liz wanted Alicia out of the picture, why did she tell us that Dr.
Levy took her? He could have done the job for her."

# CHAPTER 72

Emerson quickly sent a text to Mike Wells.

*Where are you?*

*Entrance to the O.R. waiting on word.*

Emerson's fingers flew across the keys.

*Do you have the luggage Liz brought with her and her purse?*

*Must still be in Alicia's room. Why?*

*Reese suggested they might hold a clue as to why Liz did what she did.*

Head back to the room. I'll meet you there. I'll tell Peter I'm going for coffee. Keep this between us until we find out if we have anything. No sense stirring the pot till something is about to stick to the bottom.

Mike and Emerson grabbed a pair of rubber gloves from the wall of Alicia's room.

"Could they make a large that is actually large?" Mike fumbled with the latex. Stretching it over his hand like a sausage.

"I'll start with the purse. You take on her travel bag." Emerson said.

The two carefully extracted the contents of bags.

"Detective, do you see a ring in there?"

"No, I do not. That's odd, don't you think?"

"I don't see one in her suitcase either. Wait just a minute. There is an envelope. It's addressed to, To Whom it May Concern." Mike raised an eyebrow.

"Well, we have concerns. A fucking lot of concerns, wouldn't you say?"

Agent Wells held the envelope away from his face and carefully unsealed it. It held a single, folded sheet of paper.

# CHAPTER 73

The doors to the operating room swung open, and Peter spun around to see Alicia's surgeon. Peter's eyes swelled, and his heart was ready to break.

"Mr. Andora, your daughter will be fine. The bullet barely grazed her head. Not that she won't have a scar and one hell of a headache for a while, but there is no damage to her skull or her brain. It's more like a deep cut. We used lidocaine to help numb the area we had to stitch. No other heavy drugs were used."

Peter gripped his hands to his chest and sighed heavily.

The surgeon put his hand on Peter's shoulder. "She's asleep in a recovery bay. I would leave her be for now. The nurse will stay in the room with her in case she wakes. I'd give her about an hour before you see her. Get a little rest, Mr. Andora. Your daughter will need you now more than ever."

"Thank you, doctor."

Peter texted Agent Wells to tell him the good news.

*Where are you now? I'll meet you.*

*Meet us in Alicia's room. We have something we think you should see.*

When Peter opened the door, Emerson and Mike greeted him

with a hug and a handshake.

"Glad to hear the news," Wells said.

"Me too, Wells. What have you got for me?"

"This letter we found in Liz's luggage. Read it and then you decide where we take it from here."

Peter took the sheet of paper and began to read.

*To whom it may concern:*

*I never wanted to hurt Alicia. I loved her with all my heart. You must believe that.*

"This is fucking bullshit." Peter let his hand, still gripping the letter, drop to his side. "She tried to kill my daughter." He screamed. A vein in his neck visibly pulsating.

"Just read the rest," Emerson pleaded with him.

> *To Whom It May Concern:*
>
> *I never wanted to hurt Alicia. I loved her with all my heart. You must believe that.*
>
> *The reason I did what I did was so she would not have to suffer the rest of her life with nightmares, unstable visions, mental breakdowns, the fear, the anger that overcomes his victims. The years of healing from broken bones, drug addiction, and rape.*
>
> *After all these years, I thought I was finally free of him and the pain he caused. Until I saw him with Alicia that night. I froze. All my fears of being tied up and tortured for the rest of my life flooded back. I didn't know what else to do but hide. I knew her life would be over soon, at least the life she knew before he took her. And there was nothing I could do to stop him. It was gut wrenching.*

*I gave Detective Lake the note at the restaurant out of my love for Alicia. I was hoping maybe, just maybe, they could find what he left of her. Yet, I was afraid of seeing it again. Seeing the harm he could inflict on the human body and mind. He put what was left of my body, at thirteen years old, in a barrel. Left there to die. Someone found me though. I was in rough shape. I spent some time in a mental hospital. I lied my way through that hellhole, which got me released.*

*As you read this, I am free of him and hope Alicia has joined me, if not now, in the future.*

*The man who called himself Dr. Jonathan Levy was my stepfather. My hope is, he will rot in hell.*

*I'm sorry for your pain. Mr. Andora. Truly, my love for her is real. Thank you for accepting that.*

*Liz Carter*


Peter Andora fell to his knees. The letter scrunched up and close to his chest. "No! No! God why?"

Emerson and Agent Mike Wells each got one side of Peter. Lifting him from the floor. Sitting him in Alicia's chair. Letting him cry it out. Mike went to get him a power drink to help replenish his electrolytes.

"When was the last time you ate anything nourishing, my friend?"

Peter just shook his head. "Do not know." His phone rang.

"Mr. Andora, you may see your daughter for a few minutes now."

Peter jumped off the chair. Emerson was right behind him.

"Hold on, cowboy. Get in that bathroom, wash your face, and use cold water in those eyes. You don't want her to see you like this."

"Give me the letter for safekeeping," Wells plucked the sheet from his grip.

"She's alive, my friend. Just think of that gift." Emerson led him through the doors.

Alicia lay silent, her eyes open. Seeing her dad, she smiled. "I'm okay Dad. I am. What happened to Liz?"

Peter hesitated.

"It's time for you to rest, Alicia," the nurse said. "You can talk to your dad more when we return you to your room. But for now, you need to sleep. Lots of sleep."

Peter gently kissed her forehead. "I love you. You are so strong."

"I got it from you." Alicia smiled and closed her eyes.

# CHAPTER 74

"Olivia, we need to talk."

"Well, sis, that is never a good way to start a conversation. Am I right?"

"Yes, you are indeed right. Grace Center is closing, at least temporarily. We need to do something quickly. The only place available for Mom and Dad is in Burlington."

"Reese, I can't travel to Burlington every day."

"I know. My idea is to move them into your house. I'll hire nurses and we'll get the hospital equipment needed for Dad to recuperate here. I will also see to it that anyone working here is thoroughly screened."

Olivia sighed. "Ok, yeah, I think that makes the most sense."

"And while Dad's here, I think we should talk to him about getting him a roommate when we find another assisted living apartment."

"Like whom? Certainly not Mom."

"No, I was thinking, Mr. Horton."

"That part sounds great, Reese. He will have someone to eat with and maybe find some common interest. At least have someone to talk to. It might take a little more research to find a place for Mom."

"What about the Wellington House?" Reese flipped her phone around. "Look at the photos. I think it looks nice, and it's less than a half hour from here. Five Star rating."

"Are you a wee bit off your rocker, Reese? Did you look at what it would cost to place her in there? It's a million-dollar entry fee."

"Yes, and the monthly fee will be deducted from that entrance fee. If any funds are left when she passes, they return it to the family."

"How are we going to come up with that kind of money?"

"My retirement account."

"You are off your rocker. I say we sell the stretch. That's worth a shitload of cash, don't you think? All those bells and whistles that come with that thing."

"I somehow think the federal government will have a problem with that."

# CHAPTER 75

Peter finally read Liz's note to Alicia. It was so painful to watch his daughter absorb yet another devastating shock. After spending a long while consoling her, he needed to hear a friendly voice and decided to call Olivia.

"This is a pleasant surprise," Olivia said when she answered. "Is Alicia, ok?"

"I am hoping she will be. Just wanted to tell you myself what happened."

Olivia could hear the sound of water running through a coffee machine in the background. "It sounds like you could use a shot of something in that coffee."

"You would be correct...but I don't see a place to swipe my credit card for that."

He quickly shared the events of the past 24 hours.

"My God, Peter, how is she handling all of this?"

"Right this minute? She is strong, but who knows what the next ten minutes will bring?"

"What can I do for you? I'm worried sick about you. These past few days have been an absolute nightmare."

"There is nothing you can do right now. Talking to me helps though. I just wish you were closer." Peter Andora surprised himself with that comment.

"Do you need me to fly there, be with you? I'll need that credit card though." Olivia thought she'd try to lighten the mood a bit.

Peter laughed. "No, not yet anyway. My suspicions were right about my wife. No concrete proof yet, but almost there. At least it's being investigated the right way." He paused for a few seconds.

"And what else, Sherlock? I can hear it in your voice. What?"

"Thank you for asking if you could be with me, Olivia. I needed to hear that. Can I see you when I come back?"

"I will wait for you." Olivia could feel the pain in his voice. "You can count on that. I'm sending you a warm hug."

"Liv."

"Yes."

"You don't know what that means to me right now."

"Oh, I think I do. I'm feeling your heartache, your pain, your loneliness. Stay strong Peter. I'm a phone call away. Until you return, be safe. Please."

"Yes, ma'am."

# CHAPTER 76

Agent Wells saw the Caller ID on his phone. "What can I do for you, captain?"

"I received a call from FBI forensics in NYC. I have the report in front of me."

"Why from the FBI?"

"I was hoping you would know."

"What does it say?"

"It states that the bullet came from my state trooper's gun. A bullet was never recovered from the Manhattan crime scene, Wells, how did the FBI get it? Something is fishy about this. I should have been the first one informed, agent. My state trooper is my responsibility."

"Captain, I completely agree. I will call you back in a few minutes, with answers."

It didn't take long for the return call.

"Captain, my apologies for the mix-up. The FBI didn't find that round."

"Then who?"

"A Manhattan surgeon. And also, a client of...."

"Let me guess, Craig Stockton?"

"You got it. The surgeon claims to have removed the bullet. Suggested Stockton go to the hospital. Of course, he ran before the ambulance came to get him. Luckily the smart doctor knew what a shady character Stockton is and had everything sent to the labs. Our labs."

"I'm guessing the doc had dealings with Stockton before, don't you?"

"No doubt. Also, pretty sure the doc was covering his ass. The ballistics report on the gun said it was a Smith & Wesson M&P 40 caliber. The rifling in the barrel matches the bullet."

"Figured that as well. Now, are we working together on this or not?"

"I'm going to say yes. This involves Stockton. We need to find him, and fast."

"I hardly think his capture will be fast. This guy is smart and has boatloads of dough to help him get out of the country if need be."

"That's my worry, captain, and also my job to see that he doesn't get out of the States."

"I don't know what to say about Trooper Matthews to the press. Although no one has inquired about him as of this afternoon. Something I find a little disturbing."

"Me too. Does he have any family?"

"There was only one person I was aware of. His father. He was in law enforcement at one time. Proud of his boy. He passed away from cancer-related issues from what I heard. He worked in NYC for a long time."

"This means Matthews was familiar with the city and probably encountered Stockton there. Strange, though, that he chose Vermont to be a trooper. He could have just moved upstate toward the Catskill area or Kingston and still have been a trooper."

"Trooper Matthews was not as upset with the news of his father's passing as he should have been. We had a ceremony here; the town came out with flags and tears. Not his son. I informed the crowd the family wanted to be alone. Nothing else I could say."

"Okay, you know what you have to do, and I know what my duties are. Let's find the truth. All of it. Captain, are you sure you don't want to come to work with the FBI?"

"You're an okay agent, Mike Wells, and to tell you the truth, that surprised the shit out of me. I'm fine right where I am. Thank you though, for the offer."

"Offer is always open. Talk soon."

"One more thing, agent. Any news on Judith's briefcase?"

"There is a load of info in that case, captain. It's like a full confession without being a full confession."

"Meaning?"

"Meaning, we have identified the people involved in the murder of Judith Maxwell-Andora. At least some of them. All from foreign countries."

"So, it was murder?"

"Yes, and it seems the same group was involved with tampering with the brakes in your squad car. We found fingerprints on the underside of the brake lines. One print belongs to a man here in the States legally on a work visa. The remaining prints, who knows? Could be anyone. Money. If you have a guy telling you what to do and that guy is a billionaire, you don't ask questions. You just say when and where."

"Stockton?"

"Beginning to look that way."

"There was also a print on the door of the tow truck. But doesn't prove much."

"Why not?"

"Because it belonged to Trooper Matthews. He was at the scene that day. He could have grabbed the door just by talking to the driver. So far, there is no proof that someone intentionally caused Trooper Matthews's squad car to veer off the road either. And no explanation for why he was not found after his car went over the cliff. Having him turn up dead in Manhattan just complicates things."

# CHAPTER 77

"Mr. Horton," Reese said. "I am so happy you came to dinner with us."

Leaning in for a hug, "I thank you for thinking of an old man, with nothing to do but wait to see heaven."

"Mr. Horton, that is a terrible thing to say. You have so much to offer to so many people. I wanted you to come to dinner with us so we could discuss the situation at Grace Center. Do you have a place to go, now that it is closing for the time being?"

"No, I don't have a place in mind, possibly one of those extended-stay hotels. I can afford to stay almost anywhere in the area, Reese. My pension and savings are decent. Thank you for your concern though."

"I was hoping to speak with you about moving in with my dad. He is leaving the hospital and staying with Olivia until we can find another assisted living arrangement. Our Dad is smart and funny too. He also doesn't enjoy being alone. Misses our mom. At least the way she was before. Plus, being alone weighs heavily on him."

"I certainly understand the loneliness."

"You could share expenses. Dad has a car." Olivia joined the conversation. "He just has no one to go anywhere with him."

"I still drive as well, but not as much as I used to. Let me think about it for a few days. If that is okay with all of you?"

"Of course, Mr. Horton." Olivia said. "Meanwhile, Dad will stay at my house with round-the-clock nursing care until his doctors say he is fine to go back to his normal lifestyle. You know, Mr. Horton, I have plenty of rooms in my house. If you wish, you can stay with us. Come and go as you please, even have your very own bathroom. I don't have a big enough garage for another car, but inside is plenty of space. Emerson and Reese are at the Beckham Hotel, close by. You can chip in for food and maybe you and Dad can cook for me once in a while, just until you find a new place."

"Olivia Clayton, you are just as kind as your sister."

"Well, I try, sir."

"My goodness, sis, that is a kind thing to do. Wow, I'm impressed."

"You should have known all along how kind I am. Remember the ring I gave you, the one that shines like a 100-watt light bulb?"

Reese and Olivia tried to stifle a laugh but just couldn't. "We're sorry. Reese said. "We're laughing at something that happened at Chez Dubois the other day."

"And what, may I ask, was that?" Emerson stated.

Neither one could stop laughing. "Olivia proposed to me in the restaurant. Called my engagement ring the Hope diamond. It's a long story."

Emerson shook his head at both of them as they continued

giggling.

"I see you girls have not changed in all these years," Mr. Horton said. "Still up to your old antics." He, too, was laughing. "Doesn't matter what the two of you became after high school, you are still the same two rowdy girls I remember. And, yes, young ladies, I will accept your offer to move in temporarily."

"Oh, by the way, Mr. Horton," Emerson said.

"Yes, Detective Lake."

"The reason Olivia said you could help with buying food and cooking. There is nothing in her fridge to eat." He gave Olivia a nudge in the arm.

"That's not true," she giggled. "There is a pot of something in there."

# CHAPTER 78

"Oh shit," Reese said. "I forgot all about that pot."

"What pot?" Emerson asked.

"I placed a heavy pot of water in front of the camera, so Olivia wouldn't be frightened."

"What?" Olivia was startled.

"I'm sorry, but Emerson found a camera in your refrigerator and figured the person who broke into your house placed it there. We didn't want to touch it until we found out where it was streaming from, so I placed a pot in front of it. We forgot all about it until you just said something about the big pot."

"That's right, there has been so much going on, it completely skipped my mind. You didn't put the camera there yourself, did you?" Emerson inquired.

"No, of course not, but I bet I know who did. Craig. That lunatic is always saying I need to lose a few pounds. He's been watching me?"

"Geez, why would he say that? You are thin as a rail, Liv."

"I think it's time, Mr. Stockton and I have a little chat. I'm done with his crap."

"Don't forget to get your keys to the house back?"

"I never gave the asshole, excuse my language, Mr. Horton, my house keys. But I am having the locks changed, first thing in the morning. As for that camera, I'm going to fill my mouth with chocolate cake and smile for it before I rip it out of there."

"Can I do it with you, Liv?" Reese asked. "We'll tag team Chocolate Heaven."

"Oh, that will make your dad proud." Mr. Horton shook his head, amused by both girls.

"Hold your horses, ladies," Emerson raised his hand. "And right now, I'm using that word, ladies, lightly. We still don't have any idea where the camera came from and who is watching. We need to check it for fingerprints. I'll have the forensics team check before you two decide to become the next Lucy and Ethel."

"Is he always a detective?" Liv asked.

"Yeah," Reese flipped her long hair back over her shoulders, "but I love him anyway."

Mr. Horton asked for the check. "Oh no you don't Reese scolded him."

"It's on me," he said. "All of you have been so nice to me. I want to spend my money on those that care. And I am a little tired, so I think I'll leave you to continue your good time."

"Mr. Horton, nonsense. You are coming home with me." Liv glanced at Emerson. "You must have a pair of extra pajamas, hot stuff."

"I do."

"There, settled. And give that check to my sister."

"Absolutely," Reese grabbed the folio from Mr. Horton.

"We're staying with Olivia as well, for the evening anyway. I'll have Emerson pick up some breakfast in the morning. We all need to get some sleep."

# CHAPTER 79

Emerson and Reese lay in bed at Olivia's house.

"Emerson, I'm glad you convinced me to stay here at Liv's tonight instead of going back to the hotel. Kinda feels like when we were kids sleeping down the hall from each other. Well, except we didn't have boys in our rooms." Reese wrinkled her nose.

"I know Warren would have never allowed that." Emerson leaned in for a kiss.

Reese blocked him with her palm to his chest. "Shh. Do you hear that?"

"What is it? I don't hear anything."

"Listen," she whispered. "Is that Mr. Horton?"

They heard his heavy footsteps padding up and down the hall. "Is this the right place for me?" he asked.

Silence.

Reese propped herself on her elbows, sinking into the soft mattress, straining to listen.

"But are you sure?" Mr. Horton asked again.

Emerson and Reese couldn't hear anything. But Mr. Horton

did. "You'll be fine," the voice in his head kept saying. "Don't be afraid."

Emerson finally broke the silence. "He's okay Reese, he's just getting used to his new digs. You know how lonely he's been. Probably talks to himself a lot."

"I suppose you're right." Reese eased herself back down to her pillow. "Goodnight my love." She gave Emerson the sweetest kiss.

Emerson woke first. No alarm was necessary. "Reese, kiss me," he snuggled close to her. "I love you with all my heart."

"I know," she stretched her arms over her head. "Is something wrong?"

"I'm just feeling bad for Peter and his daughter. Do you know that the same thing could happen to us if we have children someday? Did we even talk about our careers after marriage, and the possibility of having a family?"

Reese rubbed the sleep out of her eyes. "Not too much that I remember. Emerson, you understand one thing, right?"

"I understand a lot of things, babe. Can you be more specific?"

"There is a huge possibility that my age may be a factor in our having a family. But if we do, I want to get out of this career. I want to be a part of our child's life. Go to ball games or ballet or school plays...anything but live in fear of putting our child at risk."

"I agree," he pulled her in tighter. "You are beautiful."

"And, as handsome as you are, my love, I smell coffee."

# CHAPTER 80

The three of them entered the kitchen at the same time. All following the odor of freshly brewed coffee.

Olivia knew it had to come from takeout, she didn't own a coffee maker. "Emerson, that smell of caffeine, delicious caffeine, is divine. Thank you. And you bought croissants too?"

"Can't take the credit, Liv. Must have been Mr. Horton. Check to see if he's in his room."

"No way, that will not be my job."

"Oh my God, the two of you are impossible," Reese said. "I'll see if he's up. He must be, otherwise we wouldn't have this lovely breakfast. Set the table, both of you. I'll be right back."

Knocking on his door several times, Reese heard nothing. "Mr. Horton, it's Reese, are you okay? Are you coming down for breakfast?"

Nothing.

"Mr. Horton, please let me know you're okay. That was so kind of you to buy us breakfast."

Still nothing.

She carefully turned the doorknob and nudged the door

open a crack. Peeking in to see the bed fully made, but no sign of Mr. Horton. She pushed the door wide open. She could see the in-suite bathroom was unused. Towels and facecloths were still where she left them. Then, looking out his window, saw his car was gone.

"Emerson, get up here. Now!"

"What's wrong?" He bounded up the stairs. "Is he okay?"

"I have a funny feeling."

"About what?" Emerson looked around the empty room.

"He wouldn't just leave, Emerson. I'm telling you something was wrong last night when we heard him talking."

"You don't know that. Maybe he just wanted to go get some groceries or something."

"Possible, but no man makes a bed like Olivia. And nobody used his bath either."

Emerson scanned the room. "Reese, there is a note on top of the dresser." He picked it up. "It's addressed to my favorite English student. Reese Clayton. I'm getting tired of all these notes." He handed her the slip. "So far, they haven't been good news."

"What's going on up there?" Olivia yelled up the stairs.

Reese and Emerson headed down to the kitchen.

"Where's Mr. Horton?" she asked.

"He's gone, but he left a note," Reese grabbed a coffee from the carrier on the counter and began to read aloud. "To my favorite student." Reese gulped down some of her coffee and winced. "Liv, do you have any milk or maybe some of that powdered cream stuff? This is pretty strong."

"I picked up some milk the other day. I don't know how good

it is, though."

Reese continued to read the letter. "I didn't have any intentions of doing what I did."

"Emerson!" Olivia screamed, her curly long blonde hair filling the inside the refrigerator. "What the hell? Where is it?"

"If the milk's gone, it's gone no big deal. Geez, can I finish the letter, please?"

"Sis," Olivia emerged from the fridge, "the pot of water is gone and so is the camera."

# CHAPTER 81

Captain Connelly walked into the squad room full of troopers, standing at attention.

"At ease. I've spoken to FBI Agent Wells. We have concluded that Trooper Matthews did fire his weapon before falling or being pushed over the balcony. I am asking all of you to tell me what you knew, if anything, personally about Matthews, because of where the bullet was discovered."

"And where was it?" several of the troopers asked at once.

"In the shoulder of an investment broker in Manhattan."

Quiet chatter filled the room.

"We don't have eyes on the broker yet. Any info you can give me on Trooper Matthews is important. Did he visit Manhattan frequently? Did he have a girlfriend in the city? Did he talk to any of you about this broker? No detail is too small. We need to confirm if Matthews was murdered, firing his service weapon in self-defense or was it an accident, or possibly suicide? Everything is on the table. Whatever information you have, I want you to report it to me and only me, immediately. Dismissed."

Not wanting to discuss a fellow trooper's idiosyncrasies in

253

front of the entire squad, a young trooper asked to speak with the captain privately after his shift.

"Captain, I don't think Matthews wanted to be a cop at all. He told me as much at the Tap Room one night, while a bunch of us were shooting darts. He said it was his ole man's choice of a career. And he expected his son to follow through. He did not want this life and hated his old man for it."

The captain shook his head. "His father was a hero. Did you know that?"

"Yes sir, I did."

"Then have some respect for him by not calling him an old man."

"I apologize, sir. Just trying to help. Ole man is just a term we use in jest."

"I understand, and I have used that term myself, but this guy saved lives during 9/11, helping many get out of the towers before they collapsed and later, he died from a related illness. He earned some respect."

The young trooper nodded, feeling the weight of his misstep.

"Is there anything else you can remember Matthews saying?"

"I know he was investing some of his paycheck. He bragged he wouldn't be in law enforcement too long. Knew some hot-shot broker. But never mentioned his name or where he was from. That's all I know, sir."

"Thank you. If you think of anything else," he ended the conversation right there nodding his head.

Captain Connelly made a call to the NYPD.

"Hi, Shawn," the young lady answered. "Haven't heard from you in quite a while."

"I know. The incident with my trooper is something I'm sure you know about."

"Yes."

"Was there anything found at Mr. Stockton's office? Anything that may have connected the two of them? Files of any kind? Transactions?"

"From the balcony, there is nothing concrete. Pardon the pun." She chuckled.

The captain wasn't amused.

"There was, however, a file on his desk, with annotations. Listed transactions over a period of time that seemed to have earned the account holder a great deal of money."

"How much time are we talking?"

"Five years. No name on the file though. And no prints either, other than Mr. Stockton's."

"So, fake document? Perhaps to make someone believe they had a large sum of money to retire on?"

"That's what our guys are thinking, but no proof."

"Not enough proof to clear the name of my trooper."

"What are you getting at, captain?"

"Only that Matthews didn't want to be law enforcement. Just a guess he was investing for early out."

"You could be right, captain. His prints are all over the office, but just not on the document. Poor bastard probably thought he had a fortune, I'm guessing."

"And a shady broker, who didn't earn him a cent. Thanks. Keep me posted, please."

"You're welcome, captain, and just so you know, we all miss you around here."

"I don't miss the city at all; love the quiet of Vermont, or at least it was until recently. I do miss the people I worked with though."

Next, call Mike Wells. "Just a thought, Wells. In that briefcase, was there anything about Trooper Matthews?"

"Don't know, but I can't find out right this minute. I can call you back later. I'm not at the bureau at the moment. Got a hunch, captain?"

"Maybe. You have my number."

The captain called his desk sergeant. "Yes, captain, what can I do for you?"

"I need Trooper Matthews's personnel file. Address. Name of his landlord."

"Actually, I've got that info already, captain. We live in the same building. Or did. I can give you the owner's name and number."

"Thanks. Call him and ask if I can meet him there in an hour. Also, I need to get into Matthews's locker here at the station. I'll need you there when I open it."

"You got it. Bringing cutters for the lock," he said.

Turned out, cutters weren't needed. There was no lock on the door. When they opened the locker, the first thing that stood out was a large yellow envelope. Nothing written on it, but a return address. Rubber gloves in his pocket, he put them on, and carefully removed the envelope from the locker. He then photographed it and made notes as he went along. Every item in the locker was documented. Noting the other trooper with him as a witness to the removal of each piece.

"Ok, I think we've logged, bagged, and tagged everything.

Now, we have to find out who murdered Trooper Matthews. Follow me back to the office and find some camera equipment to record everything."

"Yes sir."

Once back at his desk, Connelly punched in some numbers on his phone.

"Didn't I just talk to you, Shawn? Miss me or what?"

"Lil bit, smart ass. Wells, listen to me. Opened Matthews's locker, and found an envelope, unopened, inside. Yellow manila kind. Guessing some kind of document in it."

"Are you going to open it? Or are you just telling me this, to aggravate me."

The captain laughed. "That's not a bad idea, but I will refrain from being an asshole."

"Too late."

"No, I'm waiting for one of my men to bring me some camera equipment. No mistakes on this one. He's coming now."

"Send me what you find, Shawn. Good luck!"

Before removing the top of the envelope, the captain noted the return address. Carefully he sliced through the top of the envelope with scissors, making sure the flap and the section it was glued to were intact. Holding the envelope up to a very bright light, making sure he wasn't cutting any paperwork inside. He carefully removed the piece of paper inside. "Oh shit! Son of a bitch. These are not finance documents. These are orders to have someone murdered."

"No!" the desk sergeant was blown away.

"Yes! Who the fuck is that stupid to put something like this in writing? Yet alone, leave it in trooper barracks. The return address on the envelope is probably bogus. No name, address is Orinda, California."

"I never heard of a city named Orinda in Cali."

The captain took a big swig of his coffee "Me either, but that doesn't mean it doesn't exist."

"Who was that hit man? And who is the hit?"

The captain didn't reply, he just kept rereading the names silently to himself.

"Captain, are you okay?"

He drew in a deep breath. "No name on who the hit man is, but it's not just one hit. It's two. Detectives Reese Clayton and Emerson Lake."

# CHAPTER 82

"I'm taking this to the lab myself, sergeant. I'll contact the detectives on my way. You get back on the desk after I get a copy of that video."

"Yes, sir, I can send the video to your phone now." Within a few short minutes, it was ready. "Here you go, sir."

Captain Connelly replayed the video on his phone. He didn't say a word. Just nodded his head as he left his office and dialed Emerson Lake.

"Lake here, what can I do for you captain? I'm in the middle of something here."

"You certainly are my friend."

"Huh? What does that mean?"

"Meaning you and Reese need to watch your backs. Is Reese with you?"

"Yes, she is, and we expect her mom here soon. Captain, tell me what is going on now."

"Listen carefully, there is a credible threat to the both of you. We found a hit list in Trooper Matthews's locker. And both of your names are on it."

"Seriously, Shawn what else can go wrong?"

"I'd rather not venture a guess on that one. I'm on my way to our labs to see about DNA-testing the envelope flap. Maybe we'll get lucky and get a hit of saliva if the person licked the flap."

"Do you think Trooper Matthews was the hit man?"

"It's possible, but there was no lock on his locker. So, technically, anyone could have placed the envelope there. Just be careful, Lake. If you need bodies at Olivia's house to help, let me know. And detective, I believe I have a mole."

# CHAPTER 83

"For the third time, can I finish reading this letter from Mr. Horton?" Reese hastily set her coffee cup on the counter, a droplet splashing over the edge.

"I'm afraid not yet, sweetheart. I have to talk to you first. Alone." He motioned to the door.

"Okay," she said following him outside. "What now?"

He told her they were on a hit list.

"Oh my God, Emerson, who is threatening us? How are we supposed to protect everyone else if we're not safe?"

"I don't know for sure, but guessing it has something to do with Stockton. We need to tell your dad and Olivia. Captain said if we need extra help to ask. I think we should take him up on that offer and have a trooper posted on the house."

"I think you're right." She nervously scanned the yard.

"How did we get so involved with this case, hon? This was supposed to be our vacation. A chance to discuss our plans for a lovely wedding in peace. A chance to connect with my family. Now, we have to fight for our lives. What am I supposed to tell my sister? If I didn't love them all so much, I'd be on a fucking plane back to South Dakota."

"Reese, this is all the family you have. We need to take care of them. Olivia can't do this alone. We can't let anything happen to any of them, and you know it. Now for the first time in our lives, I'm going to say something to you." He grabbed her by the shoulders. "Get the fuck over it! This is not what I expected either. Do you think I want us on the job 24/7? No, I do not. Do you think I would rather be on a plane to Hawaii for a honeymoon right now? You bet your ass I would. But shit happens. Now grow a set, and let's figure out a way to handle this."

Reese began to cry and jumped in his arms wrapping both legs around his waist. "You're taking me to Hawaii?"

"Oh boy," he stumbled, thrown off balance by her sudden leap into his arms. "I guess I am now."

# CHAPTER 84

"Are you two all right?" Olivia asked. "What's going on?"

Emerson brought her up to speed.

"What's the plan?"

Reese and Emerson just looked at each other. Neither was expecting such a cool, calm, and collected response.

Emerson hugged her. "What's that for?"

"For being a superstar."

"Oh. Okay." She pushed him away.

"Dad will be here in about 20 minutes. Are you sure you feel safe with us, Liv? If not, we can send you to South Dakota to be with Emerson's dad."

"No, I'm good. Just tell me what to do."

"Emerson, I think Olivia and I should go to get Mom. You stay here so someone is here when Dad arrives. Get any info you can about what we need to do for him daily. We'll need the nurse's schedules. Also, we need a list of names so we can background-check everyone that will be in this house."

"Bossy bitch isn't she, Liv?" Emerson joked.

"Feel sorry for you, bud, but you agreed to marry her."

Reese and Olivia left for Grace Center, completely forgetting about the missing camera and the note from Mr. Horton still sitting on the kitchen counter where Reese left it.

# CHAPTER 85

The conversation on the way was not what Reese had expected. Her baby sister was quiet. Just staring out the window.

"Olivia, what's going on? Why so quiet suddenly?"

"Every time I put my ass in this motorized army base of a car, I think of him. His eyes, his subtle smile. I don't know why I couldn't have met someone like him years ago?"

"Hmm. Could it be that my little sis is in love?"

"Is that even a possibility, Reese? Am I being foolish? I hear his voice on the phone, and I feel my heart beat a little faster. Feel like an enamored teenager with a star football player. When Peter called me, he said he just wanted to hear my voice. How sweet is that? He said he wants to see me when he returns. I told him I would wait for him. Is that crazy Reese? I barely know him, and yet I feel him."

"Not crazy at all, Liv. You have never really been in love before. You may be now. But just remember, he has a lot on his plate right now, and patience will be the key."

Reese pulled the car into a parking space at Grace Center. "Are you ready for this, sis? Best if one of us sits in the back seat with her so she doesn't escape."

"I agree. It would be just like her to find a way out of this tank."

They both laughed as they headed inside.

"There isn't much clothing to pack," Reese said as she opened each dresser drawer.

"Yeah, somehow clothing seems to disappear in nursing homes. You could find one shoe in someone else's closet. I gave up buying nice things for her long ago. I just chalk it up to the damn dryer. It eats clothing, you know."

Reese laughed. "You know it happens in my house too, always missing a sock or pair of underwear."

"That's because you're always leaving your underwear at someone else's house, I presume."

Reese gave her a light punch in the arm. "You never know."

Eve sat in her chair at Grace Center, her food untouched from breakfast and lunch.

"Mom, how are you today?" Olivia asked. "Aren't you hungry?"

"I'm starving." Eve said.

Neither of them expected a response from her.

"Well, why didn't you eat your breakfast or lunch? At least you should have had a bottle of your protein drink, Mom."

"Would you eat that shit?" Eve gestured to everything on her tray.

"Matter of fact Mom, no I would not."

"What can we get for you?" Reese beamed at her.

"A burger and fries. And an ice cream cone."

Reese and Olivia nearly burst into laughter.

"Okay, Eve Clayton," Reese said, "burger and fries it is."

"Let's go." Olivia grabbed a few items from the closet, leaving the remainder behind.

"We can buy new clothes for her later," Reese said.

"Reese, you keep paying for things and you won't have any money left."

"Not to worry, sis. I'm good."

The sisters stopped at a local joint on the way to the house. Reese ordered burgers and fries for all of them except for Dad. She ordered a big, tossed salad for him with grilled chicken on top. And iced tea for all. Decaf, unsweetened. They would forget the ice cream cone for now.

When they arrived at the house, the ambulance was in the driveway. Eve got anxious. Fidgeting.

"It's ok Mom, Dad is here. He can't wait to see you." Olivia said.

They got Eve out of the car. Her feet marching in place. "Where are they taking me? Me? Who am I? I don't remember my name. Where am I? Do I know Dad? Warren, I need Warren." Eve turned to walk toward the road. "Let's go."

Olivia grabbed her arm. "Mom, where are you going?"

"You know." The standard answer.

Reese grabbed the bags, following close behind.

Olivia led Eve into the house through the kitchen, holding onto her elbow. She pushed Olivia's arm away. Her hands stroked the granite countertops. This feels nice and cold, what could it be, she wondered. I don't remember this place. "Where am I?" she finally asked.

"Mom, you're at my home. You're going to stay here for a

while," Olivia told her. Reese will be here to help. Isn't that right Reese?"

"It is sis," as Reese tried to get her under control.

The look of fear washed over her face once again. "No! You are no good. I don't know who you are." She pulled away from Reese.

"Mom, let's go find Warren." As they started toward the hallway to the living area, Eve paused, staring straight ahead at the fireplace, placing both hands on the walls, gasping for breath.

"Mom! What's wrong?"

Reese yelled for help from the EMTs.

"We've got you," one of them replied. "Can you tell us what hurts, ma'am?"

She pointed to the mantle in the living room. The photo of Craig Stockton was still there. "He hurt me," she said as she tried to retreat backward from the room. Her eyes shut tight.

Emerson immediately flipped the photo face down. "It's ok Eve, he's gone."

Eve turned away from the living room, heading for the dining area. The hospital bed placed there by the EMTs was empty. She walked over to it. Pulled down the sheets and crawled into the bed, covering up her face with the sheet. Olivia sat on the bed with her mom, rubbing her arm for comfort.

"Where is Dad, Liv?" Eve asked. "Where is Dad?" she repeated from her haven under the sheet.

"He's in the bathroom. He's fine and looks like nothing ever happened to him. From what they tell me, this is a precautionary procedure."

"Where's Eve?" Warren emerged from the bathroom, after

hearing the commotion.

Emerson pointed to his hospital bed.

He cautiously walked over to her. "Eve, my beautiful Eve, where are you?"

She pulled the sheet down, "Warren, help me!" She jumped out of bed and held him tight. "Help me! Help me!"

"It's all right, I'm here now. It's okay, I'm here."

Her eyes looked straight at him. "Warren?" She kissed him on the lips. Something she had not done in years. Not since the onset of Alzheimer's.

The entire room fell silent. No one had a clue what to do or say, but all remained silent while they had their moment.

And their moment was brief as she let go of him and went to the mantle. Picking up the photo, she began to shake. She punched the photo, yelling obscenities at the picture. A trickle of blood escaped from her knuckle. This kind of violence was new to Olivia.

"Mom, no. You're bleeding."

The paramedics bandaged her cut. It was minor. The damage to the photo, however, was not.

Picking it back up again. Eve looked at it sternly and suddenly tossed it in the fireplace with a crash. "You burn in Hell, you fucking piece of shit!"

Everyone jumped.

"Mom, do you know this man?" Olivia was baffled.

"Oh, you know." She walked back to the kitchen. Reese followed. Eve's eyes softened back into a blank gaze, her facial muscles contracting her face into a perplexed knot. Not saying a word, like nothing had happened, she took a bite of her hamburger. Reese followed her.

Emerson stayed back, watching the tears flow from Warren's eyes. "I've got you, Dad. Come, let's get you into bed. Your nurses are pulling into the driveway now."

"Thanks, Emerson. I just don't get it." He hung his head down as he sat on the hospital bed.

"None of us do, Dad." Emerson covered Warren with the sheet. Watching the photo burn. "None of us do."

# CHAPTER 86

Reese noticed the letter was still on the kitchen counter. The letter from Mr. Horton. She took it from the counter and placed it in her pocket. "I'll be back in a minute. I have to use the bathroom." She opened the note again, beginning where she left off.

*I didn't mean to do what I did. I took the camera and the pot of water. The voice in my head told me to do it. I hate that voice. I don't think that hearing guy was replacing my hearing aid with a new one. I can't feel it or get it out. Reese, I think it's an implant of sorts. The voice told me to destroy the camera, or you would die. He said to smash the camera and place it in the water. I couldn't do it, Reese. I'm sorry, and I hope nothing happens to you. But I thought these things might be evidence of some kind. I hid the camera in the toolbox in your sister's garage. I smashed up some stones and put them in the pot of water and left it in the flower garden on the side of the house. I am sorry for causing you harm. You were my favorite student.*

*Mr. H.*

Coming out of the bathroom, she saw Emerson waiting for her. "You read the note, didn't you?"

"Yes, I just did."

"And?"

"And I think Mr. Horton has some sort of implant in his ear. He hears a voice, Emerson, one that he hates. I have not heard of this kind of creepy shit in years. He has a damn mic implanted in his ear, telling him what to do."

"Did he mention who may have planted it?"

"He mentioned a hearing guy, but no name. I know for a fact there are doctors who come to Grace Center to check patients' hearing."

"But he's not a patient there, Reese. He's just there till an apartment becomes available, remember?"

"I understand that, but he was using one of those rooms, so who's to say, he wasn't tagged as a patient? Another thing Emerson, Mr. Horton saw who killed that nurse. He's afraid. We need to find him."

"First things first, the toolbox." Grabbing a cup of coffee, they went to the garage. Sure enough, the camera lay in the toolbox.

"Emerson, can you get this over to the captain's team as evidence?"

"Of course. Meantime, do you remember where Mr. Horton was going to stay before we convinced him to stay at Olivia's?"

"No, I don't recall him saying a specific place, just an extended-stay hotel."

"How many can there be in the area?"

"Not that many, I'm guessing," she pulled up some possible locations on her cell and made a note to contact all three as soon as Emerson left for the state police headquarters. "I love you, babe," she said flipping her hair back.

"I love you more." He nuzzled his head in her neck, then kissed her goodbye. "Please be careful, and I think it's time to have a talk with Liv about her boyfriend."

"You're right. I'll tell her. You have enough on your plate."

# CHAPTER 87

Emerson dialed the captain. "Shawn, do you have time to see me?"

"What's this about, detective?"

"You do know you can call me Emerson, correct?"

"I do, but honestly, Emerson does sound a little stuffy to me."

"I know, but I come from what you would call stuffy stock. Wealthy family from back to my great grandparents. Beats the shit out of me why I work at all."

Captain Connelly let out a belly laugh. "Ok, what can I do for you, Emerson?"

"I'd like to bring you a camera that was found in Olivia's refrigerator. Check it for prints and see if we can access the images or video from it."

"Jesus Lake, that's unnerving. Bring it over. We'll get it to the lab."

"Sounds good, Shawn. I need to talk to you about something else while I'm there."

"Okay, see you in a few."

The desk sergeant waved Emerson through as soon as he

arrived. "Captain is expecting you."

Emerson dropped the camera on the captain's desk. "Shawn, I want you to be aware of something. There is a possibility at least one set of prints on this camera is from Mr. Horton. He removed the camera from the refrigerator and hid it. I don't know if he used gloves or not."

"Why did he remove it himself. Why not ask you or Reese to do it?"

"A voice told him to do it and now Mr. Horton is missing."

"A voice, really Lake?"

Emerson explained the note. "Reese is trying to locate Mr. Horton as we speak. When was the last time you heard of a covert listening device being used?"

"Geez, I don't remember ever coming across something like that, even when I worked in the city. How the hell did he allow that to happen?"

"Who knows? There's more."

"There's always more with you, Lake."

"Mr. Horton saw the guy that killed the nurse at Grace Center. He mentioned he had blonde hair."

"Do you think it's Stockton?"

"That would be my guess. Horton said the blonde man ran when our young priest showed up unexpectedly, but he got a good look."

"Hopefully, Reese can locate Horton. We need to get him back safely. Get a statement."

"Speak of the devil," Emerson picked up his ringing phone. "Hey, what did you find, Reese? I'm with the captain. You're on speaker."

"I have Mr. Horton with me in Londonderry. I brought him straight to the emergency room to get the implant removed. Just letting you know we are safe, and I'll contact you before we leave here."

"Sounds good. Take him directly to the station. We need him to make a positive ID on Craig Stockton."

"Got it."

# CHAPTER 88

Before she allowed the doctor to see Mr. Horton, she pulled him aside. "Listen to me, doctor, no mistakes here. This man is our witness to a crime. I want a copy of your credentials." She snapped a photo of his hospital ID hanging from his white coat. "Here are mine," she flashed her badge. "If you need further information about me, contact Michael Wells at the FBI."

"Unnecessary, detective. I trust you. This is a 5-minute process. You can put on a mask and come in with him if you like." He asked the desk receptionist to pull his file and make a copy for Reese.

They entered the bay where Mr. Horton was sitting patiently on the hospital bed. The doctor worked swiftly, but delicately. Pulling a tiny device out with forceps. "This is the first time I have ever seen something like this. I've read about this in books. Covert listening devices used during the war. World War I or II perhaps? Based on what you've told me, I think it's a miniature transmitter with a microphone."

"Thank you, doctor. Bag it up. I will have it taken to the FBI labs as soon as I get Mr. Horton secured."

On the drive back, Reese noticed how drawn her friend looked. "Are you okay, Mr. Horton?"

"Yes, I'm just tired and a little bit scared. But I'm happy to have that thing out of my ear. What are you going to do with it now?"

"Taking it to the police. May I ask you a question?"

"Of course."

"Did you use your bare hands to remove the camera?"

"No, I used my winter gloves. My hands are always cold. It's called Raynaud's disease. Worried about my fingerprints, Reese?"

She smiled at him. "Not anymore."

Emerson and Captain Connelly waited at the lab for the fingerprint report to come back hoping for a miracle.

"Some sort of fabric smudged most of the camera, but you lucked out." the technician said.

"How's that?" Emerson asked.

"We have a partial print still visible. Should only take a few minutes for identification. It's running now."

The ticking of the clock on the wall was deafening. All Emerson could do was pace.

"It's been nearly 40 minutes. What is taking so long?" Emerson asked.

"Do you know how many prints are in the system, detective?"

"I apologize," Emerson said just as the computer completed its search.

"See detective, patience." The technician pulled up the report. "We have a match. Craig Stockton."

"So, now what captain? We have his prints on the camera, but what good is it to our case? This is just an invasion of privacy, albeit enough to arrest him, but I'm sure his lawyers are smart enough and paid enough to have him out on an appearance ticket in 5 minutes."

"If Wells and the FBI finish their investigation of Judith's briefcase, they definitely will have cause for arrest, or at least questioning."

"But who knows when they will be ready to move forward with that. I want this guy off the streets now." Emerson rubbed his face in his hands.

"We also can connect Stockton to Trooper Matthews's death. He's a suspect at the very least."

"Have you searched Trooper Matthews's apartment, Shawn."

"Not yet. Let me contact the building owner. Set it up." He put in the number his trooper provided.

"I'm sorry, captain," the owner said, "Trooper Matthews's mother came and took all his belongings already."

"Are you fucking kidding me? Did you even think for a minute that his death might require us to search his home?"

"Hey, I'm sorry. She must have had her son's key code. She let herself in. Called me when she was done clearing the place and said she would send me the back rent. The FBI was already here too. They said the apartment was cleared for me to rent again. I didn't know I had to wait for Vermont State Police too."

"Did Matthews's mother give you any personal information? How do you know she will pay the rent he owes you?"

"Captain, I never mentioned back rent to her. I have been in the real estate business long enough to know she was not about to send me any money. They never do. And it's not worth the court battle. Besides, he was a state trooper. I wouldn't even think of bothering the family with that."

"Do you still have the phone number for her?"

"Yes, but I wouldn't count on it being real. She said her name was Emily Smith." He recited the number from his recent calls. "Sorry, but that's all I have for you."

The captain hung up.

"Now what?" Emerson asked.

"I'm thinking a whiskey, straight up."

"Is that the Irish in you, captain?"

"A wee bit. Have you heard from Peter?"

"I left him a message to call me. What do you say we go have that drink, Shawn?"

The captain gave him a thumbs up.

# CHAPTER 89

"How's everything going, Reese?" Emerson called on his way out with Captain Connelly. "Is Mr. Horton, okay?"

"He's fine, but I'm insisting he find someone to stay with for now. I just don't know who. Don't want him alone."

"See if you can convince him to go back to Olivia's."

"I'm trying to. He is a bit stubborn."

"Did you tell him that he doesn't have to worry now? The ear mic is gone?"

"Yes, like I said, stubborn. Like most of the male gender I know."

"Ouch, the woman I love just stabbed me in the heart. That's not nice."

"I'm the nicest person you ever met." Reese said.

"Absolutely, damn straight you are."

"Emerson, I don't know if the police labs can get anything from that microphone. You don't think it was also a recording device, do you?"

"Honestly, I don't know, but highly doubt it. But then again, I can't keep up with technology these days. I'll ask Peter if he ever calls me back. Left a couple of messages. Nothing yet. I don't want to keep bothering him. I'll call you later."

"Ok, sounds good. By the way, where are you? It sounds pretty noisy."

"An Irish bar with Shawn. Headed back to the station in a few minutes. If you're not too tired, can you bring Mr. Horton over to the precinct to give his testimony? If you think he's up to it."

"I'll make it happen."

# CHAPTER 90

"Thank you for coming in, Arthur. I know you've been through a lot today."

"I'm fine, captain, just glad to get that thing out of my ear." He rubbed the side of his head. "You two should take a lesson," Mr. Horton pointed at Reese and Emerson. "You should call me Arthur as well. I'm insisting on it. I'm no longer your teacher, and I'm hoping you will remain my friends, all of you."

"Deal." Reese was closer to tears than she wanted to admit. He was such a sweet man, and her heart broke for him that none of his children cared enough to be here with him. Her own guilt for doing the same thing to her family seeped in.

"Reese? Reese, are you ok?" Emerson gently placed his hand on her arm.

"Um, uh, yes of course."

Emerson slipped his hand into hers and squeezed. He whispered, "I'm here."

She flashed him a loving smile and then turned her attention to the task at hand. "Are you ready, Mr.," she paused. "I mean, Arthur?"

"I am indeed."

They asked Mr. Horton some basic questions about the day of the homicide. Date. Time. And asked him for a description of the perpetrator.

"Since we don't have a suspect in custody yet, Arthur, we are going to show you photos of blonde men. Take your time, looking at all of them," the captain advised.

"Have a seat, can we get you some water?" the captain asked.

"No, I'm good. Thank you."

Looking at the stack of photos in front of him, Arthur's heart raced. A bead of sweat formed on his upper lip. Do I want to get involved with all this? I wish I were just a plain old teacher right now, instead of a witness to a murder. His hands began to shake as he opened the folder. "I think I'll take that water if you don't mind."

"Not a problem."

A quarter of the way through, Arthur pushed his chair back away from the metal table. He looked up at Reese. "That's him."

"Are you positive Arthur?" the captain asked. "Take another look, Arthur."

"I'm positive and I do not ever want to see that face again. Reese, can you take me back to my hotel?" He was so relieved to have her with him.

"Thank you, Arthur." She kissed the top of his head. "Emerson, I'm going to take Arthur back to our hotel so he can get a nap. I'll see if the adjoining room is still open since Peter left."

"Better yet, take him back to Olivia's. She's going to need you to help with your dad. And he can also use some male company by now, I'm sure."

"What are you trying to say, darling? That I'm not good company."

"You're perfect. Now go. Grab his clothes from the extended stay before you go back to Olivia's and cancel his room, till we find the right place for him and your dad."

Captain Connelly quietly studied the photo Arthur selected. He sat at the table, the look of a forlorn puppy on his face. Rubbing his forehead, distressed. The photo was not Craig Stockton.

# CHAPTER 91

"Captain? Captain, snap out of it." Emerson snapped his fingers in front of his face. "Are you okay? What the fuck is going on? Do you know this guy?"

"I think it's time for you to leave, detective. I can take it from here."

"Fuck you, Shawn. I'm not going anywhere until you tell me what is going on."

"I told you; I've got this." Shawn stormed back to his office, a fiery look in his eyes, and slammed the door behind him.

Emerson followed, barging into the office to find the captain reaching for his gun in his desk drawer. Along with a set of handcuffs. "Captain, talk to me. Please. Tell me who is in that photo."

"Emerson, I can't believe it. I don't want to believe it. I told you I thought I had a mole in my precinct. Never put two and two together. I'm guessing you're not going to leave, so you might as well come with me, detective."

Emerson followed the captain to the front desk.

"Where's Miller, the custodian?" he asked the desk sergeant.

"The custodian?" he asked, thinking this is a weird request.

"Yes, the custodian, who else would I be referring to I said his name is there anyone else that works for us with the same name?"

"How would I know where he is? Cleaning the toilet probably. I don't keep tabs on him?"

"Pull his contact number. See if he's in this building, now! And get me the name of the company he works for."

"Yes sir." He said fumbling through some computer files surprised to see this side of his captain. "Powell Brothers Commercial Janitorial service. I have the number right here."

"Shit," the captain's face flushed red as a ripe tomato. "Damn it."

Emerson was worried. "Calm down, captain. What's the problem now?"

"Look at the number, Lake."

"What about it? I have no idea what you're showing me."

"That's a Manhattan area code, Lake. That bastard Stockton has everyone under his thumb and on his payroll. I will bet you my badge on it."

"How do you know that's a Manhattan code?" Dempsey asked. "That's a huge city and Manhattan is just one of the boroughs."

"I worked for NYPD before I moved here, sergeant. See if you can find out when Miller was last scheduled to clean the station."

"Looks like he hasn't been here for about two weeks. Why are you looking for him, captain?"

"He's a suspect in the murder of the nurse at Grace Center. We have an eyewitness."

"How would your witness recognize him?" Lake asked. "Does Miller work at Grace Center too?"

"No. I included some random photos of people who work here with the photos of Craig Stockton." The captain pointed at Sergeant Dempsey. "See if you can find out where Miller is working today. Contact me as soon as you know."

"Nice work, Shawn." Emerson was impressed.

"Be nicer if we could locate Stockton. I hope the hell the FBI is having better luck than we are. Nothing from Andora yet?"

"No. That's beginning to worry me. Just not like him."

"Captain," Dempsey interrupted. "More bad news."

"What have you got?"

"Powell Brothers receptionist claims that Miller hasn't called in for his work orders in weeks. She said they tried to call him, but the phone is no longer in service. They mailed him a letter telling him he was relieved of his duties and no longer an employee of their company."

"Did you get his home address?"

"I did." He handed Shawn a piece of paper.

"Let's go detective, we have an arrest to make."

As they drove out of the station parking lot, Shawn confided in Emerson, "I don't think this case is going to have an easy end. I can't believe this mess is happening in our relatively quiet, friendly town."

"You don't have to tell me about baffling small-town cases, my friend. Reese and I have seen enough to choke a horse."

"So much for your quiet getaway."

"I know. On top of all the crime, I think being here and seeing Eve again threw me a curve ball. One I didn't see coming and I don't know why I didn't. It's not like I was unaware of what the disease can do to someone, Shawn. She is the sweetest woman you would ever want to meet. She loved me as much as my parents. To see what her illness has done to her mind and her body." Emerson shook his head. "Just awful. She was in great shape and kept fit. Her hair and makeup were always exactly right."

"I'm so sorry, Lake. It's just awful to watch."

"Exactly. I think the worst is the facial expressions. I wonder why she scrunches up her face like that. It makes her appear so much older than she is."

"I don't understand it either. The human brain is remarkable. As sick as she is, it's unbelievable how she knew her hairdresser was abducted and that she could identify the person who took her as doctor. Almost creepy."

"It hurts to see what it's doing to Reese and her family. Fucking nightmare."

"Well, my friend looks like we're driving into another nightmare." Shawn pulled the car up to the house. "The yard is a mess. Why can't people see the grass needs cutting? Rake the leaves? The mobile home itself looks fairly new. Not bad at all."

They exited the car and cautiously approached the home. "Emerson, you take the front door. Ring the bell. I'll go around the back. Chances are he won't like seeing a cop in his front yard."

Emerson rang the doorbell. Nothing. Tried again, same results. He pulled his gun out keeping it by his side, preparing for the worst.

Shawn peeked around the corner. "Don't bother, detective. He's dead. Saw him through the window on the kitchen floor.

There's blood everywhere. I already called it in."

A mail vehicle pulled up to the mailbox. "Hold it right there!" The captain yelled. "Don't touch that mailbox."

"What's your name?" Emerson asked.

"John. What's going on?"

"When was the last time you delivered mail to Mr. Miller?"

"Yesterday. Is he hurt or something?" he asked.

Captain Connelly didn't answer him, just reached for his rubber gloves, and carefully opened the mailbox. All that was there was a manila envelope with a return address. Orinda, California.

"What's going on?" John didn't know what to do. "That's a federal offense trooper, to take someone's mail."

"This is now a crime scene young man. And it's Captain Connelly. The sirens blasted in their ears as squad cars arrived on the scene.

"Is there anything for Mr. Miller in the mail today, John?" Emerson asked.

"Just a weekly coupon flyer." He handed it over.

"Did you deliver this manila envelope to this address?"

"Probably, but he's not my only delivery. I can't remember everything I deliver."

"Listen to me, John. Give this nice trooper all of your information. Your post office info too. We will be in touch if we need you. You can leave after that, finish your route."

"You don't have to tell me twice." John did as he was told, watching as the crime scene tape was being strung across the yard. As soon as he finished providing his info, he hopped back into his mail truck and drove away. Already dialing his postmaster. He'd never believe this story.

After searching the victim's mobile home, Shawn instructed the forensics team to contact him immediately with the findings from their initial investigation.

Shawn put the envelope in his vehicle. "That's for safekeeping, Lake. We will take that to the forensics lab unopened. This was a hit. Not a suicide."

"Do you need me to go with you, Shawn? I really would like to go back to see what the girls have decided to do about their parents."

"Not a problem, I'll get you back to your car and keep you in the loop when I hear something."

# CHAPTER 92

"Wells," he answered.

"Have you seen or heard from Andora today?" Emerson asked as he drove back to Olivia's house. "I have been calling and leaving messages all day. Yet not a word. Is his daughter, okay?"

"How are you, detective?"

"Need you ask my friend?"

"I hear you. Andora is on a special assignment, you might say."

"Really? What about Alicia? Who's watching her? And don't give me a bullshit answer because we both know he would not leave her side unless he was absolutely certain someone reliable was by her side 24/7. So, who is it?"

"An incredibly good friend of yours, Lake. We put her on a special assignment as well. Does Carly Brennan come to mind?"

"No shit?"

"She is well-trained, my friend. I just checked for an update on Alicia, and they are getting along fine. Not too far apart in age so I imagine that helps. Carly mentioned Alicia's first physical therapy sessions have gone great and mental health therapy is coming along nicely too. It doesn't appear she's holding back her feelings while speaking to the therapist."

"The therapist allows Carly to listen in on the appointment?"

"Unbelievable, I know. But that's the rules by Carly. I have a hunch they are becoming friends."

"Good news for a change."

"What have you got for me?"

Emerson updated Wells about the station custodian but guessed it was nothing he didn't already know.

"What's the connection to Orinda, California, these manila envelopes, and Craig Stockton? When we first got here, Reese's sister mentioned he worked at a brokerage house on the West Coast. I'm sure he has an address there as well as Manhattan."

"He has more than an address on the West Coast. He has a wife and three children in California. Orinda would make sense. The median price for a home is over two million dollars."

"Son of a bitch! He's just been using Olivia this whole time!"

"Looking that way, my friend. Listen, I'll contact our team out there and see if he's on the radar. Maybe a post office box. Something besides Olivia's house and his Manhattan office. See if we can find out more about his wife and kids."

"Sounds good, Mike. Let me know what you find…at least some of what you find."

"I will my friend, count on it."

# CHAPTER 93

"Can I talk to you, Emerson? About Peter," asked Olivia.

Emerson threw his keys on the counter. "Sure, is everything okay?" He opened the door to the backyard of Olivia's house. They sat on the lawn chairs to talk.

"I spoke with Peter on the phone a few times. He sounds different."

"How so?"

"I think he likes me, a lot. Is that even possible?"

"I'm no pro at this Liv, but I guess the heart wants what the heart wants. How do you feel about him, and what about Craig?"

"Craig can go fuck off! There is something weird about him. Fool putting a camera in my refrigerator."

"Who told you it was him?" Emerson raised his eyebrow in surprise.

"No one, I just assumed it was him. He's done some strange things in the past that concerned me a bit. Phone calls in the middle of the night, telling me to talk to him about what I'm wearing. Telling me to touch myself. What a weirdo. And then the camera, it's not a surprise at all."

Emerson leaned forward and ran his hands through his thick hair. "Liv, there is more about Craig you don't know. He's actually a stockbroker in Manhattan, and he has a wife and three kids that live somewhere in California."

Olivia didn't even flinch, "I suspected he was married; his visits were hit and miss at times."

"Meaning?"

"It could be weeks or months in between visits. At the time I just didn't care. He was good looking, and I was so busy with Mom and Dad."

Emerson wanted to shake some sense into her. "That blonde, well-built asshole is a liar. Not only did he lie to you about being single, but we also think he's involved in some serious shit, Liv. I don't want to scare you, but he's dangerous. He's a suspect in a murder case. You need to be aware of your every move and stay close to Reese or myself at all times until we find him."

"Are you sure? I mean he was weird at times, but he never made me feel like my life was in danger."

"Do you trust me, Liv?"

"Of course I do."

"Then, pay attention to what I just said."

She teared up, but quickly wiped away the tears with her shirt.

"That no-good prick killed Peter's wife, didn't he?"

"Possibly."

Emerson's phone buzzed, and he put on the speaker. "What can I help you with, captain?"

"The manila envelope delivered to Miller, the custodian's trailer. It contained a financial statement from C.A. Stockton and Associates. It shows he lost everything he invested in. That's not all, there was a check made out to Miller signed by Stockton in the amount of five hundred dollars. The notation said for services rendered."

"We know he didn't commit suicide," Lake said. "There was no weapon found at the scene. I'm guessing a hit."

"Me too, but the check would make Stockton look like he was trying to soften the blow of losing all his investments. Get him off the hook as a suspect."

"Yes. A cover-all-bases maneuver."

Olivia sat motionless listening to the entire conversation.

Emerson ended the call. "I'm sorry, Liv. Do you believe me now?"

# CHAPTER 94

Reese and Arthur turned their car onto the lush campus of New Life Continuing Care Senior Community.

Arthur's eyes brightened. "Wow! Now this is the type of place I want to live. I wouldn't feel old living here like I do now." He marveled at the residents he saw strolling the sidewalks. They all looked healthy and so full of life.

"Hell," Reese said, "I would love it here too. It's everything you would expect of a high-end continuing care center. Lovely grounds, beautiful scenery, and a very well-maintained golf course."

"Look over there, Reese." Arthur pointed to a fenced-in area. "Now that's more my speed. Pickleball courts!"

She smiled. Silently hoping that her dad would agree. "It's lovely, Arthur."

At the front desk, they were greeted by a woman who appeared to be in her early forties, at most. "You must be Reese Clayton and this young man is your father?"

Reese grabbed Arthur's arm and smiled. "No, my father couldn't make it today, but by next week he should be able to come explore what you have to offer. This fine gentleman is my former English teacher, Arthur Horton. He is also searching for a new adventure here at your lovely property."

"Oh, my goodness, Mr. Horton, you were my English teacher too. And Reese, I remember you now, from school, but that was so long ago. We didn't hang out together, but that's probably because you were too smart for my group of friends. I'm Emily Collins. It's lovely to see you both. "Mr. Horton, is there anyone you didn't have for a student in that school?"

"Probably not," he joked.

"Well, let's get you started on that tour of our facility. Can I get either of you a beverage?"

"No, thank you."

They hopped into a golf cart, and Reese shared with Emily her mother's battle with Alzheimer's and her dad's recent heart issues. "He needs to be able to visit my mom whenever he wishes and yet have assisted care himself such as house cleaning and meals. He still drives. So independent. The reason I say meals is because he would eat cookies and drink soda if he didn't have planned meals. My sister, Olivia, lives nearby. I do not, so a lot is placed on her. Let me rephrase, *all* of it is placed on her."

Emily listened as they continued with the tour. She showed them fully furnished apartments. Heat and central air included. Housekeeping, once a week. All they were looking for in housing and ways the residents could be entertained. Residents could come and go as they wished.

Reese was more concerned about the nursing wing. They passed through a lovely entryway. Reese was thrilled to see a security guard greet them. She handed him her badge and driver's license.

"Welcome, detective. It's a pleasure to meet you." The guard waved them through.

"A detective, huh?" Emily asked.

"Yes."

"Where? I'm impressed."

"South Dakota. Cromwell, PD."

"I hope to hear more about it later, Reese. Let's continue the tour."

Reese took her time observing everything, including the personal hygiene of the residents housed there. Everything was as clean as could be, patients as well. The hair salon was top-notch. Friendly nursing staff. She asked about the doctors and what the staff provided for exercise and outdoor activities. She also asked about security and if they had any incidents with patients escaping the facility or the grounds.

Once she was fully satisfied, she turned to Arthur. "I think I've seen enough. How about you Arthur?"

"It's perfect," he gave her the thumbs-up. "When may we see the director?"

"He's waiting for you in the dining room," Emily replied. "Lunch is waiting as well. He has the necessary paperwork for you to take home. You can take your time and discuss all of this with your families, etc. And if you need to have another tour, just let me know. Here's my card." She handed one to each of them.

After a lovely lunch and chat with the director, Reese and Arthur began the trip back to Olivia's house.

"Well, what did you think, Arthur?"

"I was ready to sign on the dotted line. I know it's pricey, but sometimes you get what you pay for Reese. I do want to go over the paperwork, and I need to contact my attorney about my will and such. I'll set that up for tomorrow."

"Good idea. I'll discuss all of this with Emerson because I'll be paying for this care. Olivia can't do it. I told her not to worry about the cost."

"May I say something here, Reese?"

"Of course, Arthur, you can say anything you like to me."

"Don't try to fund this for reasons of guilt. Let your father use what money he has to help. The rest you can assist with. The reason I say this is, as parents, we have pride. And we're supposed to take charge of our lives and leave what we can for our loved ones. Don't be too quick to think your dad is helpless. He's not. This way he knows that down the road, the ones he loves will get what is left after his expenses. The way it's meant to be. I understand that Olivia is unable to help fund the cost of his care. But please don't make her feel terrible about this. Let her know how much you appreciate her doing all she has done for your parents. She is a good daughter, Reese, and so are you. Warren is one lucky bastard to have you both on his team."

"Thank you, my dear friend. Once a teacher always a teacher." She gave him a loving wink.

# CHAPTER 95

"Agent Wells," he answered. "What have you got, Peter?"

"Not good news. Stockton does have a wife and three kids, we knew that. What we didn't know is one of the children is his stepson. The wife had a baby boy long before she met Stockton."

"Was she married before?"

"I can't find any other marriage certificate or divorce papers. Guessing she may have had him out of wedlock. The birth certificate has no mention of the father. I haven't spoken to his wife, not sure I should. Don't want them to get into an argument if he's in the area. He may spook and run. Or worse, hurt her."

"Well so far, he's not attempted to leave the country. The business jet is still grounded, and there are no reports of him on commercial flights. I'm guessing he's still in Manhattan. Hiding. I say try going to the house to see if she is home. Maybe even stake it out for a while. See who comes and goes."

"Can't do that, the place is huge. Looks like a modern-day castle, just no moat. Cameras everywhere. He would know in a heartbeat if anyone was nearby. Actually, I have another idea."

He hung up the phone.

"Great," Wells slammed his cell against his head. "What the fuck?"

Peter checked the school records to find out where the younger kids attended. A private school of course. He picked a spot across the street and parked. Waiting patiently, he opened his phone and flipped over to the photos of the kids. "Thanks, Wells. FBI is on it."

He spent two of the three hours studying the children's photos, committing them to memory. He finally heard the jubilant voices of children emerging from the building. Excited they were done for the day. He rolled the window down. His eyes shielded by his Oakley sunglasses scanned the crowd until he picked them up. The two blonde children he was searching for. Beautiful children. They fidgeted on the sidewalk in their uniforms until a limousine pulled up. A woman approximately 20 to 22 years old stepped out. "Are you ready, children?" he heard her say. "Your grandmother is waiting in the car."

Both girls seemed excited to see their grandma. "Where's our mom?" Peter heard one of the girls say. "When can we see her again? I miss my mom."

"Your mom doesn't feel well. Your dad called and said to tell you mommy loves you, but she's sick. I don't want you to catch anything, so please do as I ask and spend a few more days with your grandmother."

Peter texted the plate number to Wells and dialed. "I need you to find out who rented the limo."

"Only if you tell me what the hell, you're doing this time."

"Sorry, Wells. I'm used to working alone." I'm at the school that Stockton's children attend. They were just picked up in a limo.

"Remember, you're not alone on this case. Let me run it. Looks like it's registered to Stockton's mother-in-law. By the way, his wife's name is Carolyn."

"Okay, then I guess that's a safe spot for the kids."

"What's the next move, Peter?"

"I'm going to go knock on Stockton's door."

# CHAPTER 96

Olivia was first to notice that Eve was becoming agitated as the days went by. Her angry moments were popping up a lot quicker with her husband. Taking things out on him. Yelling at him for the smallest things and sometimes for nothing at all. It was probably good that he had gone with Reese, Emerson, and Arthur today to finalize the paperwork with New Life Senior Community. But Eve still looked distressed.

"Mom. What's wrong?"

Eve stood and stared at Olivia. "Let's go."

"Where do you want to go?"

"You know," she paused for a moment. "Home."

"Mom, in a few days you will be home again." Olivia didn't know what else to say to her. Then it occurred to her. I'll bet she is bored by not having enough room to walk in the house. No long hallways. Olivia put a coat on her mom along with a knit hat as the temperature was beginning to drop by late afternoon. Made sure her shoes were tied.

The nurse looked at Olivia, "Do you want me to help you, I think this is a marvelous idea."

"Yes, thank you."

Eve was near the end of the driveway before Olivia locked the door. "Hold on a minute, Mom." She yelled to the nurse, "Stop her before she goes into the road."

Olivia was happy to see her mom quiet and walking like there was no end to the road ahead. But the face. The face was still scrunched up, like she was frustrated. "Mom, where are we going?"

"Oh, you know."

Olivia shrugged and shook her head. "Am I a bad person to want my mom to go to that facility? Will she ever be happy again?"

"That's what we will never know, Olivia," the nurse said. "She can no longer communicate what her desires are. But this is the best possible decision. She will be well taken care of, and your dad won't have to worry about her constantly. He will learn to make new friends as well. Let's hope that happens soon. Most husbands find themselves so lost when their spouses can't communicate with them. They feel as much guilt as you do."

Olivia nodded and pushed her hands deeper into the pockets, trying to warm her chilly hands.

After a long walk, Olivia steered her mom back in the direction of home. Eve allowed the nurse to remove her coat and hat, and then she wandered toward the bed. "Warren," she said before she pulled the sheet down and got in, once again, shoes and all.

Reese was thrilled everything had come together so quickly. It had been a lot of back and forth with attorneys and the director of the New Life facility Lots of finalizing transactions. Transfer of accounts, signing contracts and wills. All of it.

Reese had spoken with her dad about finances, just as her former teacher had asked her to do. He was right. Her dad felt comfortable with the help from Reese and Emerson but also felt that he had some skin in the game.

Arthur was able to take on the expense himself.

"They can move in next Monday." the director said. "Welcome to your new home and a New Life." He shook Waren and Arthur's hands. He could see Warren was a bit sullen. "Trust me, sir," he patted Warren's hand, "your wife will get the attention she deserves in this care center. I promise you that."

Warren smiled.

Turning toward Arthur, the director stated, "I hope you enjoy the pickleball courts and having your new friend Warren just a few doors away."

"I'm sure I will. How about you, Warren?"

"I am so ready for this. It's too bad Eve isn't with us today. We could have had a nice lunch together." Warren lowered his head a bit. "I mean the Eve I once knew. I do miss my wife. The one who always had a smile and a kind word. Now, it's mostly nothing at all or anger."

Reese gave her dad a side hug. "I know Dad, I wish there was a cure. It's heart-wrenching."

Emerson had to break the tension. "Okay, everyone let's go tell Olivia the good news." He paused for dramatic effect. "That she can have her house back on Monday!"

# CHAPTER 97

Peter went back to Stockton's Orinda, California house. He planned on asking to use the phone. As he approached the front door, he could see a dog barking through the side window, but no human. The dog jumped on the door, then ran in the direction of the massive garage, then back again several times. No one answered even after ringing the doorbell several times. The dog was getting more agitated with every chime of the bell, continuing to run back and forth toward the same spot. Shit, something is wrong.

He called Orinda Police for help.

Arriving in just minutes, police and EMTs were on scene. Peter greeted them in the driveway sharing his concerns. Unfortunately, they forced him to show his credentials, taking them back to the squad car to check Peter out. He knew it was protocol, but they were wasting time.

The trooper walked back to Peter, handing him his ID. "Sorry, we can't be too careful in this neighborhood, agent."

"I hear you, but I know we need to get into this garage now."

"First, we need to shut off the security, before we pry open

307

the garage door."

"Then do it!" Peter pleaded.

He made the call to the security company. Annoyed at Peter for barking orders.

Peter stood in front of the garage door anxiously waiting. Finally, after what felt like forever, the trooper yelled up to him. "It's off."

"I could use some help with this door, damn it."

The trooper scowled. "When you give me some goddamn respect, I'll be glad to give you, my help."

"Forget it." Peter gave the door another few tugs, then decided to use the crowbar in his car. He wedged it between the pavement and the door and applied pressure. Nothing. The crowbar bounced back up to its original position. He gripped the bar tight and pushed his full weight down onto the bar. He held his breath, and his muscles strained as he rocked back and forth trying to release the door. His face reddened, and beads of sweat formed on his forehead. Suddenly, the door broke free from its locked position and bounced open an inch. The crowbar clanged against the pavement, and Peter stumbled trying to catch himself from falling.

Peter grabbed the handle and yanked the wide door open.

The stench of rotting flesh rushed out of the garage, gagging Peter and the trooper.

"Oh shit!" The trooper covered his face with his arm. "How the fuck did you know something was wrong?" He yelled to the paramedics, "Get in here now!"

Peter grabbed the ladder leaning against the wall, readying it for the paramedics to check her, but like the rest, he knew she had been hanging there for a while.

The trooper yelled at him. "Stop right there. Back away from the body. We need to have the coroner here. Don't touch anything." He waived the EMT to climb the ladder to check for a pulse, knowing she was already dead. "We need a team here," giving the address into his radio, "Now!"

Peter dropped back allowing the young trooper to take over. He was a good cop, just a little taken aback by a federal agent in his neighborhood.

After the medical examiner arrived with his team and began their work, Peter approached the police trooper and extended his hand. "Great work today, sir. I apologize for being an ass earlier, but this poor young woman is just a pawn in a much larger case. Thank you for your dedication to your career."

The young man shook Peter's hand. "Can I be of assistance to you in any way?"

"I'm sure you can. Got something with your name and contact info for me."

He handed Peter his card. "My private cell is on there as well, agent."

"Do you know this woman personally?" Peter asked.

"Yes, I do. Her name is Carolyn."

Peter knew that already but wanted his reaction.

"She's a sweet, gentle kind of woman. Used to volunteer at local charity events. I spoke with her on several occasions. Even jokingly asked her about the bruising on her arms one day. I already knew what they were from, or should I say, who they were from. That prick. Baffles me why women put up this shit."

"What did she say to that?"

"It's always the same story with abuse. I fell, or I walked into the wall. Her husband is Craig. He owns a brokerage house in Manhattan. I need to contact him."

"I apologize if I'm overstepping here. I'm asking you to call this person instead." He handed him Agent Wells's info. "I'm on my way back to D.C. tonight. Carolyn's husband is a prime suspect in another ongoing investigation. Have you seen him around the city lately?"

"No, I haven't."

"The one thing I need you to do for me is take someone with you when you notify her children and her mother. See what her mother has to say about her daughter's choice for a husband."

"You got it, agent. Thank you."

Peter nodded his head. "Oh, one more thing. Can I have my credentials back?"

"Oh, shit, yes of course." The young man retrieved Peter's ID.

The medical examiner's team loaded Carolyn's body and transported her to the coroner's office. Peter followed. He wanted as many details as he could get. After leaving the coroner's office, he briefed Wells and then called Emerson.

"Lake, listen carefully."

"Hey buddy, it's about time you called."

"No time for pleasantries, my friend. This is important. I found Stockton's wife. Hanging in her garage."

"Oh no!"

"The coroner says the time of death would normally be determined by rectal temp, but even liver temperature is undeterminable because of the deterioration of the body. She could have been dead for weeks. Lots of factors are involved. Although she was not exposed to the outdoor elements, even the temperatures in the garage could impact time of death. Hot all day in California, yet it could be much cooler at night. He needs to do a full autopsy on her. The cause is most likely strangulation, but who knows at this point? He will send all the results to Wells, along with fingerprints on the body and the rope. I have a bad feeling that Stockton is involved. We haven't been able to locate him. You've got to stay vigilant, Lake."

"Got it. I'll make sure Reese or I will be with Olivia 24/7 till you arrive."

"I owe you one. Or maybe two, Lake."

"I'll have a beer. You better throw me a damn good bachelor party, Pal."

"You're on."

# CHAPTER 98

"Everything is going so smoothly moving your parents into New Life CCSC today, don't you think Reese?" Emerson asked.

"Almost too easy, Emerson. My dad was excited to meet these new people. Odd."

"Why would you say that? He's content it seems to me. He's already walking the golf course."

"I don't know, maybe I expected him to give me a hard time about moving and the price."

"Well between you and me, sweetness, I think he will be just fine here. This is what he was used to before your mom's illness. He has his head held high now; did you notice? Your teacher was right. Your dad feels he earned this type of lifestyle and has his own money invested too. Makes him feel good again."

"Mom, though. I hope she can handle the change."

"She did just fine at Olivia's house. Was just too small for her to roam."

"Well, she was off and roaming down these halls already."

"Look, here she comes again." Emerson laughed.

"Where are you going today, Mom?" Reese asked Eve.

"Oh, he wants to see me today."

"Who wants to see you today, Mom?"

"Oh, you know. Let's go."

"Oh, not again," Reese grabbed Eve's arm, and Emerson took the other. On the third lap, Reese stopped her and kissed her goodbye. "See you tomorrow, mom."

Eve just blinked and then kept on walking.

"You're right, Emerson. She loves to walk and fast I might add."

"Reese let's go out for a nice dinner then back to our hotel room where we can be alone, and I can make mad passionate love to you. That should take your mind off the events of the past couple of weeks."

"What about my sister? I don't want to just suddenly dump her."

"You want her to have a threesome with us?"

Reese punched him in the arm. "No, you ass, I just don't want her suddenly alone. I say we invite Olivia to join us for dinner before we return to her house for the evening."

"I liked my idea better, but whatever you wish."

"Emerson, I think you need a nipple twist. Worked before."

"Mean, mean, woman, Clayton."

Back at the hotel to get cleaned up before dinner, Emerson could barely wait to peel each piece of her clothing off Reese, one by one. Touching her each time he dropped an article of clothing to the floor to arouse her. Touching her neck with his tongue, running his fingers through her lavender scented hair. Then pulling her naked body toward him. He picked her up like she was the weight of a tissue, gently laying her on the bed. Making love to each other, like never before.

"I love you, Reese. Marry me right now."

"I would, but my family is now expecting a big wedding, bridesmaids, flowers, the whole works. I even have a wedding dress."

Rolling off of her. "Seriously? When did all this happen?"

"When my sister proposed in that restaurant."

"As funny as that must have been, sweetheart, I am beginning to fear we will never be a married couple."

"Not an issue with me. When you see what I have planned for our wedding night, you'll wish you never said those words."

"Really? My beautiful Reese, how could it get much better than what we just did?" He kissed her with such passion. The kind of kiss you only feel in a good romance novel. Only this was real.

"I love you, Emerson Lake."

"And I you, Reese Clayton."

# CHAPTER 99

Reese called her sister on the way to her house from the hotel. "Olivia, get into your best duds sister. Emerson and I are taking you to dinner before we crash for the rest of the night at your house."

"You mean my torn jeans and my rocking torn tee shirt?"

Emerson yelled to her over the phone. "Only if it's torn in the right places."

"Pig!" Olivia snorted she was laughing so hard.

"The two of you are impossible. We'll pick you up in 20 minutes."

The three of them arrived at the restaurant and were escorted to a table set for four.

"This is nice," Olivia said. "Thanks for inviting me."

"We wouldn't leave you alone. Arthur is no longer there to cook for you. You'd starve to death." Emerson nudged Olivia in the arm.

"Emerson Lake, do not talk to my little sister like that."

Liv and Emerson smiled at each other, both knowing they were not only becoming best friends, but family.

"Sis, he can say what he wants to me. You know I'll give it right back to him."

"That's the problem. I know the things you pull in public." Reese waved her engagement ring in the air.

The three of them enjoyed their meal. Emerson leaning back in his chair rubbing his belly.

"It was a fun, relaxing dinner," Olivia said. "What's for dessert?"

Reese looked at Emerson with a smirk on her face.

"Uh oh, I'm guessing you two already had," Olivia cleared her throat, "um...dessert. Well, I'm all alone so I'm having the apple pie a la mode. You'll just have to wait for me."

"Bullshit," they both replied at once. "Apple pie a la mode it is."

"In all seriousness, I want to thank you both for all you've done helping get mom and dad into a safe place. Taking care of the scary stuff. Introducing me to Peter of course. And for being my family most of all. I was so frustrated for so many years I just wanted someone to blame and that was you, Reese. I want you to know how proud of you I am and how much I truly respect what you do for a living. You are my superhero. I'm sorry for how I treated you, and please know how much I love you."

Reese was dumbfounded. She slid the chair back forgetting there was carpet underneath nearly tipping over had it not been for Emerson catching her.

She composed herself and walked around to the other side of the table, squatting down eye-to-eye with her sister. Before she could get the words out, she heard a pop. It was like time was standing still. Panic swept over Reese's face. A bullet pierced the chair she had just been sitting in, shattering the wine glass, spilling the liquid like a bleeding wound. A shard of glass hit Reese's face. She winced but never broke eye contact with her sister. Reese saw Olivia's eyes widen and her jaw tense as the bullet pierced her skin.

# CHAPTER 100

Instinct drove Emerson to race out the door of the restaurant as it swung closed, not catching sight of which way the shooter went. Calling for backup and an ambulance stat. Active shooter. Looking in both directions and across the street. He saw nothing. Until a white sedan sped onto the sidewalk nearly hitting him. Lost his balance and hit the brick wall behind him. He caught a glimpse of the driver. A blonde male. Craig Stockton.

His heart was beating like a racehorse at top speed as he tried to get a plate number. No luck.

He stood up and ran back into the restaurant, not expecting to see Reese on the floor, covering her sister's body with her own to protect her. "Reese move out of the way, let me see how bad it is."

"No, no, not my sister." Reese's face was covered in tears and makeup. Her clothes were bloody.

"It's okay, honey. Please let me help her." He pulled Reese off Olivia.

Diners scurried like mice in front of a flashlight, knocking chairs over, shrieking, not knowing whether to try to go out the door the shot came from. The noise was deafening.

"Reese see if you can get some control in here."

Emerson looked at where Olivia had been shot. A flesh wound on the side of her arm.

Scared and trembling. Adrenaline rushed through her body. "Don't leave me," she cried.

"I'm right here," he said. "Hey, you," he yelled and pointed to a nearby patron, "toss me some of the clean napkins." The gentleman nodded. "You're fine. I would never lie to you, Liv. Do you trust me?"

She nodded.

The patron handed Emerson the linens, and he wrapped the wound tight to stop the bleeding. Applying a tourniquet just above the wound using his tie. It was deeper than he originally thought.

Finally, Olivia was able to force words out of her lungs. "Reese? Where is my sister, Reese?" She tried to sit up.

"Ssh, Reese is right here."

"Captain Connelly," Reese said. "I'm so glad you're here."

Shawn surveyed the scene. "What the hell happened?"

"Craig Stockton is what happened." Emerson was a disheveled mess. His pants ripped. Tie gone. "He tried to run me down. I couldn't get the plate."

"How did Olivia get shot?"

"I think it was meant for Reese." He gently grabbed her arm. "Are you okay?"

"I'll tell you one thing; this shit is getting old. Why does everyone feel a need to kill me lately? I'm going to go with Olivia. I'll meet you there when you finish up here."

She kissed him quickly and followed the paramedics as they loaded Olivia into the ambulance. Emerson didn't dare say a word about the blood all over her dress.

# CHAPTER 101

Emerson Lake, frightened to think he could have lost it all in a split second, grabbed his phone and contacted Agent Wells.

"Wells, I have some news for you." Emerson said.

"I have news for you as well, Emerson. Stockton is in Vermont."

"I know that...now. What the fuck? Why didn't you tell me sooner? He just tried to kill us. I think the shot he took was meant for Reese but hit her sister instead. Both are okay. Olivia's was hit in the arm, flesh wound."

"Look at your fucking phone, Lake. I left you messages telling you he was spotted about two hours ago."

"What? Hang on a second." Emerson switched to messages and there they were. "I turned the damn phone down in the restaurant. Sorry. Do you have eyes on him now?"

"No, but I will contact you when we do. In the meantime, don't turn that fucking thing down again until you get back to South Dakota, detective. You may not have had a bride to marry. Don't let your luck run out."

Emerson had not been reprimanded in many years but knew

321

Agent Wells was right in doing so. "Got it, Wells. Thank you."

Emerson stopped at the hotel before going to the hospital to grab some clean clothes. When he arrived at the ER, he quickly found Reese.

"How is she doing?" he asked after kissing his bride-to-be.

"She'll be fine. The doctor just finished stitching her up. Going to keep her overnight. She is sedated, but I'm not leaving her side."

"I think that's a smart idea, hon. I grabbed you a pair of jeans and a sweater from the hotel. I didn't think you wanted to spend the night in that dress."

"Thanks. Can you stay while I get cleaned up a bit?"

"Of course."

She disappeared into a hallway bathroom. When she returned, she rolled the dress in a ball and tossed it in the hazard bin. "Better."

"I have to meet the captain at the station and file a report. Will you be okay? Do you have your weapon with you?"

"I do. And yes, we will be fine. I'll call you in the morning to let you know if they're releasing her. Try to get some sleep, Emerson. I worry about you too."

By the time he got back to the hotel from the police station, Emerson was ready for sleep but checked his phone to make sure he hadn't missed anything important. He found the only thing he missed was his beautiful Reese. He debated on having a drink from the bar before bed, deciding he needed to have a clear head in the morning. Knowing a drink would turn into two or more. Sleep came quickly.

Startled by his phone, Emerson jumped out of bed causing

him to have a sudden wave of dizziness.

"Lake," the voice said.

Emerson steadied himself. "Yeah, what have you got?"

"Stockton is on the run again. Reported heading south on the NYS Thruway. I'm guessing headed back to the city."

"Why? He must know the whole city is looking for him. I don't get it."

"My thoughts are on the stock market. He probably needs to tie up some loose ends before he tries to flee the country."

"I can't imagine why he would go there. The security is on overload till we catch this guy."

"He doesn't have to be at the exchange, but he does need access to his computer files. And if my suspicions are right, it's the overseas accounts he is searching for."

"Well, the asshole isn't going to escape anywhere if he stays on the radar. Jesus, he must know the thruway is all cameras."

"We'll see how far he goes before he gets off. I'll keep you in the loop. How are the girls doing?"

"Don't know yet. I just woke up when the phone rang. Haven't even had time to take a leak, Mike. Reese is at the hospital with her sister. You know my lady; she's not leaving without her. I'm going to guess that we will be staying at Olivia's for a while."

"I'll let you know if Stockton is headed back in your direction. Sorry I woke you."

"Thanks, Mike. By the way, anything from Peter?"

"Yes, a lot, but will have to keep that with me, understand? He's safe in case anyone you may know is asking."

"Got it. Thanks, my friend."

Emerson showered and headed to the station, first stopping

for a cup of coffee to knock the cobwebs out of his head.

"I'm here to see Captain Connelly. He's expecting me."

The desk sergeant nodded and made a call. Emerson sipped his cup of joe while he waited.

"Emerson, come on in. Have a seat. What have you heard about your sister-in-law?"

"Nothing yet this morning but expect to hear something soon. Anything on the bullet?"

"No, nothing. I didn't expect to. It could have come from anywhere. No prints of course."

"I heard from Wells. Stockton was last seen on the NYS thruway headed south. Possibly a last-ditch effort to get rid of some of his computer files."

"Word has probably already reached his clients, so I'm guessing they are coming for him. The crazy bastard should use his head. His type of clientele is more apt to get him before we do. When you're dealing with billionaires, especially those in countries that hate us, there is no limit to what they will do to him."

"How would he expect to get those files? Isn't the building locked down?"

"Probably learned a lesson or two from Andora's wife. Keep a copy."

"But where? He's somewhere no one can find them. I don't think he has a panic room. Do you?"

"Don't think he is *that* smart."

"Reese is texting me, Captain. Hold that thought."

*Come and pick us up. Forgot I came here by ambulance. Love you.*

Emerson's fingers floated over the keys of his cell.

*That's funny. You mean you and your cohort have no way of*

*getting home. Hmm, let me see. Do you have any money on you?*

His phone immediately started ringing.

"No," Reese answered his stupid question. "But I have ways of making you suffer my darling."

"I know better than to ask. Be right there, sweetheart."

"Thank you. The doctor said bed rest for a few days for Olivia, but she will be fine."

"That's great news. Put her on the phone a minute."

Reese handed the phone over.

"Hi, handsome."

"Hi, beautiful. I'm glad you are ready to come home. And I had a quick word from Agent Wells this morning. He said if anyone was wondering, Peter is fine. He just can't reveal his location at the moment."

"What about his daughter, what's going on with her?"

"She has round-the-clock security; someone Reese and I know well. They are getting along great."

"Ok good. Glad someone is looking out for her. See you shortly."

Reese took the phone back from her sister. "Babe, call when you get here. We'll meet you downstairs."

"Not a chance, I'm coming in to get you both. End of discussion, Reese."

"Love you," she made a playful smooching into the receiver as she hung up.

"Captain, I'm on taxi duty, so I have got to make this quick. Where would Stockton hide duplicate files? And would he have reason to even do that?"

"He would. These are not everyday investors we're talking

about, Lake. I've seen people in the boroughs brutally murdered for a lot less than this. I'm talking fingernails pulled out and limbs torn to shreds, and that's just for starters. I moved here to get away from all that gore."

"Yeah, so much for the quaint vibes in rural Vermont."

"I think you put a curse on us, Lake. Coming here with your hot-shot girlfriend digging up the dirt that tends to get deeper as the days go by." The captain shook his head. "Damn out-of-towners."

"Yeah, that's us captain, South Dakota riffraff. I have to go pick up two beautiful women now."

"You better get it in gear, detective. They could both kick your ass."

"You're right about that, my friend."

# CHAPTER 102

Once back at Olivia's house, Emerson placed an online grocery delivery order. Breakfast and lunch essentials, dessert, and plenty of coffee. Any big meal they could order in, but at least the basics would be covered. He also ordered a couple of bouquets of roses and two boxes of chocolates for his dynamic duo. He made a special request for the driver to call before delivery.

Emerson put his arm around Olivia. "Now," he said, "be a good girl and do as you're told, to heal quickly. I heard you are helping my girl plan our wedding. I can't help her with that. It's your job as maid of honor." He was trying his best to keep her mind off what she just went through.

"I just need your wallet, or at least a heavy credit card limit."

"Just like your sister, even wounded, you're a smart ass."

Olivia gave him a playful smack.

"Peter is my best man, so maybe the two of you can come up with a nice reception. And FYI, money is no object. Nothing but the best for my bride."

The groceries arrived right on schedule. Emerson whipped up a quick meal, and they ate heartily.

"Not bad for a spoiled brat, "Reese said, her mouth still half full.

After dinner, the three of them sat on the sofa watching TV.

"Hey, did anyone find out what was on the camera in my fridge?" Olivia asked.

"Just us and your wild blonde curly hair," Emerson pretended to flip his hair back and forth.

Olivia playfully threw a napkin at him. After a moment, she asked the question she had been dying to ask all day. "So, Peter is coming back?"

"I assume so," Emerson shrugged. "He promised me one hell of a bachelor party."

Olivia's eyes beamed at the thought. "Bachelor party, huh? Reese, be prepared. We have to one-up these guys. Las Vegas here we come."

"Right now, the only place you're going is to bed. Take your medication and go to your room young lady."

Olivia was more worn out than she thought. "I know, I am kind of tired." It was time for her to call it a night. "But I feel perfectly fine." She knew the big sister response she would get.

"Too darn bad. Go. Now!" Reese shooed her sister toward her bedroom.

"I wouldn't mess with her, Liv. You know what a bitch she can be."

"I love you both and thanks for everything. I'm going to bed now."

"Me too Liv. I don't think I've slept in a week."

"Beginning to feel the same," Emerson said. "Good night."

"If you need anything during the night," Reese said to Olivia, "just yell. We will hear you."

Reese and Emerson couldn't wait to climb those stairs after checking the security. "It's time we had a good night's sleep. I'm exhausted, Reese yawned as they climbed into bed. "If I promise you better things for tomorrow, will you rub my back?"

"Kiss me good night first," he said.

She gave him a smooch and laid on her stomach. She was snoring in minutes. Emerson smiled rolling over on his side.

# CHAPTER 103

Emerson's phone pinged, startling him awake. His first thought was Wells. When he saw the photo, he sat straight up in bed. A tidal wave of fear washed over him. It wasn't Wells. It was a photo of Craig Stockton. His arm around Eve Clayton's waist. They were standing in her new bedroom.

Emerson pulled on a pair of pants and a shirt, being as quiet as he could be. Not wanting to scare Reese. And knowing someone had to be here for Olivia.

A thought raced across his mind. Was Eve trying to tell us something the other day when she told us **he wants to see me.** Who wanted to see her? Was this just her mixed-up thoughts, or did someone really ask to see her? How the fuck did he get in there?

He jumped in the stretch and took off for New Life Continuing Care Senior Community, not once looking at a speed limit sign. He called Wells on the way.

"I'll call ahead to the facility, Lake. Watch your back. It might be a trap. But we do know he was headed to Vermont again. Just got that information."

Lake hung up and not three minutes went by, and the phone rang again.

"Turn around, Lake. Go back!

"What are you talking about, Mike? No, I have to get to Eve."

"No, Lake, I confirmed Eve is perfectly fine. Stockton is headed toward Olivia's house. Step on it. I'm on Route 7 now. Meet you there."

# CHAPTER 104

"Wake up!" she whispered. The faint smell of chloroform clouded her brain. "Emerson, someone is in the house." Reese reached for her pistol, which she always placed on the nightstand. It was gone. She whispered again. "Wake up, damn it," giving him a shove. Only now realizing what she thought was Emerson was only pillows.

Reese could still smell the faint odor lingering in the air. She scrambled to find her backup pistol. Panic took over her body. She felt weak. "Emerson? Where are you?" She swung her legs over the side of the bed, her feet dangling. She attempted to stand. Her legs wobbled. She tried to catch herself, but instead fell to the floor.

"Shit, what the hell was that?" Olivia sat up startled by a thud. "Reese?" she yelled. "Are you guys, okay?"

"It's just me, sweetheart." She recognized the voice.

"What the hell are you doing here? How the hell did you get in?" She could just make out his silhouette in the dim light of the room.

"Emerson let me in. Said he was going for coffee or

something." Craig leaned over the bed to kiss her.

She turned her face away and stood up pushing him away with her good arm. This only angered him.

"What the hell is this about? Who the fuck do you think you are, pushing me?"

"For starters, you tried to kill my sister, but the bullet hit me instead." She raised her bandaged arm.

"I did no such thing. Who the hell do you think you're talking to?"

"Well, how about your wife and kids? Emerson? Reese? I need you!" she yelled.

No one answered.

"We are done. Get out now!"

"Oh, you think we're done? I say when, not you bitch." He slapped her across the face, causing her to fall back on the bed.

"Reese!" she screamed, "where are you? Emerson, help me!"

Craig moved closer to the bed.

"Get the fuck away from me! I'm not your fucking as-needed whore." She screamed for Reese again. Nothing.

He slapped her harder. Her lip split open; a trickle of blood appearing at the opening. "I am the boss here!" He began to tear off her pajamas. "You know I hate these fucking things. I like sexy nighties on you and lace underwear."

He grabbed her bad arm, and she screamed. It felt like a lightning bolt searing her skin. "Reese, help me!" Fighting with every inch of her body, her arm felt like it was broken. She was kicking, biting, punching him. He was just too big for her 128-pound body. "Emerson," she continued to scream. "Reese, help me!"

"Emerson isn't here. And your cop sister can't hear you. I made sure of that."

"No, that's not true." Olivia began to sob. "No! No! No! You didn't." Olivia fought hard to save herself from being raped, or worse, by this madman. "I said no! Get away from me, you bastard!"

An unknown voice came from the other side of the room.

"Get off of her, or I put this bullet right through your fucking head," said the young man wearing the collar.

Craig Stockton spun around. "What?" A 357-Magnum aimed right between his eyes. "Give me that thing before you hurt yourself."

"Not a chance."

"What the hell are you doing here? Get the hell out before I kick your ass too," Craig said.

"I'm the one holding the gun."

"And so am I," a second voice said. "Father Gregory, I got it from here. Put the gun down." Peter appeared in the room and tossed Olivia a robe from the back of her armchair. "Get out of here. Now! Go, check on Reese."

She fumbled to cover the front of herself with the robe. Her face streaked with tears and blood. She pushed past Peter, nearly on a dead run to find her sister. She was not stopping for anything.

A brief look of surprise flickered across Craig's face as he realized two weapons were trained on him. He quickly masked his emotions but knew this was likely not to end well.

"Why should I lower my weapon?" Father Gregory cried. "He's no good. He's no fucking good!"

Peter took a small step toward Gregory. "I know that, but he will pay for his mistakes. I promise. You know that, right?"

Gregory gripped the gun handle tighter. "There is no punishment harsh enough for him." The bead still perfectly aimed at Craig Stockton's head.

"What are you talking about?" Craig asked. "I did nothing to you."

"It's what you did to my mother. You drove her to suicide. You beat her, you raped her for years, not to mention the infidelity. Her blood is on your hands. I'm guessing this poor woman did not know what a prick you are."

"And what makes you so almighty? That collar? Don't make me laugh."

Greg's index finger depressed the trigger ever so slightly. "No. Because God is the almighty. You, old man, are going to hell."

"Gregory, no!" Peter rushed at Craig Stockton, tackling him to the floor as the gun fired. The bullet hissed above them embedding itself in the wall above Olivia's headboard.

Peter placed his knee on Craig's back. Grabbing the cuffs from his cargo pants, Peter secured Craig Stockton, thinking, I hope this kid doesn't decide to shoot again. "Give me the gun, Greg. You didn't hurt anyone." Peter kept his hands down by his side to show he wasn't a threat to him.

Gregory's outstretched arms began to tremble. Peter slowly approached and gently eased his arms down. Gregory allowed him to pry the weapon from his grip.

"How old are you?" Peter asked the priest.

"Twenty-seven," Greg replied.

"And how do you know this man?"

"He's, my stepfather."

Captain Connelly burst into the bedroom door; gun drawn. Three armed troopers were behind him. "Hold it right there!"

"It's okay, captain," Peter raised his hands. "All is secure in here. I need your men to check the house for Reese and Olivia."

"Olivia, called 911. Paramedics are on the way."

"Gregory, what are you doing here? What did you do now?" The captain made an aggressive move toward the priest.

"No, captain." Peter shielded Father Gregory from the captain. "He didn't do anything wrong. I will come down to the station and give you a statement. But first, I have to speak to my friend Emerson."

Gregory was caught off guard. Not too many people would stand up for him. "Who are you?" he asked.

Craig licked his bloody lip. "I know who he is. His wife Judith was a surprisingly good lay before I fried her ass. She knew too much."

Peter gritted his teeth. "Captain, could you maybe go check on the girls for me and give me a moment with this asshole?"

"Of course." The captain headed out of the room.

Peter bent down, unlocked the handcuffs, and grabbed Craig Stockton by the back of his shirt. "Get on your feet! Let's see just how brave you are hitting a man instead of a woman, you no good piece of shit! Go ahead, take your best shot."

Craig swung, his fist sailing through the empty air as Peter avoided the punch. Peter coiled his arm and landed a stiff uppercut to Craig's stomach, then a jab to his face. One punch after another. By the time he was finished, Craig's face was barely recognizable. "That's for what you did to my wife. You coward!" Peter gave him one last brutal kick in the testicles. Craig fell to the ground in agony.

Peter turned to the young Gregory. "That one was for your mom."

Craig groaned, writhing in pain on the floor before he vomited.

The captain knocked on the bedroom door. "What happened to him?" he motioned to Craig's body curled in the fetal position.

"Captain, he was trying to escape. Isn't that right, Gregory?"

"Uh, yes. Yes sir. That's right. He was trying to escape, and this man stopped him."

"Get on your feet." The captain grabbed Stockton by the armpit and yanked him up to a standing position. "You're coming with me." He placed the handcuffs on his wrists.

"Actually, he's coming with me, captain." Agent Wells stood in the bedroom doorway.

"You're under arrest, Craig Stockton."

"For what?" Craig spat blood to the floor.

"Illegal stock trading, real estate fraud, and the murder of your wife for starters."

Gregory gasped. "You murdered her?" Gregory clenched his fist and lunged at Stockton, being shoved back by Peter.

"Don't ruin your life by taking his. Your mom wouldn't want to see you go to prison because of this piece of shit."

"I want a lawyer." Stockton spit again, this time expelling a tooth.

"Sure. We'll see if anyone wants you as a client." Wells took Stockton by his elbow, leading him outside. "You have the right to remain silent."

"Fuck you," Stockton said.

"Oh, I do believe you will receive a lot of that in a prison cell. That's before your clients overseas find out you screwed them over."

"I didn't screw anyone over."

"How about the investments you made on hundreds of clients' behalf? You're a broker, not an investment manager. Maybe you shouldn't have used Stockton and Associates as the name of your firm, asshole."

"If they're that stupid to not check on how much is in their accounts, well that's on them, not me."

"Ha! I can't wait to see what some of those foreign dignitaries have to say about that. They're likely to cut you up bit by bit. You think they don't have connections in prisons? Think again."

# CHAPTER 105

Emerson slammed the brakes of the stretch. It skidded to a halt in front of Olivia's house. All the activity in the yard sent his heart rate through the roof. "Reese." He ran toward the house pushing past everyone to get to her. Coming to a halt when he saw Wells emerge from the front door with Stockton.

"Where is Reese, you son of bitch?" He took a swing at Craig before he could respond.

"Hey, aren't you the law?" Stockton laughed at Emerson. "You're not supposed to hit a man under arrest."

Emerson tossed his shield and his gun to the ground and hit him again. "I'm not the law anymore, dickhead. Just a law-abiding citizen visiting relatives."

"Ok, that's enough," Wells intervened stepping between Emerson and Craig. "Reese is with her sister upstairs. Go!" Wells motioned him toward the doorway.

Wells looked back at Peter standing in the doorway. "Pick up his badge and gun. After he quiets down, give him back his belongings."

"Is it okay if I take Gregory with me, sir, for backup?" he gave the kid a wink.

"Sure, we have nothing on this kid, do we?"

"No, we don't agent." the captain replied.

"Take a break, Peter," Wells told him. "You've had enough. I'll speak with you next week sometime."

Peter put his arm around Gregory. "Let's go kid." As they headed back into the house, Peter asked, "Hey, I've been wondering. How did you get the car from the Manhattan brokerage garage? The one you were seen driving from Grace Center."

"I took the keys. It belonged to that asshole. He never used it. It wasn't fancy enough for him. I've been in the Manhattan building before with my mom. Security knew who I was. They probably never gave it a second thought if they saw me on the security cams taking the car."

"Ah, that makes sense. Listen kid, I'm really sorry about your mom. How did you find out she was dead?"

"My grandmother called me. My mom's mother. She has my two little sisters with her. My mom is better off and in a better place. I just wish she valued herself more when she was alive. Her choices weren't always good ones. But I loved her more than any son could."

Emerson took the stairs two at a time, falling to his knees at Reese's side. "I'm right here sweetheart." He gently kissed her cheek.

"Emerson, I couldn't find you. What happened? Where did you go?" She tried to get up, but the paramedic insisted she stay still while he was evaluating the lump on her head. "Why weren't you here with me?"

"You needed to stay with Olivia, in case she needed help."

"Yeah, damn it. How the hell did that work out?" Reese rubbed her head. "Where the hell did you go so early, and don't try to lie, because you suck at it."

There was no sense in keeping it from her. He pulled out his phone and showed her the photo. "My phone woke me. This is the first thing I saw. And then I got a message to meet at the New Life Senior Community."

Worry filled Reese's eyes.

"Don't worry," he patted her hand. "Your mom is fine. Wells confirmed it, She's with your father for now. I was on my way there when Wells told me Stockton was on his way here. Peter got here first."

"Actually, this young man beat me here." Peter entered the room, followed by the man with the collar. "I want you to meet my new friend, Greg Collins. His mother was Craig's wife. I think he saved your life, Olivia. I am forever indebted to him for that."

"Hey kid, you're not really a priest, are you?" Emerson asked.

Greg removed the white collar from the black button-down shirt. "No, sir, I'm not."

"Why impersonate a priest?" Peter asked.

"Because it allowed me to get in and out of places without question. I've never seen a man of the cloth stopped from entering or exiting a building, have you?"

Peter nodded, impressed. "Smart tactic, kid. Not too sure the man upstairs would agree though."

"The captain?" Gregory asked.

"No, way up!" Peter pointed toward the sky.

"Oh! Yeah, right. Probably not," Gregory said.

Until this moment, Olivia had not understood how Craig had been involved with this kid, but now it all made sense and she was grateful for the distraction Greg had caused to allow her to escape. She looked deeply into Peter's eyes and then walked over to hug the boy. "I am very sorry about your mom; I swear I didn't know Craig was married. Honestly, I didn't." Greg buried his head into Olivia's shoulder and cried his heart out. Staying there until Peter led them both down to the living room.

"Emerson," Reese said. "I don't know what to say, except thank you."

"You can say you still love me, even though I left you."

She smiled, her heart beating heavily in her chest, pulling him toward her to kiss him. "I love you, Emerson Lake."

"Hey you two, stop it. You're setting off the monitors." the EMT joked. "We need to send her for some scans to make sure there are no issues, but it looks good from here."

"Emerson, stay with my sister. Make sure she's okay."

"Oh, I think the last person she needs with her right now is me. I think Peter has everything under control. Wells has taken Craig Stockton into custody. Anything else my lady? Because I'm coming with you."

They started to load Reese on the gurney. "Wait," Reese said to the EMT. "Emerson, didn't Mike Wells say they still hadn't found Stockton's files for his overseas clients?"

"They confiscated his computer from his Manhattan office. Mike thought he might have a copy somewhere, like Peter's wife did."

"How much do you want to bet those files are hidden right here in this house? The hidden camera in the fridge might have been just one of many to keep an eye on who was coming and going."

"Shit! You're probably right Reese." Emerson yelled from the top of the stairs, "Peter, come up here now."

Peter came, Captain Connelly in tow. "You need to search this house."

"For what?"

"Files. Could be paper or electronic. We think Craig hid something in this house. What better place to hide something than in his girlfriend's home. Inform your colleagues. Captain, can you help till Reese and I get back?"

"Yes, I'm all for it. This guy has made a mess of my quiet little town."

"We're on it, Emerson," Peter escorted him out. "Now go take care of Reese. Call when you're ready to come back, and I'll pick you both up in the stretch. It's my job. I'm your chauffeur, remember?"

# CHAPTER 106

Peter returned to the living room. There she was. Olivia. Battered, but still beautiful.

Despite all the commotion, they somehow found themselves alone. Her eyes met his across the room. His heart skipped a beat.

"Are you okay, Liv?"

"I'm fine. I'm just so embarrassed, Peter," her gaze fell to the carpet. "I knew Craig was a jerk, but he was never abusive toward me. I had no idea how diabolical he was until tonight. And the fact that he could have hurt my mom and Reese," her voice trailed. "I would never have forgiven myself if anything happened to them."

"It's not your fault. There is no way you could have known how ruthless he was. We need to search this house to see if we can find his files so we can put this guy away for life."

"Can I help?"

"I think you should rest. What about your arm?"

"Are you going to baby me? The paramedic said the arm was fine. He re-bandaged it. Feels good."

"Really? How good?" His fear of losing her was beginning to settle in. He blinked back tears.

"Stand right there. Don't move." She took two steps back and then ran toward him, leaping into his arms. She locked both arms tight around his strong muscular neck. Her eyes glued to his.

"Whoa, that was some leap. I guess you are okay."

"I told you, Sherlock."

"You are indeed beautiful Olivia Clayton." For the first time since he lost his wife, he could feel it again. That raw teenage energy. The butterflies you get when you have that special first moment. He held her tightly. "Olivia." He kissed her gently as he slowly let her down. "I think I may be falling in love with you."

"I already know I'm in love with you." She reached up to pull his mouth towards hers. Flinching a little from the ache in her arm.

Peter pulled back. "Let me help you." He pulled her up toward him and kissed her with all the passion of a movie star. His leading lady.

When they finally released, she looked at him lovingly. "Come on, Sherlock. Let's find out if that asshole hid files in my house. The group is waiting outside. They're probably staring at us through the window right now, aren't they?"

"Don't know. All I see is you."

# CHAPTER 107

The captain was getting frustrated. "This search is going nowhere. Olivia, do you remember Stockton bringing anything work-related into the house? Papers, flash drives, a laptop, anything?"

"The only thing he ever brought here was a zippered garment bag with a few changes of clothes."

"Where is that bag now?"

"I assumed it was in my closet." She decided to look for herself and quickly returned. "Huh, nothing in it. I guess he wasn't planning on staying long then."

"That's all he ever brought with him?" Gregory asked.

"As far as I know."

"I think you should come with me and take a look at this."

They followed him out the kitchen door into the garage.

"What are we looking for, my friend?" Peter asked.

"Those." He pointed to a set of golf clubs in the corner. "Those are his golf clubs."

"Did you know about these, Olivia?" Peter asked.

"No, I never saw him with golf clubs. He must have brought

them with him the last time he was here, but I never heard him mention playing golf. Isn't one of the first things golfers do is talk about the course conditions and how they played that day? Never once mentioned the game to me, ever."

Peter cautiously moved the bag to the center of the garage. "Let's have a look."

"Wait a minute," the captain grabbed Peter's arm. "Look at the bag tag hanging off the back."

Peter held it up so it was in view.

"Oh my God," Olivia clasped her palm over her mouth.

The tag read: New Life Senior Community.

# CHAPTER 108

Carefully, Peter removed each club with his gloved hands. The side pockets contained packages of new golf balls and tees too. A zippered case inside one of the pockets revealed more golf balls. Peter lifted one of the balls out of the bag and immediately noticed it was a much lighter weight than the others. "Don't touch anything else," he yelled. "Back out of the garage. Now! Everyone! Captain, call the bomb disposal unit. We need them to X-ray these golf balls."

The bomb unit arrived. Peter gave them a quick rundown on the situation as the team began to set up outside the garage.

"So, how does this all work?" Peter asked. "Sorry, I didn't catch your name."

"It's J.D.," the state trooper technician replied as he stepped into the heavyweight bomb suit. "First, we'll X-ray it to see what we're dealing with. There are three things we look for. A load (an explosive), a power source (like a battery), and a switch (to initiate)."

"Fascinating." Peter watched as the team got the machine in position.

The X-ray only took a couple of minutes to show the balls were inert, clear of explosives. "There is something in there, but it's not a bomb."

"That is incredible. Thank you, J.D. Oh, and by the way, nice outfit." They both laughed.

Peter lifted one of the lightweight golf balls. On closer inspection, he could see a seam around the middle. He carefully twisted and the top released from the threads revealing a black device. "The latest in file storage technology, I assume."

# CHAPTER 109

The captain put a hand on Peter's shoulder, "I'm guessing we just found everything we need to convict Stockton. Never saw anything so tiny, but I would stake my career on this being his files."

"I agree. I will get these into Mike Wells's hands, immediately."

"Now we know how he got into the New Life facility." The captain grabbed the bag tag. "Looks like he's a member at the golf course on the property."

"But he's not a resident. How could he be a member?"

Gregory and Olivia joined the men in the garage now that it was all clear. "I have a feeling his money and influence have something to do with it." Gregory said.

"You may be right," Peter replied. "It makes perfect sense. His investors might live there."

"Peter, I can go to New Life," Captain Connelly said. "I can ask around. See if anyone has any investing tips. See if Craig or Stockton and Associates comes up."

"Can I go with you, captain?" Gregory asked. "I could say you are my grandpa and we're looking into what it costs to live there."

Liv and Peter did the best they could to stifle a laugh at the mention of Shawn Connelly being a grandpa, but it didn't work.

"I'll deal with you two later," Connelly said. "Let's go kid." He grabbed Gregory by the shoulders and escorted him out of the garage.

Arriving at the resident's entrance, they were greeted by security. The captain showed his credentials.

"Can I ask what this is all about, sir? I don't think anyone on campus called the police. And who is this kid with you?"

"This is my grandson. My wife is going to need a place like New Life soon. I was hoping to speak to the director and possibly take a tour."

"Well sir, we usually require an appointment, but I know you must be a busy man, let me see if we can arrange at least a tour."

It was only a short wait.

A young woman greeted them, "Hello, my name is Emily Collins." She stopped mid-sentence when she saw Gregory.

"Hello, Aunt Emily. Long time, no see."

Emily was speechless.

"Captain Connelly, I think I know who let Craig Stockton into see Eve Clayton. This woman is my late mom's sister. Dear Aunt Emily. She was banging Craig Stockton on the side."

"What do you mean 'late' mom?" Emily's face was puzzled.

"Sorry to have to tell you this ma'am," Captain Connelly said. "She was found hanging in her garage."

Gregory gritted his teeth. "He strung her up like she was a piece of meat. You lousy piece of shit! You knew what he did to her for years and never stopped it. Now that cheating, lying bastard is on his way to prison."

Emily's eyes widened, and the blood drained from her face.

The captain placed a calming hand on Gregory's shoulder. "Emily Collins, did you allow Craig Stockton to enter the building this morning?"

"I think I should have my attorney answer any questions you may have."

"No problem, Miss. I will have an arrest warrant in my hand. That will look wonderful to the press. And what a boost for future sales. Don't you think? Gregory, I think it's time we had a conversation with the director. Let's go."

They headed down the hall leaving Emily to stew.

"I'm guessing Emily won't have a job when we finish speaking with the director. What do you think?"

"Thank you, Captain Connelly," said Gregory. "For always looking out for me. Why did you, by the way? No one ever really cared except Mom, but she lost her ability to think for herself when she met Craig. I'm a grown man, but I still felt the hurt."

"I think that over the years I've learned a lot about people. You begin to see the good and the bad. You were headed down a slippery slope as a teen. That's why I think it was great the judge gave you a chance. If you remember, none of those punishments involved jail time, just community service to help others. She could see, as I did, the good in you. I still see it. As hard as it is to deal with your mom's untimely death, you will get through this and I'm proud of you for listening to Agent Andora and not shooting Craig Stockton."

Gregory sheepishly glanced up at the captain. "How did you

know?"

"I'm a trained professional, kid. I saw the hole in the wall. Pretty sure that didn't come from the tooth fairy."

They both had a good laugh at that.

"You know, I think I might like a career in law enforcement, not the stuff that you do, but maybe on the computer side of things. I'm going to read up on what degrees I need to do that."

"I believe you can do it, Greg. We are all here to help. Nothing would make me happier."

"Captain, can I ask you a question?"

"Of course."

"What about Trooper Matthews? What are you going to tell the press?"

"How do you know about Matthews?"

"I was at the press conference. I know about his father being a hero as well. What do you do in a case like that."

"I'm not sure yet son. It's a difficult situation. I'm going to discuss it with the upper echelon. He was involved in a serious crime. It's not my call to make. I'm guessing it won't be good. Another wasted life."

# CHAPTER 110

Peter dialed Mike Wells on his way to pick up Reese and Emerson from the hospital. "Agent, I hope you haven't left the area yet."

"Just waiting for transport for our guest of honor here, Stockton. Why? What's going on now?"

"I have a gift for you. We found some interesting items hidden in some fake golf balls. Where are you?"

"I'll send you, my location."

"This looks like a job for Carly Brennen. After I pick up Reese and Emerson from the hospital, I will head back to D.C. and relieve Carly from her assignment to watch over my daughter. Alicia is stable now."

"That's great news. Make the arrangements to get me those files, and I'll see you back in Vermont for the wedding."

Peter hung up and pulled up to the curb at the hospital entrance where Emerson was hovering over Reese in a wheelchair.

"There's our chauffeur, right on time." Emerson opened the door and Reese slid in.

"How are you, Reese?" Peter asked.

"I'll be better when I get rid of this headache."

"Oh, you mean Emerson? Yeah, he's a royal pain in the ass. Hey Emerson, maybe I should call Wells and tell him your lady is trying to get rid of you."

"Smart ass!" Emerson shook his head as he loaded himself into the backseat. "You know, you're a little chipper given everything that has gone on. Is that a smile on your face? Did a certain young lady cause that to happen?"

"Now who's the smart ass?"

Peter brought the detectives up to speed on the golf bag and the files. "Captain Connelly called from New Life. We know who let Craig into the facility. Gregory's Aunt. Emily Collins."

"Emily the tour guide?" Reese asked.

"The same. Apparently, she was sleeping with Craig for years. That guy makes a booty call everywhere he goes. She lawyered up of course."

"Thank you, Peter," Reese said. "I'm so glad this is over."

"We might need you back here on the east coast for court, but besides that, I think you're finally all set to head back home to South Dakota. I can't thank you enough for helping me find my daughter. I hope we remain friends forever."

"We feel the same, Peter." Reese gave his hand a gentle squeeze. "Thank you for all the help with my parents and Olivia."

"Just doing my job, ma'am. When you see your dad again Emerson, you can tell him I'll be back in town once Alicia is on her feet. I want to see how things go with Olivia. I think I'm in love with her."

Emerson caught Peter's eye in the rearview mirror. "We know

you are. We can see the change in you."

Peter cleared his throat. "Now about this wedding of yours."

"Small. Court House is fine. Just the four of us," Emerson said. "Then, Reese and I are headed to Hawaii. For a long honeymoon. Is that okay with you Reese?"

"Sounds perfect to me sweetheart."

# CHAPTER 111

"Olivia, you look beautiful," Reese said. "I'm so happy to have you as my maid of honor."

"And you look stunning, Reese. That dress is going to knock the pants right off that man of yours. Thanks for buying my dress, sis." Olivia did a twirl. "I feel great in it. I hope Peter likes it as well."

"Seriously? After the ceremony, I'm guessing you won't have it on long."

"I hope not." They both giggled like teenagers. "I'm in love with him, Reese."

"I know you are honey. He loves you too. Be patient. It's a huge transition to leave his career, but he knows it's the right time to retire. And Alicia is working so hard at getting better. It could take years. She's a strong young lady. You know Peter just beams when he is around you."

Olivia blushed and gave her sister a loving hug.

Emerson and Peter waited patiently for Reese and Olivia to arrive at the courthouse. Late of course.

Peter Andora felt his heart skip more than one beat as he saw

Olivia walk into the room ahead of her sister. He offered his arm for her to hold as they made their way to their places of honor. "You are absolutely beautiful," he whispered.

Olivia couldn't contain her smile. "You are everything I expected Peter. Handsome as could be."

Emerson, his heart filled with love, saw Reese. Her dad by her side. Mom was left at New Life. It was a sad decision for everyone, especially Reese, but it was the right one.

Her dress, shimmering white satin, fit every curve of her amazing body. Low-cut back and front. An elegant slit flowing down one side, revealing just a hint of leg with each graceful step. She carried a single long-stemmed red rose. Her hair cascaded to just below her shoulders. One diamond butterfly barrette was perched on the left side of her hair, representing the flutter she felt in her stomach for Emerson. Instead of a veil, just a gorgeous face.

Emerson's eyes wet with tears. Peter handed him a tissue.

Warren kissed his daughter, whispering, "I love you. Reese, your mother does too. I know how hard this has been to accept what has happened to her. I finally can let go of the times she doesn't know me and focus on the times that she does. I can see her failing and I'm sure you can too. No matter what, she is my wife, and I will be with her till the end, whenever that may be. We are so very proud of who you are, and I will never forget what you have done for our family."

"I love you both, Dad. I wish she was here with us." Reese, for the first time, cried into her dad's shoulder. "It's not fair, Dad. I miss my mom. And I wish she could have seen us in our grown-up clothes. I wish she could have gone shopping with Olivia and me to pick out my gown. Things mothers and daughters do."

"Shh, here, take this tissue and wipe your eyes carefully. You don't want to look like a raccoon on your wedding day, do you?"

She smiled and dabbed her eyes gently so as not to smear her makeup.

"You know, I showed Mom the photos I took of you and Olivia when you were getting fitted for your gowns at the bridal salon. You know what happened? She held my hand and said we created two stunning daughters."

Reese held her hand to her heart. "Really, Dad? She remembered?"

"Yes, sweetheart."

"But how? It's so perplexing how one minute she knows us and the next she doesn't. I wish we knew how she remembered the things she did to help us find Peter's daughter."

"Honey, I see it as a gift. And not ask questions. Maybe it's not for us on this earth to know."

Reese smiled. "I like that idea, Dad. A gift."

He patted her hand. "Now I see a young man up front, waiting for his bride."

They walked down the short aisle, and Warren handed her off to Emerson, hugging him. Emerson's dad stood close by dazed by Reese's beauty, stepping out of the line to also hug and kiss his new daughter-in-law.

The ceremony was noticeably short.

Emerson could barely get through his words. "I've never loved anyone as much as I love you, Reese. Will you be my wife for as long as we both shall live?"

Reese spoke from her heart as well. "We have been through so much sadness together, but we have survived. Our love has survived and always will. Yes, my dear Emerson, I will be your wife for as long as we both shall live."

Together they said, "Forever and a day."

The judge nodded with a smile. "By the power vested in me by the State of Vermont, I now pronounce you husband and wife. You may kiss the bride."

And that he did.

Peter and Olivia arranged a small reception at Chez Dubois. They included a few of the friends, old and new, they had made during this visit to beautiful Vermont. Captain Connelly, Arthur Horton, Agent Michael Wells, Alicia Holmes in a wheelchair, her psychiatrist in tow, Gregory Collins, and Carly Brennen. Also, one special guest couldn't be left out.

A bald server, with a white towel over his arm, approached the wedding couple smiling from ear to ear. "Welcome," he said. "And congratulations to you both. My name is Carmine. May I pour you some champagne?"

Reese stood and gave the man a huge hug. "Thank you, Carmine." She kissed his cheek. "It's a pleasure to meet you, sir. This is my actual spouse, Emerson Lake. It's not her." Reese pointed at her sister who was laughing uncontrollably.

"I know," the man said. "Your sister filled me in on the misunderstanding the last time you were here. Now I can really do this." He removed the towel from his arm and swung it around his head. "She said yes!" The restaurant, packed with patrons dining, was in an uproar. Everyone raised their glasses and yelled, "She said yes!"

# CHAPTER 112

Barely making it on time, they boarded the flight bound for
Hawaii with a layover in California.

"Ah," they both said slipping into their luxury first class seat-
ing. Still in their wedding clothes.

"It's been a rough and long visit Emerson. Makes me wonder,
do we want to continue doing this job? We never did get that
chance to discuss what's next."

"We did not, but right now, I just want to enjoy our
honeymoon."

Nearing California, daylight still streamed into the cabin
with the time change. Wobbling down the aisle, a man who
obviously couldn't handle his alcohol, was wreaking havoc with
some of the passengers and pushing his way toward the cockpit.

"Open that door, or I will take down this aircraft," he slurred.

Reese whispered, "Emerson we have to do something. He's
headed our way toward the cabin."

"Are you fucking kidding me right now?"

"Emerson please, we need to do something. All these people
could die if he gets in there. Including us."

"Kiss me," he said. "Now!"

She planted her lips on his. His leg spread across the aisle.

The drunk never saw it coming. His head hit the armrest knocking him out cold. Emerson handed the flight attendant his zip ties. "Can you handle this?"

"I certainly can, sir," she whipped out her own set of zip ties. "By the way, congratulations to you both. Lovely wedding gown."

Emerson winked at Reese. "Case closed. Now, where were we?"

## THE END

# EPILOGUE

Stopping at her wing of the New Life Continuing Care Senior Community before he left for the golf course, Waren placed a stack of wedding photos on her bed. He looked dashing in his golf shirt.

Eve held his hand, staring at him. "I love you, Warren."

"I love you too, Eve." Kissing her ever so tenderly, a tear falling to his rugged cheek, before he walked away.

Eve sat on her bed staring at the stack when a nurse entered her room.

"How are you today, Eve? I see you haven't eaten very much of your lunch. Would you like a drink of your protein shake?"

No answer.

"Not feeling chatty today? That's okay Eve. Let's give this shake a try." The nurse placed a straw in the bottle and held the straw to Eve's lips. Eve leaned in and took a few sips. She grimaced and pulled away shaking her head no.

"Aw, you don't like it, Eve?"

Her face slowly retreated to a vacant stare.

The nurse moved the lunch tray aside. "Ok, we'll try again later."

She attempted to straighten the bed linens while Eve remained perched in the middle, sneakers on, a look of anxiety washing across her face. Tears pooled in her eyes, revealing the turmoil within.

"Are you okay, sweetheart?" The nurse placed a gentle, caring hand on her thin, wrinkled arm.

The question lingered, unanswered.

Eve picked up the stack of photos Warren left and scattered them all over the bed.

The nurse glanced at a few. "Who are these beautiful girls, Eve?"

Silence.

Eve picked out one photo, slid herself down off the bed, and headed toward the door to take her usual stroll. She paused in the doorway holding the photo to her chest. She turned to the nurse, a hint of a smile, and raised the photo in the air. "Family. I must have done something right." She turned and placed the photo back on her chest, humming a tune as she began her ritual walk down the hallways of New Life.

# ACKNOWLEDGMENTS

My genuine thanks to all those who play a huge role in my writing endeavors.

My closest friend and reason to keep writing is our incredible daughter *Crystal Dovigh*. Without her, none of this could happen. She is kind, giving, exceptionally intelligent, and un-afraid, to take a red pen to this manuscript. That takes courage when you are my developmental editor and I am your mom. We love you. We are so proud of who you are and what you have become. Our Angel on Earth. Our gift from God.

To my husband of 53 years. *Al Fournier*, who knows, if something is not going right when I am creating, to either hug me or stay out of my office. I love you. Forever and a day. God sent you to me and I thank him every day for allowing you to be my husband. I do not know what I would do if you were not in my life.

*NY State Trooper, Jeffery Dovigh*, Our son-in-law. You are

always there for me. Ready to answer my police questions and willing to send me in the right direction when I don't have the answer. A treasure for sure. We love you. (Fave)!

**The FBI** for taking my calls and for the advice. Always a pleasure to speak to those who will pick up the phone and kindly answer my questions.

**Manchester State and local police.** Thank you for your patience in answering my questions. I appreciate **law enforcement and first responders everywhere.** God Bless all of you for the risks you take every day, for your patience with the public when you try to do the right thing and get criticized in the process.

**Vermont Medical Examiner's Office.** Thank you for your expertise in explaining the process of identifying the ashes of a burn victim.

**To John,** (the mail delivery guy) thank you for wanting to be a part of this Novel. Where would the world be without the dedication of the US Postal Service?

**To David Michaels,** your knowledge of finance was incredibly helpful, I appreciate the time you took to explain just a bit of the terminology used in the world of investing. The do's and don'ts of Broker and Investment Manager.

**To Author David K. Wilson,** Sam Lawson Series, and *Red Dirt Blues*, his latest *Murder in Spa City*. Always available to answer questions night or day. Great friend, my buddy, a wonderful writer, a screenwriter the list goes on. I am blessed to have met you in this writing world. I can count on you to be truthful when reading my manuscript. That's a task in itself.

*To AnnMarie Piche*, author of Journey Through Magic River Series. Time travel Historical Fiction. Thank you for knowing this journey we share not only in writing but as former hairstylists. Our lives have crossed paths for a reason. I will never forget you. I will always love you my dear friend.

*Joan Michaels*, My new copy editor. Senior technical writing editor for a pharmaceutical company and before that Senior writer/ editor for academia (2 different colleges). 42 years' experience. How lucky am I too to have discovered such a treasure. You are intelligent, kind, and gentle with a heart of gold and soul to match. I am thrilled to have found you. A friend for life. Thank you for all your advice. A new and needed addition to my endeavors as a writer. Many thanks for your time and patience. My husband and I both think you are the best thing since chocolate. We love you.

*Caroline Teagle Johnson*, you are the one who makes my novels come to life. Thank you for taking on this task once again. Cover designer, formatter. No matter what the trend in novels happens to be, a reader most often will be drawn to a book by its cover. You hold a special place in my heart, thank you.

*Erin Malcom* @Erin Malcom photography. Very proud to call

you friend and always confident you will make my author photo incredible. My family and I think the world of you. Your professionalism, kindness, and love for your chosen path shows through every photo. You and your husband have a gift. It's called love.

***Deborah Lyman*** Retired East Greenbush N.Y. School Teacher/ Librarian, MLS, DAR member of Rensselaer's Fort Crailo Chapter, Troy New York. Thank you for seeing the importance and the need for further discussions and research on the topic of Alzheimer's. I also thank you for reading and reviewing my work.

A forever thank you, ***to all my readers.*** Without you, I would not have had this amazing journey and a second career as a writer and published author.

***Last but not least, our families.*** Thank you for your support, ***Family is the backbone of our existence, hug and kiss them whenever you can.***

It wasn't until **BARBARA FOURNIER** retired from a 35-year career as owner /operator of two hair salons, that she realized it was time to put her lifetime of knowledge and real-life experiences, into a different format. That of writing mystery novels.

Barbara grew up in a small town in upstate New York. As one of eight children living in a house with little guidance on how to handle life's difficult moments, she and her siblings learned on their own how to navigate the world around them. Not an easy task, but every one of them managed to make very good life choices for themselves, in spite of, or possibly because of, the struggles they had to endure.

One thing Barbara always says. It's not always a good idea to give your children everything. Allow them to learn how to handle life's ups and downs. Allow them to know the value in having a job, even if it's not what they want to be in the future. Give them the right to learn how difficult it is to be fully capable of making a great life for themselves. The tools that will make them proud of themselves and thank you later for the lessons learned.

Barbara and her husband of 53 years have one daughter, the beacon of light in their lives, and a son-in-law whom they admire greatly as well.

Check out these other titles from Barbara Fournier:

*Now Say You're Sorry*
*Death in My Reflection*
*After Our First Hello*

You can order Barbara's books at your favorite bookstore or on Amazon.com.

Visit her website at barbarafournierauthor.com

Facebook: Author Barbara Fournier

Instagram: barbarafournier54

Leave a review on Amazon, Goodreads or Google Reviews.

Made in the USA
Monee, IL
03 September 2024

64561321R00225